PECULIAR TREASURES

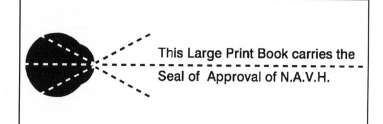

This Large Print Book carries the
Seal of Approval of N.A.V.H.

PECULIAR TREASURES

ROBIN JONES GUNN

THORNDIKE PRESS
A part of Gale, Cengage Learning

GALE
CENGAGE Learning

Detroit • New York • San Francisco • New Haven, Conn • Waterville, Maine • London

GALE
CENGAGE Learning

Copyright © 2008 by Robin's Ink, LLC.
Most Scripture quotations are taken from the *Holy Bible, New Living Translation,* copyright © 1996, 2004. Used by permission of Tyndale House Publishers, Inc., Wheaton, Illinois 60189 USA. All rights reserved. Quotations taken from 1996 version.
Other Scripture quotations are from:
THE MESSAGE: Copyright © 1993, 1994, 1995, 1996, 2000, 2001, 2002 by Eugene Peterson. Used by permission of NavPress Publishing Group.
The King James Version.
The New King James Version © 1982 by Thomas Nelson, Inc. Used by permission. All rights reserved.
The Holy Bible, New International Version®, NIV®. Copyright © 1973, 1978, 1984 by International Bible Society. Used by permission of Zondervan. All rights reserved.
The New American Standard Bible. Copyright © 1960, 1962, 1963, 1968, 1971, 1972, 1973, 1975, 1977 by The Lockman Foundation. Used by permission.
Thorndike Press, a part of Gale, Cengage Learning.

LIBRARY OF CONGRESS CATALOGING-IN-PUBLICATION DATA

Gunn, Robin Jones, 1955–
    Peculiar treasures / by Robin Jones Gunn.
        p. cm. — (Thorndike press large print Christian fiction)
    (Katie Weldon series ; bk. 1)
    ISBN-13: 978-1-4104-1798-5 (alk. paper)
    ISBN-10: 1-4104-1798-0 (alk. paper)
    1. Self-actualization (Psychology)—Fiction. 2. Female friendship—Fiction. 3. Large type books. I. Title.
PS3557.U4866P43 2009
813'.54—dc22   2009013673

Published in 2009 by arrangement with The Zondervan Corporation LLC.

Printed in the United States of America
1 2 3 4 5 6 7 13 12 11 10 09

For my Rachel,
with endless love and thanks
for all your beautiful touches to this
story.

And for all the Peculiar Treasures
who begged me to write more books
about these characters.

This story is for you.

ACKNOWLEDGMENTS

Many, many thanks go to two openhearted Peculiar Treasures, Shannon Kubiak Primicerio and Danae Jacobsen Yankoski for dreaming with me about how we could tell a new story about Katie and the gang. You are women of extraordinary words. I owe much to your willingness to step inside this mysterious process and wait on the Lord with tender hearts. Thank you.

After the dream of this story came affirmation from the people I hold closest in my heart: my husband, Ross; our son, Ross; our daughter, Rachel; and my agent, Janet Kobobel Grant. Sometimes I think the fictional characters are as real to the four of you as they are to me. I couldn't do any of this without you guys. Thanks for your decades of unfaltering encouragement, love, and support.

The superb staff at Zondervan turned this dream into a reality. I know I speak for many readers around the world when I say thank you for all your extra efforts. Creating this story has been twice as happy an experience because of the pleasure of your company every step of the way. Sue Brower, thanks for coming to California to tour the Biola University campus with Janet, Rachel, and me to get a feel for the story's setting. I highly value your insights.

Warm thanks to Ali, Meaghan, Saira, Taissa, and Rebecca for suggesting Psalm 121:8 as Katie's verse for this book.

Working with the whole team at Zondervan has been a delight. I'm so glad we have more projects ahead of us. You guys are wonderful. Many thanks to Jackie Aldridge, Marla Bliss, Scott Bolinder, Karwyn Bursma, Karen Campbell, Michelle Lenger, Beth Murphy, Joyce Ondersma, Joe Questel, Becky Shingledecker, Karen Statler, Nikki Taylor, and Ray Wadle.

Much appreciation goes to my critiquers, starting with the first critique group I ever attended at the home of Ethel Herr; receiving insights years ago via email from Tricia Goyer, Cindy Martinusen Coloma, and Sandra Byrd; my ever-kind sister, Julie Johnson; my favorite troubadour, Paula Gamble; my soul-twin, Anne deGraaf; my assistant, Rachel Zurakowski: my prayer pals, Cindy Hannan and Carrie Dishner; and the PPC's, Meg Wilson and Jaynie Roberts.

And a final huge thank you to all the readers who have written to me over the years. I still get choked up every time one of you shares with me how God has used these stories to draw you closer to his heart. That's all I've ever hoped for and pray for each time I sit down at the keyboard.

1

Katie picked up the skirt of her bridesmaid dress and playfully elbowed her way through the gathering circle of female wedding guests. "Pardon me. Coming through. Woman on a mission, here! Make room."

Most of the guests knew Katie and responded with equally high-spirited comments. Katie planted herself front and center and took her softball outfielder's stance as demurely as she could before flipping her swishy red hair behind her ears and calling out, "Right here, Christy! I'm ready for ya' now."

The other young women crowded closer and called their own directions to the bride.

"No playing favorites, Christy!"

"Over here. On your left. Throw it to me on your left!"

"No! Throw it to me, Christy! Me! Here!"

The bride kept her back to all of them as her ever-efficient aunt bustled into the mo-

11

ment. Aunt Marti adjusted Christy's position so her profile was just right for the photographer's lens.

"Keep your shoulders back, Christy-darling," Aunt Marti directed. "Turn your chin slightly to the right. No, not so far. Back . . . there. Just like that."

The camera flash captured the pose before the bride could breathe or blink. Another flash came, aimed this time at Katie and the other restless women. Katie was a little taller than many of the high school girls bunched beside her. So far the competition didn't look too challenging.

"Maid of honor, right here!" Katie called out. "Follow the sound of my voice, Christy!"

From the sidelines, someone called out, "Throw it high!"

Katie knew that voice. It belonged to Rick Doyle, her "almost" boyfriend. Rick had joined the rest of the groomsmen on the edge of the crowd of women. The other guys, all surfers at heart, had removed their ties long before the toasts were offered an hour ago. They were ready to more comfortably enjoy the warm southern California afternoon. Rick was the only one who had remained "camera ready," as Aunt Marti called it. She indicated she was pleased with

12

Rick but exasperated with the others, including the groom, Todd, who had peeled off his tux coat right after he and Christy had cut the cake.

Tall, good-looking, brown-eyed Rick cupped his hand to his mouth and called out again, "Throw it high, Christy!"

Why is he saying that? I'm right up front. Katie turned her head to see who Rick was looking at in the back row of the eager bouquet catchers. Before she could spot anyone in particular, something smushy and fragrant hit the left side of her head.

All the women around her screamed.

Katie's quick reflexes prompted her to pull the flying object close to her side. A young woman bumped against Katie in her attempt to make her own crazy, off-balance lurch for the flowers.

"Hey!" Katie felt herself topple and knew the bouquet was about to be snatched from her haphazard grasp.

Just then, Sierra, a friend of Katie's, swung her arm forward without making clear trajectory calculations and unwittingly launched the bundle into the air. The bouquet was back in play!

From the sidelines the guys yelled. From inside the huddle of surprised women a chorus of squeals rose. All arms were up in the air.

The runaway bouquet seemed to enjoy its moment of flight and tagged the fingers of one eager-reaching wedding guest, who batted at it like a badminton birdie. With a hop and a skip the white ball of mischief released a single white rose to the woman with the longest arm before Katie regained her balance, leaped forward, and seized the bouquet. *Carpe bouquetum!*

The tall girl beside Katie blinked at the single rose in her hand. Katie raised her arm and let her cheer be heard across the meadow. "I caught it!"

"I almost had it," muttered Sierra.

Christy, who had turned around to watch the momentary circus act, broke into a wide grin when she saw where the bouquet had landed.

Katie echoed her best friend's delighted expression, beaming back at her. The two of them had speculated about this moment for years. Many years. Both of them seemed to know that Christy would be the first to marry. Katie always maintained that Christy's groom would be Todd, even during those seasons when Christy had her doubts. To boost her friend's confidence during those dreamy-yet-doubting moments, Katie's best cheer-up line for Christy had been, "Just promise you'll throw the bouquet to me."

That line always caused the two of them to smile at each other the same way they were smiling at this moment.

Mission accomplished.

Spinning around once in a twirl of triumph, Katie caught Rick's gaze. Whomever or whatever his "throw it high" comment referred to no longer mattered. Rick was watching her with his chocolate brown eyes, and she felt herself melting a little inside, just as she had ever since her first, puppy-dog crush on him in junior high.

"Look over this way, please," the photographer said.

Katie tilted her head and gave him her widest smile.

"One more. This time a bit more subdued."

Drawing the fragrant, gardenia-and-white-rose bouquet up to her nose, Katie dipped her chin and took a lingering breath of the pure white sweetness.

So this is what getting married smells like.

The photographer captured the shot, readjusted the camera's angle, and took another. "Great. Thanks."

Katie glanced up, ready to twinkle one of

her bright, green-eyed looks of alluring charm at Rick, but her smile fell. Rick was no longer watching her. He had turned his attention to the single guys, who were lining up to catch the garter. She ambled over to join the group, brushing her hair off her forehead.

Being so dressed up and having her picture taken felt strange. Yet it was a nice sort of strange. An improvement over how she usually ran around. Katie's clothing selections had long been in the realm of jeans and a T-shirt or sweatshirt. During the past year, however, she had done what she called a "Katie-version" of a makeover. It started with a haircut that gave her swishy, red mane a more sophisticated, yet easy, wash-and-go style. She added some fun skirts to her wardrobe and went in search of comfortable but feminine tops. This bridesmaid outfit was way beyond anything she would normally wear, but Katie liked how sophisticated she felt in it.

A casually dressed guy with a trim goatee and distinctive, rectangular sunglasses leaned toward Katie as she stood to the side of the group of guys. Without turning to look at her, he said in a low voice, "Your halo is slipping."

She squinted into the late afternoon sun

and blinked at him, not sure if his comment had been aimed at her. The guy kept his face forward. He didn't repeat his comment or return her glance. Behind his left ear she noticed a thin, white scar in the shape of a backward "L."

Ignoring him, Katie turned her attention back to the group of guys that was now heckling Todd, the easygoing groom. Todd had positioned Christy's garter between his two thumbs in a slingshot position and impishly aimed backwards. If he let go, the garter undoubtedly would land somewhere in the palm trees that bent over the wedding party like gentle giraffes sheltering their young.

One of the guys called out, "Hey, wrong way, dude."

Doug, a groomsman and the only married guy in the group, stood beside Todd to direct him in the garter launch. Doug turned Todd back around to face the pack. "Just aim it this general direction. It'll fly off crazy, so you don't need to have your back to them the way Christy did."

Todd looked as if he was enjoying this as much as he had clearly enjoyed the wedding and the leisurely paced reception. For all the arguments that erupted among Todd, Christy, her parents, and her eager-to-be-

17

involved Aunt Marti during the planning of the wedding, it had turned into Todd and Christy's special day. The wedding and reception had only a few touches of Marti's influence here and there — most of the day had been quintessential Todd and Christy. Katie couldn't be happier for her friends.

The guys stood back with nonchalant postures, indicating by their expressions they were too cool to go after the garter. But Katie knew this group well enough to realize that the competitive streak in them would spring into action the second Todd launched the ball of lace.

True enough. Todd jutted his determined chin forward. On Doug's command, he launched the lacy white elastic band into the cluster of too-cool guys.

Mayhem broke out.

Katie noticed that Rick was one of only a few guys who didn't spring into action. The garter seemed to make a beeline for the guy with the goatee next to her. But before he could secure his grasp on the flimsy, fluttering piece of lace, another hand reached out and snatched the prize.

Katie's shoulders involuntarily slumped when she saw who caught the garter.

David, the little twerp.

Christy's fifteen-year-old brother broke

into a spontaneous victory dance. Sadly, the dance was too clever for his large feet to maneuver and too painful for Katie to watch. She lowered her head and made her way to the other side of the crowd where Rick had ended up. He was talking to Todd's dad.

"Great save on the bouquet catch, there, Katie." Todd's dad tipped his plastic punch cup her direction and added, "Way to go after what you want."

"Thanks." Turning to Rick she said, "I didn't notice your making any heroic efforts to catch the garter there, Doyle."

Rick gave her a grin and a shrug. "It wasn't coming my direction."

That is such a Rick-Doyle-philosophy-of-life statement!

In the past six months Katie had watched Rick roll through several challenging situations without lurching forward with the sort of aggression he had displayed during their high school years. He had mellowed. Maybe too much.

She gave him a long look. This was her friend. Her "almost" boyfriend, according to their last "DTR" — Define the Relationship — conversation. They had been around each other nearly every day for the past seven months, and yet she felt she didn't really know who he was or what he was thinking at any given moment.

Of one thing she was sure. She was glad she had "come his direction" on the night Todd had proposed to Christy at the Dove's Nest Café. Rick was the manager of the Dove's Nest, and although they had known each other since junior high, their paths hadn't crossed for several years.

After they reconnected that night, Katie and Rick fell into a steady, side-by-side rhythm of being together. She even took a job at the Dove's Nest. The past half-year had been the most stable stretch of her life, and she didn't want anything to change. All she wanted was a label for their relationship. She wanted to be established once and for all as boyfriend and girlfriend.

"Katie!" Christy's aunt motioned sharply from her staging position next to the wedding trellis. David already was posed, holding up the garter. The photographer was checking the fading light with his meter.

"You're being summoned," Todd's dad said.

"So I am. You want to come with me?" She reached for Rick's arm.

"You go ahead. I told Doug I'd help him with a little, ah . . . project."

"You guys aren't going to mess with Todd

and Christy's car, are you?"

Rick only smiled.

Todd's dad stepped away. "I didn't hear that. I'm not in on whatever you guys are planning."

"Rick, Christy doesn't want you guys to do anything to their car. You and Doug know that, right?"

"Katie!" David's voice interrupted them. "Aunt Marti says to hurry up!"

"Promise me you won't do anything to their car, Rick. I'm the maid of honor. I'm supposed to protect Christy. Help me out here. Please don't —"

"You'd better go." Rick pointed her toward Aunt Marti and the photographer. "Your flowers are crooked, by the way."

She took off for the trellis, glancing at the bouquet in her hands. What did he mean the flowers were crooked? They didn't look out of balance to her. A little fluffed up and missing a rosebud, maybe.

"For goodness sake, Katie, bend your head down." Aunt Marti reached up and repositioned the headband of white baby's breath Katie wore as the crowning touch of the bridesmaid's outfit.

Suddenly Goatee Guy's comment made sense, as did Rick's. Her halo had slipped. Katie made her own adjustments with the

21

two remaining bobby pins after Marti finished her attack. Smoothing back her silky red hair, Katie asked, "Better?"

"It will do." Marti stepped aside and gave an irritated snap of her fingers, as if she were in charge of giving directions to the photographer.

David moved closer to Katie and put his arm around her shoulders.

"What are you doing?" Katie asked.

"Posing for the picture."

Katie wiggled out from under his lumbering arm. "Just smile, David. That's all you have to do. Smile. Like this." Katie gave the photographer her best, cheesy-faced grin.

The perturbed photographer looked up from behind the lens. "A little less exuberance, if you don't mind." He took another shot. "Now give me a casual pose."

David stretched his arm in Katie's direction. The scent of his adolescent sweat was strong enough to wilt the flowers in the bouquet — and the trellis that surrounded them. "I'm warning you, David. Keep your paws off me." Katie's words leaked out through her closed-mouth smile. David lowered his arm.

"That's it." The photographer gave them a nod and walked away with his camera.

Katie tossed out a "thank you" and noticed Goatee Guy standing at the end of the aisle next to Tracy, the other bridesmaid. Tracy was married to Doug, and the two of them were expecting their first baby in a little more than a month.

"Are Christy and Todd preparing to leave?" Katie called to Tracy across the rows of empty chairs.

Tracy nodded, her hands folded on top of her round belly. "I came to find you. They're in the chapel signing the marriage license, and they need you to sign as a witness."

Katie scurried across the grass toward the small prayer chapel located on the corner of the university property. The chapel was one of Katie's favorite hidden treasures on the Rancho Corona campus. This grassy meadow on the high mesa that encompassed the university campus usually was used for long strolls along the trail. Having an outdoor wedding in this gorgeous space had been Todd's idea, and it was a great one. No doubt the meadow now would become a frequently requested wedding location for other Rancho Corona students.

Taking a shortcut past the palm trees, Katie caught a glimpse in the distance of the flaming sun making its nightly trek into the hazy blue field of the Pacific Ocean. The air was cooling already. Thick, atmospheric layers of peach and primrose hinted at a touch of glory soon to be viewed in the sunset.

Katie smiled. She found it easy to believe that God, in his not-so-subtle way, was adding his celebration touch to the end of Todd and Christy's perfect day. In a whisper, Katie said, "Will you bless them, Father God? Bless all their years to come. You have been so good to them."

With a catch in her throat, she added, "I don't know exactly what you have in mind for me, but would you bless me too? If Rick isn't the right guy for me, would you make that clear pretty soon? I don't want to convince myself that becoming Rick's girlfriend is one of your God things if it's really only a Katie thing."

Arriving at the chapel, Katie paused before she opened the door and added a P.S. to her prayer. "If you don't want Rick and me to go any further in our relationship, then will you break us up? This unsettled thing of being his 'almost' girlfriend is killing me. Especially today."

2

"Good timing," the minister said when he saw Katie step inside the chapel. Todd had a pen in his hand and was signing a document attached to a clipboard. Christy signed next. Then Todd's father, Bryan, who had stood as Todd's best man. The pen was handed to Katie, and she felt her heart swell for a sweet moment.

"You guys are married," she said with a grin, as she penned "Katie Weldon" on the form.

Todd leaned over and kissed Christy on the cheek. He whispered something that only Christy heard. By the way her eyelashes lowered and her face warmed with a glowing smile, Katie guessed he must have said something pretty wonderful. Something Christy probably had waited half a decade to hear him say. Something out of the ordinary for the noncommittal Todd of days gone by.

"You two about ready to go?" Todd's dad asked.

"I am," Todd said. "Are you, Kilikina?"

It seemed fitting for Todd to call Christy by her Hawaiian name — his nickname for her. They were on their way to Maui for their honeymoon.

Before Christy could answer, the chapel door opened and Aunt Marti blustered in, red in the face. Her husband, Bob, was with her.

"Come, come! We're ready for you," Marti instructed. "Everyone is in place. Big smiles. The photographer will be on your left as you head for the car so make sure to —"

"The car!" Katie burst out. "Christy, I almost forgot to tell you guys! I'm pretty sure Rick and Doug are trying to do something to your car. I tried to stop them, but —"

Todd gave a relaxed shrug. "Doesn't matter."

"Katie, they're not taking their car to the airport." Aunt Marti's sharp retort was a little too loud for the small chapel. Even the pastor raised his eyebrows, and Bob took a step closer to his wife.

"How are they getting there?" Katie asked.

"In the limousine, of course. Now, why are we standing here? Come. Please.

Christy, you could use more lip gloss. Katie, where is the lip gloss? You were supposed to be in charge of freshening her makeup for the photos."

"My lips are fine, Aunt Marti," Christy said firmly.

"Your lips are more than fine." This time Todd's comment wasn't a whisper. That he said aloud what he must have been thinking seemed to surprise Todd as much as the rest of them.

Uncle Bob was the only one who laughed. Clearly, he was enjoying every moment of today's celebration. Opening the chapel door for the blushing bride and grinning groom, Bob said, "Couple of final details for you two. The limo driver has your airplane tickets, car rental papers, and two keys to the condo. You have my cell number if you need anything else."

"Thanks so much, Uncle Bob." Christy gave him a big hug and a kiss on the cheek.

Marti jutted out her chin slightly, making her cheek more accessible for a thank-you kiss from Christy on her way out the door.

A few yards away the wedding guests had formed two lines with a pathway down the middle leading to the parking area. As soon as the group saw Todd and Christy emerge from the chapel hand in hand, they went to work with the wedding favors that had been provided at the tables. The guests released a volley of bubbles rather than the traditional yet messy shower of rice. At one point, Katie had tried to convince Christy to release butterflies. The bubbles now seemed like a wiser option.

Katie charged ahead of the newlyweds, who were taking their time, strolling toward their tunnel-of-love bubbles. She wanted to make sure they reached the limo with no problems. Tracy was already in position at the very end next to Christy's mom and dad.

Christy's mom handed Katie an extra bottle of bubbles. Instead of opening it and joining in the bubble fest, Katie looked around for Rick.

"Do you know where the guys went?" she asked Tracy.

"No, I was hoping they were with you."

Todd and Christy entered the path that led to the parking lot. Hundreds of iridescent bubbles rose around them and danced in the air. Todd stopped and reached out his hand, allowing the enchanting moment to fall on them. He kept his palm extended the way a child would to catch a raindrop or a snowflake.

Katie opened her bottle of bubbles and

added to the shower of glistening wishes.

The first agreeable bubble that came to Todd's palm burst on impact. He kept his hand out for a second bubble, and a third and then a fourth. The guests stepped up their bubble production, each of them eager to be the one who could supply the singular, resilient bubble that would float into the open clam of his hand and become the elusive pearl he was waiting for.

Two more bubbles landed and collapsed before Christy put to use her newly endowed wifely persuasions. She leaned toward Todd and reached over, placing her hand in his. Todd turned to look at his bride. A slow smile grew as he closed his hand around her fingers. The real enchantment of the moment was clear; Christy was the pearl of Todd's heart. He had no need ever to try to grasp wishes as thin as soap bubbles. He had his treasure in his hand, and she would be the gift that made him a wealthy man.

As Christy and Todd came to the end of the passageway of friends, they stopped and gave Christy's mom and dad one last hug and kiss. Katie choked up when she saw Christy's dad tearfully give his all-grown-up daughter a big bear hug.

A thin razor of pain sliced through Katie's

heart when she realized she never had received a hug like that from her father. As quickly as the razor showed its edge, she fled from it. She was good at moving away from pain in record-breaking speed. "Call us when you can," Christy's mother said to the newlyweds.

"We will." Todd gave his new mother-in-law a hug.

Christy paused in front of Katie, and the two of them reached for each other's hand. The warm smiles they gave each other were all that was needed for these two best friends to convey their feelings for each other at this moment of farewell. Then, with quick hugs for Tracy, the new couple waved to the rest of the guests and hurried to the open door of their waiting limo.

"I wish Doug and Rick weren't missing this," Tracy said.

"What do you mean missing it? We're right here." Doug came up behind them. Rick was with him.

"Where were you guys?" Tracy asked.

Rick slipped his arm around Katie and murmured in her ear, "You look nice with bubbles in your hair."

Rick was good with words. A little too good sometimes.

Katie pulled back, trying to more clearly

see his expression. "You're just trying to distract me so I won't find out what you did to their car."

Rick gave her a fake look of shock.

"Don't worry," Doug said. "We didn't do anything to the car. Besides, did you see the limo driver? Or should I say the limo gorilla?"

"Hey, we could have taken him down if we wanted to," Rick said.

"But we didn't want to, did we, Rick?"

"Nope." Rick's grin had turned into a smirk. Katie knew that meant trouble.

"What did you guys do?" She looked to Doug for a truthful answer. "You have to tell me. I know you did something."

"It was nothing bad, Katie." Rick placed his hand on her shoulder. "Just relax."

"I'll relax after you tell me what you did."

"Man," Doug said, "she's relentless, isn't she?"

"You have no idea." Rick adjusted his tux jacket. "All we did was add a little parting gift to their luggage."

"What kind of gift?"

"A honeymoon survival kit."

"A what?"

Tracy jumped into the conversation. "It's okay, Katie. I helped them put it together. It's a bunch of little items with notes on them. Like a bottle of mouthwash that says, 'Open in case of morning breath,' and a pair of socks for each of them with a note that says, 'In case you get cold feet.' "

The limo slowly rolled through the gravel parking area. The guests waved and sent bubbles in the couple's direction.

"It's nothing to be upset about, Katie," Doug said. "When they get to Maui and Christy opens her suitcase, they'll have something fun to laugh about."

Katie still wasn't convinced. "Christy's suitcase? Why didn't you put the stuff in Todd's luggage?"

Rick laughed. "Todd's luggage is an old nylon bag with one side held together with duct tape. We couldn't fit anything else in there without the bag exploding. We had to make a little room in Christy's suitcase, but everything fit."

"Make a little room? What did you guys take out?"

"Just some papers."

"What papers?" Katie and Tracy said in unison.

Rick pulled from the inside pocket of his tux a stack of neatly folded pages tied with a beautiful lace ribbon. They looked like a collection of handwritten letters.

Katie froze. "Rick, you didn't!"

32

"Doug!" This time Tracy's shriek was louder than Katie's.

"What?"

Katie grabbed the bundle of letters and took off running after the limo. "Wait! Stop!"

Her left shoe came off, but she kept running. Behind her a swell of laughter rose from the onlookers. She knew how ridiculous she must look, a one-shoed bridesmaid frantically chasing the getaway limo. But none of them understood. The letters in her hand were Christy's heart.

From the time Christy was sixteen, she had been writing letters to her future husband, telling him she was praying for him and saving herself for him. Todd knew nothing about the letters, and he wasn't supposed to. These carefully preserved words were Christy's wedding gift to him. Rick and Doug had no right to steal them.

"Stop!" Katie yelled. She waved wildly and tried to catch the driver's eye in his side mirror. "Wait!"

The limo slowed and then came to a stop. Katie flung open the side door and breathlessly lurched inside only to see Todd and Christy kissing.

"Katie!" Christy said.

"Sorry!" Katie blurted out, quickly hiding

the bundle of letters behind her back.

"What are you doing?" Todd asked.

"I'm sorry. This is really, really important. Todd, could you turn your head the other way? Just for a minute."

Katie had rarely if ever seen Todd angry. At this moment he definitely was angry.

"I promise, Todd. I'm not messing around here. This is extremely important. If you could just, yeah, just like that. Keep your head turned and close your eyes."

"Katie." Christy's voice was firm. Her expression stretched tight. "This better be —"

"It is. I promise." Without another word, Katie pulled her hand from behind her back and revealed the bundle of letters.

Christy's eyes opened wide. Her jaw dropped.

"I know," Katie said. "I'll explain it all later."

Christy snatched the letters and quickly sat on them, tucking them under the folds of her wedding dress.

"Katie, you have no idea . . ."

"Yeah, I think I do."

"Thank you, Katie!" Christy's voice cracked.

"Sure. All in a day's work for a brides-maid."

Todd turned and questioningly looked at both of them.

"Okay." Katie brushed the hair out of her eyes. "I'll be on my way now. I know, I know, you guys really wish I could stay, but, well, hey. I need to unleash my superpowers elsewhere. Love you guys."

Katie paused with a grin and added, "See you later, Mrs. Spencer."

Todd gave Katie his usual chin-up gesture. "Later."

"Yeah," Katie said, climbing out of the limo. "Later."

She turned her head and bumped into the chest of the limo driver, who was now standing guard by the open door. Katie caught her balance and looked up at the not-so-amused, gorilla-sized man.

"Whoa, Doug was right!" She turned and hobbled back down the gravel lot looking for her lost shoe.

One of the amused wedding guests had retrieved Katie's shoe. She held it out for Katie as if it were payment for getting inside information. "What happened? Is everything okay? Did they forget something?"

"Everything is great. Perfect, actually. Excuse me, will you?"

She was, once again, a woman on a mission. This time her objective was to hunt down two certain pranksters and give them a piece of her mind. Not a piece exactly. More like a slab. Or a chunk. A chunk of her mind so big both of them would choke on it.

A tall woman in her thirties fell in stride beside Katie as she began her trek across the meadow. "Katie, do you have a minute?"

Katie paused and glanced at the woman. She was pretty sure she had seen her around campus. Katie's lack of recognition must have been evident on her face because the woman introduced herself. "I'm Julia Trubec. I'm the women's resident director at Crown Hall."

"Oh, right! Sierra lived on Crown Hall North this year. You guys had the best Christmas party of all the dorms last December."

"Thanks. The Christmas parties are becoming our tradition."

"Well, keep up the great tradition." Katie started to walk away.

"Actually, if you have a minute, I was looking for you."

Forgetting her objective of hunting down Rick and Doug, Katie turned and said, "If it's about the smell that was in the kitchen on Crown Hall North two weeks ago Friday night, I can explain."

Julia looked surprised and intrigued. Her complexion hosted a galaxy of freckles that weren't obvious on first glance because they blended so well with her warm skin tone. Her sandy brown hair was flecked with a similar sprinkling of highlights. She gave Katie the impression of someone who had crossed the Pacific Ocean in a sailboat and now carried with her the effects of endless sunshine in her hair and on her skin.

"I admit I was the one who put Vicki's shoes in the oven," Katie said.

"Vicki's shoes?"

"We were just having fun. Playing a little joke on her before her big date. Sierra and I only planned to hide them there for, like, ten minutes. We never expected anyone to turn on the oven. I mean, who starts to make cookies and turns on the oven without first looking? You know what I'm saying? And obviously we never expected the soles to melt the way they did and form those weird, non-eco-friendly stalagmites, but Sierra said she was able to clean the oven, and I already paid Vicki for a replacement pair of —"

Julia held up her hand. "What I was about to ask you had nothing to do with the oven. Thanks, though. I appreciate the inside story."

Katie pressed her lips together. *Sierra is going to strangle me for telling!*

"What I actually wanted to ask is if you might consider being an RA in the fall."

Katie blinked. "A resident assistant? Me? Are you sure you have the right Katie?"

"Yes, I'm sure you're the right Katie. Here's the deal. We had another RA lined up for Crown North, but she just let us know she won't be returning in the fall. We asked around for recommendations, and your name kept coming up."

"It did? By whom? Sierra?"

"Actually, the recommendations all came from staff and faculty. You have quite a reputation in the biology department."

"Okay, well, whatever they told you about the time three out of five botany students broke out in hives after testing my herbal tea, well . . . actually, that's pretty much true. Or maybe it was three out of five reported stomach disorders and only two out of five had hives. But —"

Julia grimaced. "Are you saying we need to keep you away from the organic gardens on lower campus as well as from the kitchen?"

"Yeah, basically. I'm much better with people than I am with plants and appliances."

"How are you with animals?"

"Animals?"

Julia smiled as if Katie should get her joke.

"Okay, well the first goldfish I had last fall was really old when I bought him. I think they had a special geriatric tank that wasn't labeled as such, but they charged me full price. Rudy was so old he should have come with a cane. Or a walker. Seriously. And the second goldfish, well —"

"Katie, I'm only kidding!" Julia laughed while Katie wished she could find a way to end the conversation gracefully.

"Listen, Katie, the job description for an RA doesn't have anything to do with fish, tea, or oven maintenance. You're good with humans, and that's what matters."

"Oh, okay." Katie realized that if she hadn't bungled Julia's first impression of her, she might actually have a chance to obtain a lucrative, on-campus position for her senior year. She listened with her lips pressed together while Julia gave her more details. It sounded pretty good.

"Could you come by Crown Hall Monday afternoon around three o'clock?" Julia asked. "Craig, the other RD, will be there."

"Sure."

"Perfect. I'll see you then. Oh, and Katie?

Your confession about the oven is safe with me."

Katie smiled. "Thanks." Somehow she had the feeling any confession would be safe with Julia. She also realized this RA position could be an answer to a prayer she hadn't even had time to pray.

3

With a determined stride, Katie hitched up the now frumpled and soiled skirt of her blue bridesmaid dress and set her chin forward.

"Hey," a male voice beside her said. "Your halo is —"

"Yeah, yeah. I know. Slipping again."

"No, this time your halo came off." Goatee Guy held out her fallen wreath.

Too agitated to take the baby's breath hair band and try to position it on her head, Katie swatted at the air and kept walking. "Just throw it away for me, will you?"

Heading for the reception area where the remaining guests had gathered, she spotted Rick and Doug standing beside the cake table. Both of them were enjoying thick slices of wedding cake while the caterers cleared the head table.

Katie marched toward them with a frown. Doug volunteered, "Hey, I know you're really upset about what we did but listen. Trace just told us about the letters. We didn't know."

Rick stepped in. "Katie, we had no idea what the letters were."

"That's not the point." Katie placed her hands on her hips. "Regardless of whether you guys knew, you shouldn't have taken them out of her suitcase. As a matter of fact, you shouldn't have messed with Christy's stuff at all. That's just rude."

"You're right," Doug said.

"You do know that we were only trying to do something fun for them, don't you?" Rick said. "We weren't trying to sabotage their honeymoon."

Katie scrutinized Rick. Then she glared at Doug.

"Whoa!" Doug said. "I haven't seen that expression on your face since the houseboat trip when I accidentally gave you that bloody nose."

Repressing the grin that would have accompanied that long-forgotten memory under other circumstances, she said, "Yeah, but if I remember correctly, I smeared your face pretty good with a brownie on that trip."

"A brownie with whipped cream," Doug added. "And you're right. You got me pretty good that time. I didn't see that one coming."

Katie noticed Doug still was holding the plate with his bonus-sized piece of wedding cake. Taking a step back before Doug got any ideas, Katie felt her fiery indignation drain away. She had marched over, ready to give Doug and Rick a lesson in wedding etiquette, yet history had proven that she was a fine one to lecture anyone on such topics.

"Is all forgiven?" Rick asked.

Katie nodded. She had had a little practice in extending forgiveness to both these guys over the years. Especially to Rick Doyle. She knew she couldn't stay mad at him.

"You were quicker at accepting our apology than my wife," Doug said. He made a grimace as if he were still in trouble with Tracy.

"Where is Tracy?" Katie asked.

Doug motioned to a chair a few yards away. His petite, pregnant wife was awkwardly stretched out, pressing her hand to her middle.

"Trace?" Katie called out. "Are you okay?"

She nodded and attempted a smile.

"We should get going," Doug said. "I know she's tired. During the reception she said the baby was kicking a lot." He inhaled

43

two more bites of cake and handed the plate to one of the caterers before leaving with Tracy.

"Would you like a slice?" the caterer asked Katie.

"No, thanks." Katie looked around at the deserted reception area. "I feel like we should help you clean up. Do you need us to do anything?"

The young woman chuckled. "No, we've got it covered."

Katie noticed Rick was giving her an "are-you-serious?" look.

"What?"

"I think you've been working at the Dove's Nest too long."

"Why do you say that?" Katie frowned and tried to read his expression.

Is this Rick's clever way of telling me I'm fired? He isn't saying he wants to break up, is he?

"Why are you looking so worried?" Rick asked.

"Why did you say I've been working at the Dove's Nest too long?"

"Well, why else would you offer to jump in and assist the food service staff?"

"Oh, that." Katie looked around again. "I just don't know what else I'm supposed to do as the maid of honor."

"I think you officially went off maid-of-honor duty when the limo disappeared from view. You're off the clock now."

"I guess I am."

Sometimes the sporadic nature of her thoughts drove even Katie a little nuts. She often felt like a zookeeper in charge of four-dozen monkeys. When the monkeys stayed in their cages, all was well at the Katie Zoo. A little noisy sometimes, but manageable. Whenever those monkeys escaped, well . . . she had to give Rick credit for the many times he had kept up with her while she ran around with a monkey net.

Playfully dipping her finger into the frosting on Rick's piece of cake for a taste, she asked, "What do you think? Do you want to leave now or stick around some more?"

"I'm ready to go." Rick touched his fork to the fluffy white frosting and dotted the end of Katie's nose. He leaned back and smiled at his work.

Katie crossed her eyes, trying to focus on the dot.

Just then Aunt Marti bustled over to them. "Katie, you forgot the bridal bouquet. This is yours to keep."

"Oh, thanks." She didn't remove the frosting from her nose. It was too much fun waiting to see if Marti would notice.

45

Marti already had turned her attention to Rick. "Did you get the serving trays the caterer borrowed from your restaurant? I specifically told them to return the trays to you cleaned. Did they do that?"

"Yes. They're already in my car."

"Marvelous. Now, I have a little something for each of you." Marti held out two small envelopes for Katie and Rick. "A token of my appreciation for your assistance today."

"You didn't have to give us anything," Katie said.

"Yes, I did," Marti said. "You both have been instrumental in Christy and Todd's lives for many years, and you should be acknowledged on this day."

"That's very kind of you," Rick said, receiving the envelope. "Thank you."

"It's only a small token," Marti said. "I hope you enjoy it."

Katie leaned over and gave Aunt Marti a kiss on the cheek. With a mischievous tone in her voice she said, "I don't care what Rick says about you, I think you're a peach."

With a soft smugness Marti said, "If you think I'm going to fall for that comment or that I didn't notice the frosting, you're mistaken. You'll have to try harder than that to ruffle my feathers after a day like this, Miss Katie Weldon."

Even though Katie liked the thought of taking Christy's aunt up on that challenge, she left the opportunity alone and smoothed their exit by dabbing away the icing and saying, "You did a great job with everything, Marti. The wedding, the reception, all of it was perfect."

"It was, wasn't it?"

Rick and Katie left Marti basking in the lovely success of her planning and walked to Rick's classic, cherry red Mustang where he opened the door for Katie. She rolled down the window to let the hot air escape. By the time Rick walked around to his side, Katie had opened her envelope.

"Wow," she said. "This is pretty nice. You like this store, don't you?" Katie held up the plastic gift card for Rick to see.

He nodded.

"Too bad they only sell clothes," Katie said. "If they sold gas, my summer transportation expenses would be covered."

"You can buy yourself something nice." Rick started up the engine. "I like that shade of blue on you."

Before she could wonder about whether Marti and Rick were in league, trying to improve Katie's wardrobe, a beat-up, white Toyota Camry rolled past them. Katie noticed a circle of tiny white flowers hanging from the rearview mirror.

"Hey, my flowers! What is he doing with my flowers?"

"What are you talking about? You're holding the wedding bouquet in your lap."

"No, not these flowers. My halo."

"Your halo?"

Katie couldn't see the other car anymore. She turned back in her seat and blinked. *Why would he keep my flowers?*

"Hey, Angel Girl, what are you thinking?"

"Angel Girl?" Katie made a face at Rick. "That has to be one of the worst so far."

In the almost seven months that Rick and Katie had been hanging out together, Rick had tried without success to come up with a nickname for her. In high school he had dubbed her "Speed" after a sledding incident. Katie had quickly vetoed "Speed" as a nickname in this new season of their relationship. But Rick was determined to come up with something for her.

"You looked gorgeous today, by the way," he said. "Even if you don't want to be called 'Angel,' you looked like one."

"Oh, yeah, right. I'm sure I looked divine running after the limo in Cinderella-fashion, wearing one shoe and with my halo slipping."

Rick grinned. "You have no idea how cute

48

you looked. Trust me, all eyes were on you."

The song playing in the background on the radio seemed to catch his attention. He cranked up the music.

You're the one for me, Sassy Girl.
You leave the others in the dust.
Come along with me, Classy Girl.
I'm the man you can trust.

Katie never liked that song. But she did like Rick. Especially at moments like this, when he was grinning at her and telling her she was gorgeous. Her doubts about him from earlier in the day flitted away.

He might not be the best at romantic gestures, but he does have his moments of charm. And those are the moments I've never been able to resist.

"How about Sassy Girl?" Rick suggested.

"Ah, that would be negative to the one-hundredth power. And don't even try Classy Girl as a runner-up."

"Okay, I'll keep working on it. Hey, I have to take the serving trays back to work. Do you want me to drop you off at the dorm, or do you want to run over to the Dove's Nest with me?"

"I'll go with you."

"I was hoping you would say that."

"I was hoping you would ask."

They exchanged comfortable grins, and

Rick turned up the music again. He liked the stereo nice and loud while he drove. Especially on warm evenings like this one, with the car windows rolled down. He would hang his arm out the open window and use the door to keep beat with the song.

Her habit was to sing along, which made Rick smile. Actually, it was a toss-up whether his expression was more of a smile or a smirk. Either way, the two of them had their rhythm down and had spent many hours on the freeway with the music bridging the gaps in conversation. Neither of them seemed to mind the musical interludes.

But this time Katie didn't slip into her routine of singing along. Instead, she leaned back and wandered into a happy corner of her heart where she could rewind the day and go nice and slow through her favorite parts.

I wonder what my wedding day will be like. Do I want to get married outside? Will my wedding be as large as Todd and Christy's?

She let out a contented sigh. *Who will I end up marrying?*

Glancing at the eligible bachelor beside her, Katie let her mind ask the obvious question. *Could it be Rick?*

She knew she was jumping way ahead of

where their relationship was, but today was the kind of day any young woman with a tinge of romantic inklings was bound to ask such questions.

She studied Rick's profile as if the answer to her never-before-whispered-aloud question could be found in the lines of his strong jaw.

Rick seemed to sense her gaze. He turned briefly to look at her. "Did you say something?"

"No." Katie smiled to herself.

4

When they arrived at the Dove's Nest, Rick got out of the car, but Katie didn't.

"I think I'll wait here," she said.

He looked surprised. Katie didn't usually pull back from a potential social opportunity. "You okay?"

"Yeah, I just want to sit for a minute. I'll come in if I get bored."

"Okay. I'll be right back."

She thought if she sat alone for a few minutes some answers would come to her regarding several life questions that were pressing in on her.

Her relationship with Rick was always on the "up for discussion" board in Katie's mind. Second was the unexpected offer from Julia for the RA position. The third dangling decision was her major.

Earlier that week Katie had a not-so-great conversation with her advisor. When she had started at Rancho Corona University, Katie had transferred in with a variety of credits from community college and had declared botany as her major. After her not-so-successful attempts at creating her own herbal teas, she had changed to biology with the thought that she might become a teacher. That option stopped appealing to her about four months ago.

Now that she was about to complete her junior year, her advisor had presented several possibilities in the sciences. None of the options struck Katie as desirable or as a good match. She had walked away from their meeting registered for two summer school general ed classes. She also left with the word "undeclared" written on a form where a major needed to be listed before she could complete registration for her senior year.

Twice Katie had talked with Rick about what she called her "major dilemma." He suggested she become a business major, but Katie couldn't picture that. She didn't want to run a café like Rick did. But then, she couldn't see herself fitting into any particular major.

Maybe I shouldn't even be going to college. Maybe I should pull out now and wait until I know what I want to be when I grow up.

She leaned against the warm frame of the

car door and smoothed her thumb over the petals on Christy's bridal bouquet. Katie had kept her major dilemma out of her conversations with Christy during the past few weeks. Her best friend had been up to her ears with finals, graduation, and wedding plans. She didn't need to help Katie solve her problems. Katie was determined to figure this one out herself.

Just not right now.

Rick didn't return to the car as quickly as Katie had expected. And she didn't like being alone as much as she had thought she would.

Leaving the bouquet in the car, Katie went into the Dove's Nest. She found Rick in the kitchen, lying on his back on the floor with his head under the sink.

"Tell me you're not doing what I think you're doing."

"Katie, look at this, will you? Carlos said he thinks the ants are getting in through the wall here where the plumbing connects."

Katie gingerly got on her hands and knees and twisted her head to look under the sink. She didn't see any ants. "Rick, it's time for you to call a professional. Seriously."

"An exterminator?"

"Either an exterminator to kill your imaginary ants or a professional therapist to convince you the ants don't exist."

"They exist. You just haven't been here when they've come en masse."

"If you say so. And by the way, you're still wearing a rented tux. Just in case you forgot."

He got up and offered Katie a hand.

She stood. "What's next? Were you planning on heading out to the dumpster to see if you could find any rodents?"

Rick lowered his chin. "Rodents, huh?"

"Yeah, because, you know, it seems you're dressed for a little dumpster diving."

"If I'm going in, you're going in with me."

"Oh, yeah? I'd like to see that happen."

In one swift, quarterback motion, Rick grabbed Katie around the knees and hoisted her over his shoulder as if she were a sack of potatoes dressed up in bridesmaid blue.

"Rick!"

He crossed the kitchen in four strides and said, "Duck," as he exited and marched to the dumpster.

Katie laughed and pounded her fists on his back. Before she could spout a threat, two girls from Rancho Corona called out to her. They were parked next to the dumpster shed.

Rick put Katie down quickly, as if suddenly realizing how unprofessional he was being at his place of business. Katie brushed back her hair; her face felt rosy. The two girls got out of their car and greeted Katie, but their eyes were on Rick.

"Hey, Carley, Tiffanie," Katie said nonchalantly. "Nice night, don't you think?"

Both the girls were wearing pink sweatshirts. Carley's blond hair was pulled back in a ponytail, and Tiffanie wore her blond hair in two loose braids.

"We came for study-break food. What are you guys doing?" Carley asked.

"We're taking a study break too." Katie gave Rick a sideways grin. "One of us was studying ants, and one of us was about to collect data for a special report on rodents."

"Ants?" Tiffanie asked.

"Rodents?" Carley echoed. "Dressed like that?"

"We were in a wedding earlier today," Rick explained.

"You're Rick, aren't you?" Carley asked. "You're the manager here, right?"

He nodded, sporting a funny look that seemed to be a mixture of embarrassment over being caught in the frivolity and pride for being identified as the manager. Katie realized it probably wasn't good that she was mentioning ants and rodents at Rick's restaurant.

"We love your San Felipe pizza," Carley said.

"Yeah, that's our favorite," Tiffanie agreed.

Carley listed her favorite espresso beverages from the Dove's Nest menu, with Tiffanie adding her agreement to everything.

Rick kept grinning, which made Katie want to slug him and say, "Don't overdose on all the flattery, Doyle." She was familiar with his friendly manager routine and would be the first to say that Rick excelled at public relations.

"I have to go back inside and get my keys," Rick said. "When you two order, ask for Andrea. I'll make sure she comps you a couple of espressos as my contribution to your study break."

"Wow, thanks!"

Rick sprinted back to the kitchen door, and Carley said to Katie, "Your boyfriend is the nicest guy ever."

"My boyfriend," Katie repeated, liking the way that sounded.

In the awkward silence that followed, Carley added, "He is your boyfriend, isn't he?"

Before Katie could come up with some sort of answer, Rick returned and said, "All set. Andrea is expecting you. Ready, Katie?"

"Yup, I'm ready."

Katie could feel the girls' gaze as they

watched her leave with Rick. She would have loved it if Rick had put his arm around her or held her hand. Any sort of affectionate gesture to show Carley and Tiffanie that Katie and Rick were together. But Rick kept his hands to himself. He and Katie walked side by side, behaving like respectable, overdressed employees of the Dove's Nest.

As they drove up the hill to Rancho Corona, Katie twirled Christy's bouquet in her lap. She drew in the fragrant scent of the wilting gardenias and smiled, thinking of Christy and Todd. They were on the airplane now, winging their way to Maui.

"Why are you grinning?" Rick asked.

"No reason."

Rick gave her a skeptical look.

"Okay, I can't lie. I was thinking about Todd and Christy and the wedding and, you know, a bunch of mushy stuff."

"Mushy stuff, huh?"

"Yeah, mushy stuff."

"Do you want to know what I was thinking?" That was a rare question from Rick.

"Of course. What were you thinking?"

"I'm pretty happy with where our relationship is. I think things are going well."

Katie waited for him to add something a little more promising. He didn't.

So Katie added her own thoughts. "I think

we've been in the slow lane for a really long time."

Rick glanced at her, looking confused. "This road only has one lane going up the hill."

"I meant the slow lane of the freeway of our relationship."

Rick still looked confused.

Katie rolled her eyes. "Rick, you and I have been taking things slow in our relationship for a long time. I mean, s-l-o-w. Not that I have any major complaints. I just thought maybe you were going to say you're ready to put on your turn signal."

"And the turn signal would mean we're ready to move into the fast lane?"

"Right. Or at least thinking about making a lane change. And it doesn't have to be a change into the fast lane. It could be to the middle lane. Or if we're on a six-lane relationship highway, then it's an even smaller lane change. It's just that we've been in this slow lane so long that we're wearing a rut in the road."

Rick kept driving. Same lane. Same speed. No comments.

Katie looked out the window and wished she hadn't said anything. At least not the whole lane-change, rut analogy. She didn't like the way her thoughts had tumbled out.

The truth was, she didn't want to be the one to push things forward. She wasn't even sure she was ready to make a lane change in their relationship with all the other decisions she had in front of her. But today felt like a day for declarations of love — or at least affection. Rick's things-are-going-well statement was just blah.

"Here's the thing." She turned to face Rick. "When you went back for your keys, Carley asked if you were my boyfriend."

"What did you tell her?"

"I didn't say you were, but I didn't say you weren't. I wanted to say, 'Yes, Rick Doyle is my boyfriend. Isn't he great?' But I can't say that. I mean, I can say you're great. But ever since we decided not to go with the boyfriend-girlfriend labels until we were both ready for that next level of commitment —"

"Are you?" Rick asked.

"Am I what?"

"Ready for the next level of commitment?"

Katie didn't have an answer. That surprised her.

Rick rephrased his question as if she hadn't understood what he was asking. "Are you thinking we're ready to make a lane change? Are we ready to be boyfriend and girlfriend?"

Katie's immediate, off-the-top answer was "I don't know."

The spontaneous response surprised her again. She believed it was honest, so she stuck with it even though she knew that if he had asked her the same question earlier that day she probably would have squealed, "Finally! Yes!"

Katie tossed the hot potato back to Rick. "Are you?"

"Am I ready to officially be boyfriend and girlfriend?"

"Yes. Are you?"

Rick paused. "Almost. See, I don't think ruts are a bad thing. Ruts are routine, and routines are good. They're steady and predictable. Routines get you where you're going. We need to keep praying about what's next for us. We have the whole summer ahead of us, and next fall you'll be —"

"A resident assistant. Possibly. Or maybe a college dropout. I'm wavering between the two."

Rick laughed.

"Don't laugh. I'm serious. About the RA position, mainly."

Katie filled Rick in on her conversation with Julia and concluded with, "I haven't decided, but I'm seriously thinking about it.

And I'll pray about it. And you're right about us praying about what's next for us. I need to pray about that some more."

The car pounded over the highway with neither of them speaking for a few minutes. When Rick spoke, his tone was low. "This is a pretty big decision, you know."

"Which decision? The boyfriend-girlfriend one or the resident assistant one?"

"Both."

"I know. Add those to the shopping cart with my major dilemma, and I have three big-ticket items going through the life scanner at the moment."

Rick pulled into the parking lot of Katie's dorm and turned off the car's engine. He leaned against the door with his arm over the steering wheel. "If you take the RA position, it would mean you would work fewer hours at the Dove's Nest. That could be a problem since you've been saying you need to make more money next year."

"I know. But that's the good thing about the job. If I take the RA position, my room and board will be covered. Room and board, Rick! I can't make enough working part-time at the Dove's Nest to cover room and board. And I can't work more hours than I already do because, even with summer school, my advisor said I'll probably

have to take eighteen units in the fall regardless of my major. Once I decide on a major,
that is."

Katie was feeling exhausted. She didn't
want to end this glorious day examining all
the unfinished decisions in her life. It was
depressing.

Rick's jaw shifted forward and back as he
chewed on Katie's words.

"You realize you and I would see each
other a lot less," he said.

"Not necessarily," Katie countered.

Obviously Mr. I-Like-Being-in-a-Rut
didn't like Katie's potential leap out of their
established routine. Maybe it was a good
thing their relationship was still going
slowly. If it changed radically, it could be
their breaking point.

As soon as Katie realized the potential
outcome of her decision, her throat tight-
ened. She didn't want to break up. She
would take the slow lane over no lane any
day.

Sticking with routine, Rick returned Katie
to her dorm, gave her a hug, and said he'd
call her later.

She sighed. "Later" was always one of
Todd's favorite words. Katie realized it was
also the word that was keeping her relationship with Rick from bursting into a big,

mushy romance. "Later" would never be her favorite word.

5

Katie opened her dorm room door and stood there in her bridesmaid dress. She didn't walk right in. She hated, hated, hated entering her room alone that night. She hated that Christy was married and gone and would never again be her roommate. For the past nine months Christy had been only a few feet away every night, and they had the luxury of talking for hours in the cozy comfort of their beds. That era was over forever.

Katie tossed the bouquet onto Christy's vacant bed and let the door slam behind her. She hated being alone. She hated being stuck in the slow lane. She hated that she had so many unresolved decisions in her life.

Right then and there, Katie decided she was going to take the RA job. She wanted the position. She liked the thought of partnering with Nicole, the other RA who would be on her floor. She liked the possibility of reporting to Julia. Plus, the wages would meet her financial needs for room and board.

There, one problem solved.

Just declaring the decision to herself felt like a huge relief.

Leaving her bridesmaid dress draped over the back of her desk chair, Katie put on her fuzzy yellow robe and headed down the hall for a shower.

As soon as the warm water pelted her back, she wondered if she had decided too quickly. *Is this what you want, God? Because if you don't want me to take this job, then close the doors. I'll do something else for the money. Whatever you work out is fine with me. This just makes sense, and I love the thought of being around a lot of new people next year now that Christy is gone and Sierra will be in Brazil. That is, if you want me to keep going to school here. I need to figure out a major. What do you want me to do with my life? With my relationship with Rick? I'm yours. I'm ready for you to roll out your plan for this next stretch of my life. I really will try to be patient, but don't forget about me, okay? I know you won't.*

Katie turned off the water and sighed in the quieted shower stall. She wrapped her hair in a towel, put on her robe, and padded down the hall to her room. Entering the space that was now void of any evidence of Christy except for the wedding bouquet, Katie closed her door and cried. She didn't cry often, but when she did, the cascade could be significant. One of the good things about Katie and her all-out-front emotions was that once a moment was over, it was over. Rather than saving up her feelings and luxuriating in a bad mood for an extended period, she considered herself to be more of a pay-as-you-go sort of emotionalist.

As soon as her tears were spent, she was done. Katie crawled into bed and fell asleep with her wet hair still wrapped in a towel.

Her cell phone woke her the next morning. She could tell by the customized tune it played that Rick was calling.

"Hi." Katie sat up and tried to focus her eyes to see the time on the alarm clock on her desk. The towel fell off her head and toppled to the floor.

"I wanted to see if you were doing anything today."

"I don't know. I think I was planning to go to church later. It's pretty early, Rick."

"I know. My parents called and asked me to come down to their house today. I wondered if you wanted to go with me."

"When are you leaving?"

"Around seven-thirty."

"That's in, like, twenty minutes."

"I guess it is. Listen, I know you're not a morning person, but I wanted to get down there in time to go to church with them. I need to clean the rest of my stuff out of the garage this afternoon and bring it back to my apartment. Their house goes on the market Monday."

Katie threw back the covers and tried to jumpstart her brain. "Is their new house done yet?"

"No, but they think it will be by the time they sell the Escondido house."

Rick's parents lived a little more than an hour away from Rancho Corona. They had built the Dove's Nest and the adjoining Ark Christian Bookstore almost a year ago in an area where the rents for business property were much less than near their home in Escondido. Business had been so good they decided to build a new house near the café and bookstore.

Katie walked past the mirror and let out an involuntary, "Whoa!"

"What's wrong?" Rick asked.

"Nothing." Katie didn't want to explain what she looked like at the moment. Her hair had "set" itself during the night, and

68

now the right side stuck straight up to form an entertaining curl at the top like a woodpecker.

Intrigued, Katie leaned to the right. The wave remained in place. She tilted to the left, and the crimson wave crested and fell. Katie cracked up.

"What's going on?" Rick asked.

"It's my hair." Katie be-bopped her head back and forth in front of the mirror and watched her hair perform all kinds of tricks. She laughed at the antics of her hilarious hairdo.

"What's so funny?"

"You're not going to believe this. Actually, this is too good to miss. I'm going to take a picture and send it to you. Hang up and call me back when it comes through."

Katie hung up. She held out her phone, dipped her chin to get the full effect of her wild hair, and snapped a picture. She cracked up again when she saw the shot and sent it to Rick.

A moment later her phone played Rick's song.

"What in the world did you do to your hair?"

"I went to bed with it wet. Is that just the most hilarious thing you've ever seen?"

"Katie, you are the most . . ."

"What? Go ahead. Say it. The most whacked-out woman you've ever met?"

Rick neither agreed nor disagreed. "So what did you decide? Do you and your whacked-out hair want to go to Escondido with me in ten minutes?"

"I think my super-sonic hair and I should stay here. I have a final on Monday, a seven-page paper due Tuesday, and two more finals Wednesday. If I go with you, I know I won't get any studying done." Katie returned to bed and pulled up the covers.

"Okay. I understand."

Katie thought she detected disappointment in his voice. That was good. She liked that at this moment she wasn't officially Rick's girlfriend. If they had decided to make a lane change last night, she had the feeling she would have gone with him because it would have seemed like something an official girlfriend would do.

"I'll call you later tonight," Rick said. "Maybe you'll be ready for a study break."

"Sounds good. Have a great time at your parents'. Oh, and if you do come by later tonight, bring food." Katie flopped back in bed and stared at the ceiling. Within two minutes she fell asleep and didn't wake up until noon.

Whoa! I must have really needed that sleep.

After a quick shower to tame her wild tresses, Katie dressed and set about organizing herself. Her first order of business was a jaunt to the vending machine at the end of her hall where she emptied her quarters into the slot and stocked up on study snacks.

When I move to Crown Hall, I'm buying a little refrigerator so I can keep snacks in my room. And milk!

The thought of dining on a bowl of Cocoa Puffs with cold milk while jumping back under the covers on any given morning made Katie smile.

She realized she hadn't told Rick about her decision to take the RA position. Her hair had distracted her. She would tell him tonight.

However, when Rick called that night, he was the one who had a surprise for her. "Do you feel like going for a walk?"

"Sure."

"I'm about three minutes from your dorm, and I have Max with me."

"You do? You have Max in your car?" Katie knew Rick's family's Great Dane was too old and too big to be comfortable for long in the backseat of Rick's Mustang. She never had seen Rick let Max ride in the meticulously cared for car.

"Max is staying with me for awhile since

he's not exactly a selling feature for my parents' house."

"I knew you were looking for a roommate, but the question is, can Max cover his part of the rent?"

"I wish. So are you ready to come out of your study cave? I thought we could take Max for a walk. Oh, and I brought pizza."

"Well, in that case, I'll be right there."

Katie slipped her feet into a pair of flip-flops and zipped out to the parking lot. Rick was just pulling in. He wasn't driving his Mustang. He had a rented truck, and Max was in the passenger's seat, hanging his head out the open window. Katie was greeted by a slobbery kiss that covered half her cheek and half her neck.

"Max, you are such a flirt." She wiped her cheek and neck with her sleeve and pulled on Max's ear, which was her signature hello to the old dog. "Do you want to go for a walk?"

Max knew the word "walk" and woofed loudly at Katie's offer.

"He's sure glad to see you," Rick said. "All the way here he was moaning like a baby."

"That's because he is a big baby, aren't you, Max? You are just a big baby, and you know it."

Rick latched the leash on Max's collar,

and the stiff old dog clambered out of the truck. They took off at a brisk pace, with Max leading the way by curiosity and necessity. A few moments later his pace slowed, and Rick said, "I have to say I'm disappointed."

"Why?"

Rick gestured toward Katie's hair. "You don't look like your picture."

Katie laughed. "Learn to live with disappointment. Speaking of which, you lured me out here with pizza, and I'm not seeing any pizza."

"I left it in the back of the truck. I didn't want to share with Max."

When he heard his name, Max sat down.

"Come on, Max, that wasn't much of a walk."

"He looks pretty tired out," Katie said.

"It was a crazy day at the house. I have some water for him in the truck. We can go back."

"Come on, Max." Katie patted her leg. "Get up. Let's get some water."

Max panted as he meandered back to the truck, then gladly lapped up the water Rick poured for him in a plastic bowl. Katie smiled at the way Rick thought of everything, including his dog's necessities. He also had brought everything they needed for a tailgate pizza picnic, including Katie's latest favorite beverage, cream soda.

"You remembered," she said.

Rick seemed pleased that she noticed.

"What's on the pizza?" she asked as he reached for the large, flat, white box.

"Everything. No bell peppers, though."

"Good. I hate bell peppers."

"I know. I remembered that too."

"I especially don't like those waxy, shiny yellow ones. Name one other food that's sunshine yellow. It's unnatural, I tell you!"

Rick opened the box and showed Katie evidence that no "unnatural" colored foods had been included on their pizza.

They were only two bites in when a car pulled up beside them. Carley leaned out her open window and called, "Hi, you two!"

Max gave a rumbling, "Woof."

"Are you moving out early, Katie?" Carley turned off her car's engine and got out.

"No, this is Rick's stuff. I'm here all summer."

"You are?"

"Yeah, I decided last week to stay for summer school."

"I'm supposed to go home to Texas. I don't want to go." Carley's eyes were on the pizza, which Katie decided was better than Carley's eyes being fixed on Rick.

"Would you like some?" Rick offered. "We have plenty."

"Sure." Carley reached for a slice and jumped up on the tailgate next to Katie.

Before Katie could slide another bite into her mouth, two more students came around the side of the truck and greeted Katie and Carley as if they were long-lost friends. Everyone seemed to be out on a study break at the same time, and the pizza was like a homing device. Rick had brought plenty and his PR skills made him eager to share. Between bites, the small gathering talked about finals and the last week of school.

All of them expressed the same sort of stress Katie was feeling. She wasn't as alone as she had thought the night before.

Once the pizza was gone, the party dispersed. Rick closed up the back of the truck and helped Max into the cab. Then Rick turned, and Katie held out her arms, offering a good-bye hug.

"I'm pretty sweaty and dirty from cleaning out the garage," he said, opening his arms to her.

"Hey, I've already been slobbered on by your dog. You can't be half as disgusting as Max. No offense, Max, baby." Katie wrapped her arms around Rick's middle and leaned her cheek against his chest.

She could hear Rick draw in a deep breath, and she felt the air slowly release through his nostrils and into her hair. A hopeful corner of her heart wondered if Rick had reconsidered his decision from the night before. Perhaps he'd decided to move out of the slow lane. What if he realized they had a good thing going for them and was ready to make a lane change?

Looking up, Katie pulled back and tilted her chin in his direction. If Rick wanted to change lanes, all he had to do was seal this moment with a kiss. No words would be needed. Rick and Katie had been saving that telling kiss for when they were ready to establish themselves officially as a couple. Katie still wasn't sure she was ready, but she was open to the possibility. Her lips were available.

Rick smiled at her, keeping his lips to himself. "Not yet," he whispered.

"I know," she whispered back.

Pulling slowly out of their hug, Katie said, "I'm glad you came by."

"Me too."

"Thanks for the pizza."

"Any time. I'll see you tomorrow." Rick leapt into the truck and started the loud engine.

Katie waved as he drove off. Then she

crossed her arms in front of herself, trying to hold in the warmth of Rick that had been there a moment ago. As much as she agreed with their wait-on-the-kiss decision, Katie hated this feeling of non-conclusion every time Rick drove away, leaving her lips untouched.

They were doing the right thing. She knew that. She also knew her stress level was affecting her thoughts. Her emotions were all over the place. Finals week was not the week to make major decisions.

But at moments like this, all the self-control was killing her, because Katie already knew what it felt like to kiss Rick Doyle and to kiss him more than once.

6

Instead of going back inside her dorm after Rick left in the rental truck, Katie decided to walk over to Crown Hall and "do a Nehemiah." A year ago one of Katie's Bible professors had used that expression, and she had liked the concept but hadn't done it. The premise was to walk around a new situation and evaluate it before jumping in. The Old Testament prophet Nehemiah took a late-night walk around the broken-down walls of Jerusalem before he began the huge task of rebuilding them.

Katie realized she might be using the Nehemiah spy trip as a reason to avoid studying. If she was, she wasn't alone in her procrastination. Even though it was after ten o'clock, every student on campus seemed wide awake and looking for anything to do rather than study for finals.

When Katie passed the fountain at the center of campus, two girls sat on the edge, playing guitars. A guy walked past and greeted the musicians. He was carrying two cardboard trays loaded with large espresso beverages. Eight of his study buddies would be cheering him in a few minutes.

Katie gazed up at the dark sky overhead. A few faint stars peeked back at her from behind their bedtime cloud covers. *They* didn't have finals in the morning, so they could go to sleep if they wanted.

Katie wasn't ready to sleep. She realized how much she loved this school, this campus, this community of people. Even with Christy gone, Katie still wanted to be here another year. No, she wanted to be here another ten years. The rest of her life! This campus felt more like home than her parents' house in Escondido ever had been.

Approaching the open glass doors of Crown Hall, Katie saw Julia standing inside to the right. She was talking to Craig, the resident director for the guys who lived in Crown Hall. Julia looked up at Katie and waved.

Katie stepped closer. Julia introduced her to Craig, and Katie said, "Well, I'm in."

Craig nodded as if it was obvious that, yes, she was inside the lobby.

Julia, however, read Katie's meaning and broke into a wide smile. "Really?"

Katie nodded. She loved that Julia understood her quirky communiqué.

"Fantastic, Katie. That's great."

"I've decided to take the RA position,"
Katie said for Craig's benefit.

He looked impressed with her decisive-
ness. "I'm glad to hear that. We were just
talking about meeting at three o'clock
tomorrow. Would that time work for you?"

"Sure."

Katie realized again that she hadn't told
Rick about her decision to take the position. With Max and all the impromptu
picnic pals, Katie had forgotten to bring up
the subject. She didn't feel she needed his
clearance or blessing or whatever, but it
would have been nice if she had talked to
him before committing to take the job. But
there it was: she just had declared that she
was "in."

Feeling compelled to offer an escape
clause, Katie said, "I guess I should say that
even though I know this is what I want to
do, if God closes the door, then, well . . . I'll
understand."

Julia narrowed her gaze. "And what is it
that you will understand, exactly?"

"I'll understand that this isn't God's will
for me."

"The ol' hinge theology." Craig grinned.

"Listen, I hate to go, but I need to run upstairs. I'll see both of you tomorrow."

As soon as Craig ducked out of their conversation, Katie turned to Julia. "What did he mean by 'hinge theology'?"

"Every college student we've ever counseled has at one time or another said the same thing, about God's opening and closing doors. Craig's theory is that for most young adults, God's will seems to hinge on which way the door of opportunity swings."

"And what's wrong with that?" Katie asked.

"God isn't limited to expressing himself through open or shut doors."

"I know. He uses open and shut windows too. I saw *The Sound of Music*."

Julia laughed.

" 'When God closes a door, he opens a window.' " Katie quoted and then gave her mouth a twist. "Or is it when he opens a door, he closes a window?"

"I think it's closed door and open window."

"Okay, but if you're saying hinge theology isn't cool, then what would be a better theology?" Katie asked. "I mean, if it's presumptuous to limit God to opening and closing doors, then what would be a better way to figure out what he wants when you have to make a big decision?"

Julia smiled. "I like you, Katie."

"That's nice," Katie said with her usual playful, flippant attitude. "I like you too. But you didn't answer my question."

Julia laughed again. "You're right, I didn't. Do you really want to hear my opinion?"

"Yes."

"Okay."

Without adding any further information, Julia turned and walked away. She wove a path through the other students gathered in the lobby and sat down on one of the couches across the room. Then she moved her lips, but Katie couldn't hear her.

Katie stood by the door with a "huh?" look on her face. Obviously, if she wanted to hear Julia's answer, she better follow her path across the lobby.

Katie plopped on the couch with an expectant expression. "So?"

"So, that's it," Julia said.

"That's what?"

"That's my visual demonstration of what I think it's like to figure out God's will."

Katie wasn't tracking. "All you did was walk over here and sit down."

"Right. I did. Then I said, 'So, that's it,' but you didn't hear me the first time I said it. And you wanted an answer from me, right? You wanted to hear what I had to say. So you followed me." Julia raised an eyebrow as if she had just unveiled an ancient secret.

Katie nodded slowly. Very slowly.

"Craig calls it my 'hot on his heels' theology," Julia said. "That's what I think it's like with God. If you want to know what he has to say, you just follow him. You stay close. You ask and keep asking, and you listen. He'll make it clear. The closer you are to him, the easier it is to hear what he's saying."

Katie let the thoughts sink in.

Julia leaned back, looking comfy. The settled-in image didn't come from the way she was sitting, what she was wearing, or any other external influence. Julia simply seemed comfortable in her own skin and in what was happening in the moment. Her focus was on Katie, not on herself or what was going on around her. Katie didn't know if she had ever been around anyone so tranquil before. It was nice.

"Have you ever thought about the way Christ led the disciples around during the three or so years they were together?" Julia asked. "When you read the Gospels, it seems they are all over the place. One day Jesus would be out on a boat with them; the next day they would be hiking through the hills. The journey looks random. If you tried to map their path, it would look like a bunch of wiggly lines intersecting and going nowhere. But Jesus obviously had a plan. He said he accomplished everything the Father sent him to do. All the disciples had to do was follow hot on his heels and trust him."

Katie had never thought of following Christ that way.

Julia smiled as if she could read Katie's thoughts. "That's my theology. You stay close to Christ. Remind yourself that being one of his disciples will feel like an unscripted adventure most of the time. The journey is definitely not a one-size-fits-all. But he has a plan. He is fulfilling his objectives in your life."

"I agree with that," Katie said. "My verse for this past year was, 'The Lord will fulfill his purpose for me.' And I know he has. He is. It's just that right now certain things in my life aren't moving forward and that might affect my RA decision."

"What kinds of things?" Julia asked.

"I need a major. Majorly. It's a major dilemma."

"Ah," Julia said with a knowing dip of her chin.

"I'm finishing my junior year this week,

and I'm majorly majorless. I'm taking summer school to catch up on basic units, but I can't register for classes in the fall until I declare a major. That's why I said God might close the RA door for me. Do you see? No major, no registration, no classes, no fall semester, no RA job."

Julia nodded.

"When I met with my advisor, he handed me a list of majors in the science department and asked me to select one on the spot. None of them felt right. So I told him I couldn't choose any of them."

"What did your advisor say?"

"He said, 'If you can't make a decision, then I can't help you.'"

"Sounds like an honest answer," Julia said.

"Honest or not, it didn't help me a bit." Katie chewed at the cuticle beside her thumbnail. Pulling her hand away, she asked, "So, what's your advice on my major dilemma?"

"What's your passion, Katie?" Julia asked.

No immediate answer popped into Katie's thoughts.

"Think about it," Julia said. "I'll ask you again tomorrow. Think about what energizes you and makes you happy. If you answer those questions, your major probably will be right in front of you."

Katie thought Julia's response was a little too organic. Too airy and lacking the promise of fulfillment. But she said she would give it some thought.

"I have to check on a couple of women," Julia said. "See you tomorrow? Three o'clock at the office on the third floor?"

Katie nodded, and Julia left her on the lobby couch with her thoughts.

Katie's pondering lasted about two minutes. She didn't want to be alone right then. So she headed down the familiar hall that led to Sierra and Vicki's room, the hall where Katie would be an RA — if she found a major, that is. She debated whether she wanted to stop by to visit her friends or just keep going and finish out her Nehemiah spy walk. The spy walk option won, and Katie continued down the long hall.

Several doors were open along the way, spilling out a variety of fragrances, music, and voices. At the end of the hall was the room Katie would live in. Dual RAs usually were positioned in the rooms located at each end of the hall.

Katie looked at the decorations on the wall across from the front door of her room-to-be. A variety of students' artistic expressions covered the walls of most of the long halls in the dormitories. However, by this

86

time of year most of the decorations and posters were bedraggled, with only a few more days of their beautification duty left before being tossed out. The walls usually were painted or repaired during the summer months to be ready for the next round of decorations with the incoming infusion of residents.

Katie hadn't seen this wall before, but then she never had walked all the way to the end of the hall. The design was well done and gave the impression of a large picture frame with the outline done in black, rectangular, corrugated cardboard. At the top of the wall was a hand-painted sign that read "The Kissing Wall."

Katie laughed to herself. *Not exactly the same wall as the one Nehemiah walked around. I don't imagine Nehemiah discovered a kissing wall on his tour of inspection!*

Inside the frame were dozens of pictures of people kissing. Most of the pictures appeared to have been cut from magazines or printed off the Internet. Some of the pictures were photos. Scattered among the photos were various verses from the Bible on kissing.

"Love and faithfulness meet together; righteousness and peace kiss each other." Psalm 85:10

" 'May God give each of you a new home and a new husband!' She kissed them and they cried openly." Ruth 1:9

"Then Jacob kissed Rachel and began to weep aloud." Genesis 29:11

"An honest answer is like a kiss on the lips." Proverbs 24:26

Katie recognized a few of the girls in the photos and knew they lived on this floor. One photo showed Sierra with her wild mane scooped up on top of her head in a humorous fountain of cascading, untamed blond curls. One of Sierra's little nephews was kissing her on the cheek while Sierra was trying to stifle a yawn. It was a great candid shot.

All of the pictures on The Kissing Wall were sweet, tender, appropriate, and representative of everything that was innocent and beautiful about a kiss.

Katie felt like crying.

Less than an hour ago, Rick was inches away from her, but he hadn't responded to her invitation to kiss her. Something primal, womanly, and sad inside Katie had been awakened. She longed to be loved.

Pressing her unkissed lips together, Katie read more of the quotations.

"Let him kiss me with the kisses of his mouth — for your love is more delightful than wine." Song of Solomon 1:2

"You did not give me a kiss, but this woman, from the time I entered, has not stopped kissing my feet." Luke 7:45

"Greet one another with a holy kiss." Romans 16:16

That was it. Kate couldn't take another image or verse on kisses — holy or otherwise. She felt as if she were torturing herself standing there and taking it all in.

Striding back toward Sierra's room, Katie was ready for a heart-to-heart talk with a girlfriend. Years ago she and Sierra had commiserated while on a missions trip to England. Their angst then had been that neither of them had a guy pursuing her the way Tracy and Christy did. The irony to Katie was how little had changed. Her feelings of longing and desire to belong were stronger than ever.

When does a heart finally feel at home and content? When are these unending passions fulfilled? In marriage?

The person Katie really wanted to talk with was Christy. Or should she say Mrs. Todd Spencer? Christy would have a whole different take on this discussion once she returned from her honeymoon, and Katie would be eager to hear it.

With a string of taps on Sierra's door,

Katie waited for the usual "Enter at your own risk" invitation to come from Sierra on the other side.

However, no voice responded. She knocked again. No answer. Sierra and Vicki evidently had joined the ranks of other Rancho Corona study postponers who, like Katie, were out roaming the campus instead of sticking close to their rooms.

You might as well go study, Weldon. You are too emotional right now to ponder any of your passions. Get on with what you need to finish tonight. This is finals week, remember?

Katie trekked across campus. With each step she thought of Julia's acknowledgment that sometimes following Christ could seem random.

"You're here, aren't you?" she whispered, as if Christ were physically walking her back to her dorm. "Yeah, you are. I know you are." She kept walking, aware that there never is a time when the Lord isn't close to his children.

"Okay," Katie breathed in a resolved sort of prayer that encompassed everything unsettled in her life. "Lead on. I'm in."

7

Katie's exam the next day went better than she had expected. She left class a little before noon. Her plan was to skip lunch and zip over to the Dove's Nest before her 3 o'clock meeting with Julia and Craig. She wanted to tell Rick face-to-face that she had decided to take the position.

For some reason, though, she lollygagged around campus, talking to people and checking her mailbox and then stopping to talk with more people. Time ran out, and she didn't end up going down the hill to the Dove's Nest. She knew if she wanted to ponder the meaning behind her actions she could come up with a pretty good analysis of why she was avoiding talking to Rick about the RA job. But she didn't want to know.

If she was miffed about not yet being his official girlfriend or anything else related to the lowly feelings she had struggled with when she stood before The Kissing Wall, Katie didn't want to know. She didn't want to think about those things when she met with Craig and Julia.

At 2:55 Katie entered Crown Hall and headed for the resident directors' office on the third floor. Julia and Craig were already there.

Katie took a seat on the couch. "I should have mentioned this before, but I have to work this afternoon. I don't know how long this meeting is supposed to go, but if I could leave by 3:30, that would be great."

"That shouldn't be a problem," Craig said. "Do you work on campus?"

"No, I work in town at the Dove's Nest Café. Which brings me to another question I should have asked earlier. Will I be able to work part-time at the Dove's Nest or is the RA position full-time?"

"It's full-time and then some," Craig said. "We've had a few RAs over the years try to put in hours here and there at various jobs, but it never has worked out for them. The hours you need to be on duty in the dorm vary each week, and that makes it hard to mix in a work schedule from another job."

Katie nodded. Now she knew her conversation with Rick later this afternoon would be even more difficult. She had been thinking she could promise him that she still would work a few hours here and there so things wouldn't be radically changed in their relationship. But that wouldn't be the case.

"I'm going to go ahead and start our official interview time now with prayer," Craig said. "Then I have a question for you."

Katie had a hard time paying attention during Craig's prayer because she was too involved thinking about what his question was. As soon as he said "amen," Katie looked up.

"We ask every applicant this question. Even though we pursued you instead of the other way around, Julia and I thought it would be good to hear your answer."

"Okay."

"Why do you want to be an RA?" Craig asked.

Katie's immediate answer was, "I get my room and board covered." To her chagrin and surprise, her answer was spoken aloud rather than in her head. She pressed her hand to her mouth and said, "Did I just say that aloud?"

Julia nodded, and both she and Craig grinned.

"An honest answer," Craig said. "You don't know how refreshing that is."

"There is another reason," Katie said quickly. "I like people. I thought about applying for RA when I first came to Rancho, and my main reason is the same now as it was then. I love being with people."

Julia smiled as if Katie had said the right thing.

"I also like the idea that I could make dorm life fun and maybe a little easier for some freshmen women. I feel happy when I think about that."

"Good." Craig seemed satisfied with her answer because he dove into a brief overview of what the position would entail. Twenty minutes later, he handed her a binder labeled "RA Manual." Everything suddenly was official.

"Do you have any questions?" Craig asked. "I realize this is a lot of information all at once."

"I don't think so. Your numbers are in here if I need to call, right?"

"Yes, and why don't you leave your cell number with us too?" Julia said.

Katie was ready to go when she stopped at the door. "I do have one small request to add."

"Sure," Craig said. "What is it?"

"I haven't told anyone about my decision. Could you wait until tomorrow before saying anything? I need to tell a few people before they hear it through the grapevine."

"Totally understandable. How about if we don't say anything until Thursday? The next meeting will be here at 7 o'clock Thursday evening. We'll announce your position so everyone will hear at the same time."

"Thanks. I appreciate it."

Katie knew she was scheduled to work at the Dove's Nest on Thursday from 3:00 to 9:00, but all that was about to change. She could ask to get off early. Then she realized she would be giving Rick her notice; she would be quitting. The thought launched her into a new level of funk.

Change is awful. I really don't like this. Maybe Rick had the right idea about ruts being our friends.

Katie walked a little faster to her car, knowing the sooner she had this conversation over with the better.

The thickening clouds seemed to shrink the landscape as Katie left Rancho Corona campus and drove a little too fast down the hill. The low-lying marine layer of chilling dampness usually hovered along the coast during the "June-gloom" days of late spring. Inland, where Katie was from, the warmer air from the southern California desert generally pressed the clouds back out to sea.

Today the ocean forces were prevailing against the desert winds. With the dulling skies a padded hush came over the afternoon.

Katie wondered which of the prevailing forces of her life were going to take control once she stepped into work and told Rick about her decision. She tapped her thumbs on the steering wheel of her VW Thing, which she affectionately called "Baby Hummer." Not that her low-slung, cute VW bore much resemblance to the hulking SUVs sold by General Motors. No, Katie called her car Baby Hummer because, despite its age, it kept humming right along down the road. Katie loved having a one-of-a-kind car. She also loved the ridiculously low price she'd paid for Baby Hummer. Today, though, she was reminded that Baby was best suited for sunny days. As the damp breeze came through a dozen not-so-sealed-tight-anymore openings all over the car, she wasn't feeling the love. She only felt the cold.

Part of Katie knew she was focusing her discomfort on Baby Hummer and the weather instead of what really had caused the slow adrenaline siphon. She was nervous about telling Rick her decision. She didn't want their relationship to change.

Pulling into her usual parking space alongside the café, Katie hurried in the back door and found herself face-to-face with Rick.

"Hey, you're here! Good. We're slammed out front. Jared called in sick, and a group of Beanies showed up. We have a back-up on pizza orders."

"Okay." Katie wasn't sure what Rick meant by "Beanies." "Rick, I need to talk to you."

"Can we do that later? We're seriously behind." Rick took off for the front of the café without waiting for an answer.

Katie reached for a clean apron, tucked up her hair under the less-than-flattering hairnet, and washed her hands.

Carlos, the assistant manager, was alone at the food prep station. He had six individual pizza crusts lined up ready for toppings.

"Here, Katie," Carlos said. "Cheese only on these two. The next three are Hawaiian and then a pepperoni with extra cheese."

"Got it."

"We have nine more after these."

"You're kidding. What's going on out there? A Beanie convention?"

"Beanies?" Carlos asked.

"Yeah, Rick said a bunch of Beanies

showed up."

Carlos laughed. "It's not a bunch of Beanies. It's a troop of Brownies. You know, those little girls with the brown uniforms and the funny hats."

"They're not funny hats. They're little acorn tops. At least that's what we used to call them when I was a Brownie. I didn't know Brownies still wore uniforms."

"Katie, you forgot the extra cheese on that one."

"Sorry."

"You didn't by chance earn a speed-it-up merit badge when you were a Brownie, did you?"

"Why? Am I going too slow for you, Carlos?"

"Everybody goes too slow for me."

Katie caught a glimpse of Rick out of the corner of her eye and said, "Nobody likes being stuck in the slow lane when they think they can keep up in the fast lane. But you know what? I'm beginning to think differently about the slow lane."

"What are you talking about?" Carlos asked.

"Nothing. I was just starting to miss my favorite rut."

Carlos ignored her. The next three hours went by in a blink. Katie barely saw Rick since he was working out front at the cash register where café guests came up to place their orders. She did notice when he came in the back to start going through his manager closeout routine. He had a series of checkout tasks when he was about to leave for the day. Today Katie noticed he was doing them earlier than usual.

She decided to take her break and followed Rick to the back office. "You on your way out?"

He nodded and put his initials on a page clipped to a board next to the freezer. "Max has been locked up in my apartment since eleven this morning. I should have left an hour ago. I only hope I don't find a disaster. I'll call you later, okay?"

"Rick, I need to talk to you about the RA position."

"What's to talk about? You took the job, right?"

"How did you know?"

"Carley was in here an hour ago. She said someone she knew saw you leaving the RDs' office this afternoon with the training manual."

The surface temperature of Katie's face shot to blazing. "Carley had no right to tell you! I wanted to talk to you about it. That really ticks me off. Sometimes Rancho is a beehive of busybodies buzzing into everybody else's business."

Rick gave her a long look.

Katie furrowed her brow. "I put too many 'b's' in that sentence, didn't I?"

"Maybe one or two, *honey,*" Rick said.

"Cute." Katie let out a huff.

"Relax," Rick said with a tone of authoritative stability in his voice. "Carley didn't tell me anything I didn't already know."

"What do you mean?"

"I knew on Saturday when you talked about the position that you were going to take it. The numbers added up. It's as simple as that. You can get your room and board covered. I can't match that with enough hours or wages here at the Dove's Nest."

"I thought you might be . . ."

"What?"

"Upset. Or disappointed in me or something."

"Katie." Rick took a step closer and drew her gaze into his with his warm brown eyes. "You are in the final stages of a long-term goal. I get that. You have to do whatever you need to so you can graduate. You know how hard I was hit with student loans after I graduated. You miraculously have managed to stay out of debt so far with the scholarships and the long hours you've worked. You've gotten this far without any help. Katie, that's a major accomplishment. If you need to go for the job that gives you the best financial benefits, then that's what you should do."

Katie stood still for a moment, soaking in his words. "Is that it? Is that your final thought on the topic?"

Rick nodded. "You need to make your own decision, and obviously you have. Would it help you if I said I understand your reasoning and I support your decision?"

"Yeah, that would help a lot. Thanks." Katie scanned Rick's face, making sure she was reading honesty in his expression. "This means a lot to me, Rick."

"I know it does."

"You said on Saturday that we wouldn't see each other as much if I took the RA position, and that's true. I won't be able to work here at all."

Rick's shoulders slumped. "Not even a few hours a week or on Saturdays?"

"No. The on duty hours are different every week, and it's full-time. Plus, as far as my classes for next semester, I don't know . . ."

"Katie, it's okay. Relax. I'll hire someone to cover your hours, and if it does work out for you to come back at some point, we can always fit you into the schedule." He picked up his car keys and headed for the back door.

"Oh, Rick? One more thing. I need Thursday off."

"Tell Carlos and put your schedule change request in my box." Rick lifted his arm in a farewell gesture as he walked out.

Drawing in a deep breath, Katie thought, *That went well. I think. One down and one to go.*

She needed to tell her parents about her decision. Telling them would be much more difficult but for different reasons.

Because of those challenging reasons, Katie didn't call her parents until Thursday after dinner. It was her last possible opportunity to tell them before her position was announced at the staff meeting. She knew she needed to honor her parents by giving them the update, even though at twenty-one she was independent of them and capable of making her own choices, legally and personally.

On her way across campus to Crown Hall, Katie made the phone call. Her mother answered. Pulling up her brightest voice, Katie said, "Hi, Mom. It's Katie." It killed her to have to announce her identity each time she called. The necessity came about after several years of her calling and saying, "Hi, it's me," and every time the response on the other end was "Who?"

"How are you, Mom?"

"Well, the sink backed up in the bathroom last week. We had to call a plumber."

"I bet that was a mess."

"No, not too messy. They have machines, you know. They make a terrible noise, but they aren't very messy. It sure was expensive, though."

"That's too bad," Katie said.

"The sink works fine now. Did you know your Great Aunt Mabel died?"

"No." Katie paused. "Did I know I had a Great Aunt Mabel?"

"Of course you did. Mabel was Edith's sister. You know, my brother's sister-in-law, Edith."

Katie tried to make all the connections in her head. She only knew a few of her distant relatives by way of photos that came occasionally with Christmas cards. She knew she had some cousins in Missouri. Or maybe it was Michigan.

"I'm sorry for your loss, Mom."

"Wasn't much of a loss for me. I never met the woman. I just thought you might be interested to hear the family news since I never know when you're going to call."

Katie recognized the jab but dodged it and kept going. "Well, I'm calling now because I have some news."

"Are you getting married?"

"No."

"You're not already married, are you?"

"No, Mom."

A pause on her mother's end of the line was followed with, "You better not tell me you're pregnant."

Katie clenched her jaw and fought the urge to hang up and never dial this number again. "No, Mother, I am not pregnant."

Katie was walking past a trio of freshmen women who stopped their conversation and stared at Katie. She lowered her head and steered off the main path to keep the rest of her conversation a little more private.

"Listen, I have to go to a meeting in a few minutes, but I wanted to tell you my good news. I have a new job for the fall. I'm going to be an RA. A resident assistant. I'll work in the dorm where I'll be living in the fall."

A pause followed. "Is that like a janitor job?"

"No, it's more like being a counselor. A peer counselor. I'll oversee the women in one of the wings of the dorm."

"Sort of like an apartment manager? Is

that it?"

Katie gave up. "Sort of."

Her mom paused. Katie knew something random would follow and braced herself for the hit. "Now, if the sink backs up there in the dorm, if you're the manager, you don't have to fix it or pay for it, do you?"

"No, Mom."

"I'm only asking because our sink backed up last week. In the bathroom. Did I tell you that?"

"Yes, you told me. I need to get going now. I just wanted to check in and tell you about the RA position."

"The what?"

"The RA position." Katie translated for her sixty-three-year-old mother. "The manager job at the dorms."

"Yes, you already told me about your apartment job. Was that it? Was that why you called?"

"Yes, pretty much. That was it. I have to go now . . ."

"Katie, you did check into doing janitorial work, though, didn't you? The pay might not be as good as the apartment manager job, but you could work nights, and the hours would be more flexible, I would think. Did you consider that?"

Katie swallowed and switched her cell

phone to the other ear. She didn't think it was possible for her insides to cringe any more than they were at this moment. No words came out of her mouth, which was probably a good thing.

When she didn't respond to her mom's suggestion, her mother said, "Hello? Katie? Are you still there?"

"Yes, I'm still here."

"I thought you said you had to go to a meeting."

"I do. I'll talk to you later. Bye, Mom."

She heard a click on her mom's end of the phone. No final, "Good-bye, Katie." No "thanks for calling." No "congratulations on your new job," and certainly not now or ever a sweet or affectionate "I love you," "I miss you," or even an "I'm proud of you."

Only a click and an unemotional dial tone.

8

Katie clenched her jaw and fought to hold in the emotions she felt about her conversation with her mother. The last thing she wanted was to step into her first RA meeting looking as if her face had just gone through a car wash.

She noticed a stone bench off to the side of the front of Crown Hall. Behind the bench was an outcropping of purple bougainvillea that climbed the wall and stretched out forming a protective canopy. Katie took a detour for the shaded bench of refuge and sat with her back to the door of the busy dormitory. With effort she convinced her breathing to return to a calm and steady pace.

Note to self: Do not call your mother right before anything important. Better yet, stop calling your mother altogether!

Katie knew her mother had no idea what an honor it was to be offered this position.

Sadly, it was one of the many things her mother would never know or understand about her.

Katie had spent years trying to explain the emotional disconnect she had with her parents. She attributed their detachment to her being a surprise baby who showed up when her parents were well into their forties. Her two older brothers were a pack of adolescent trouble, and then boisterous baby Katie was added to the mix. In many ways she had raised herself.

That rationale didn't make it any easier to accept that her parents never would know how hard Katie had worked to make it this far in college. If she managed to graduate, she would be the first person in her immediate family — and extended family, for all she knew — to graduate from college. That accomplishment alone was reason for her to keep going.

Katie understood, however, that her friends rather than her family would truly celebrate with her on graduation day. Christy, Todd, Doug, Tracy, and especially Rick were the ones who grasped what an accomplishment her college degree would be.

That is, once she decided what her major was.

One issue at a time. I got the phone call to my mom over with. I'm through finals week, and right now, I should concentrate on the RA meeting.

She walked into the meeting with her chin up and was met by a rush of welcoming comments from the group of seven other Crown Hall RAs.

Nicole greeted Katie with a big smile, hugged her, and said, "They wouldn't tell me who my new RA partner was. Then you walked in the door, and I was so happy! I'm glad it's you!"

Nicole was someone Katie had misjudged on first meeting her. Nicole's thick, dark hair appeared always to cooperate. Her smooth skin, beautiful round eyes, and wide smile had put her into a pageant princess category in Katie's mind. However, once Katie got to know Nicole, she discovered her to be down-to-earth, kindhearted, and occasionally hilarious. Katie felt confident they would get along well.

In the glow of Nicole's warm welcome, Katie entered the meeting and felt at home with her new pals. They spent some time connecting and getting a feel for what their responsibilities would be in the fall.

Afterwards Julia invited the women to her apartment, but Katie was the only one who didn't have previous plans for the evening. At first she felt a little awkward taking Julia up on the invitation, but in the end she was glad she did.

Julia's apartment was located at the end of the hall on the third floor, at the opposite end from the RDs' office.

"Craig and his wife have the RD apartment that connects with the office. I like it better down here," Julia said as she opened her door. "Usually when someone comes to see me in my apartment, it's for socializing. When they see me in the office it's more for straightening out problems. Do you like tea, Katie?"

"Yes, I love tea, and wow-oh-wow, where did you get all this stuff?"

With a sweeping gesture to the collection of artwork scattered around the apartment living room, Julia said, "Around."

"Around where? Around the world?"

"Yes, more or less."

"Where have you been?"

"I've been in a few corners of creation. I'd like to visit a few more one day." Julia headed for her tiny kitchen and put some water in the teakettle, plugging it into the wall. Katie started with the first wall in the living room and examined a picture of a sandy beach that curved around a calm bay.

Colorful fishing boats lined up in the sand, and tattered grass umbrellas fluttered in the afternoon breeze.

"Where is this corner of creation?"

"That's Playa de las Canteras."

"Where's that?"

"Las Palmas in the Canary Islands."

"And where is that?" Katie grinned at her hostess. "I hate to show my lack of geography skills, but . . ."

"It's okay. I can't say I knew where the Canary Islands were located until I went there. They are a province of Spain, and they're located about fifty kilometers off the coast of West Africa."

"I never would have guessed. What about this picture? Is that you?" Katie pointed to a framed photo on the end table. It was a desert setting with a brightly colored tent in the background, and a woman in sunglasses riding a camel in the foreground.

"Yes, that's me."

"In the Sahara Desert?"

"No, they have camels in the Canary Islands. That was a fun day."

Katie had seen parts of Europe the previous summer when Todd, Christy, and she had traveled around together, but she couldn't picture a place in the world where you could walk along a beautiful beach and ride camels in a desert setting on the same island.

"The Canary Islands' claim to fame is that Christopher Columbus set sail from there on his voyage to discover the New World." Julia pointed to the large picture of the fishing boats and the bay. "Some things on the island seem similar to how they must have been when he was there outfitting his ships for the journey."

"Okay," Katie said. "I'm officially in awe. So where else have you been?"

"I lived in Austria for awhile. Then New Zealand and Brazil."

"How very, very cool. I think I'm jealous of your life. I have a friend who's going to Brazil."

"Are you talking about Sierra?" Julia asked.

"That's right. Sierra lived in this dorm. Of course you know Sierra."

"She's staying with some of my friends while in Brazil."

The teakettle whistled. "I'm guessing herbal tea is your preference," Julia said. "Unless you're still recovering from your herbal experiment."

Katie smiled. "I was hoping you had forgotten that piece of information from our first meeting."

"Do you like honey or sugar with your tea?"

"Neither. I'm a purist."

Julia handed Katie a china mug that was sprinkled with purple and yellow flowers. "I bought that cup in London at the airport."

"Heathrow?" Katie asked. "They have great shopping there, don't they? When I was there I wished I had money for souvenirs."

Julia lit a candle in the center of a trunk that doubled as a coffee table. "I love to celebrate conversations by lighting a candle. If the fragrance is too strong for you, let me know."

Katie took a sip of the tea. "This is nice."

The air around them now was laced with a calming vanilla-almond fragrance. Julia settled into a corner of her love seat, leaving a snuggly chair open for Katie. It was the sort of chair that beckoned weary souls from across the room and turned into a world of ministering coziness by the time the person sank into it.

"Tell me about when you were in London," Julia said.

For the next two hours Katie and Julia compared travel experiences and even discovered they both had been to the same youth hostel in Amsterdam at different times and knew some of the same people.

Long after the tea was gone and the candle had burned low, Katie asked, "So how did you end up here?"

"I love this school. I love this campus and this community. I graduated from here fifteen years ago. After lots of ministry around the world, I ended up back at Rancho in a season of brokenness. I came on campus to spend some time praying in the chapel. The first person I saw was Craig. He knew me from way back and told me about the opening. The minute he told me, I knew this was what I was supposed to do next." Julia smiled. "This is my passion. This makes me happy."

Katie remembered their conversation from Sunday night and said, "In case you're about to ask me what my passion is, I should tell you that with finals and everything I haven't had time to figure it out."

"I already know what your passion is. You told me earlier this week."

"I did? When?"

"At our meeting with Craig on Monday. You said you love people."

Katie hadn't considered "people" as her passion, but she didn't disagree with Julia's summation.

"So now I have a question for you," Katie

said. "What was your major when you were at Rancho?"

Julia smiled. "Which semester?"

"You too?" Katie asked. If she didn't feel kinship with Julia already, Julia's changing her major more than once bonded Katie to her freckled resident director forever.

"Yup. I changed three times before I ended up majoring in sociology." Julia stretched out her legs and rested her feet on the edge of her coffee table. "At that point in my life, I knew I liked humans, and I wanted to do something that would keep me interacting with people."

"Sociology," Katie repeated. At that moment it sounded to her like the title of a lovely song. A song she had been humming for a long time but never knew the words to.

Could it be that simple? You send me here to have this conversation with Julia, and I decide on a major just like that?

"Would you think I was a copycat if I decided to major in sociology?" Katie asked.

"Does it feel like a fit?"

"It could be. I'm interested in checking it out. I know I can do that online. It won't be hard to find out which classes transfer. I'm going to check it out tonight."

"Do you meet with your advisor again soon?"

"Next week."

"Tell me how it goes."

"I will. Thanks. I should get going. Thanks for the tea and conversation and everything. You are such an encourager."

"Email me or call me after you talk to your advisor, okay? I'll be gone for most of the summer, but I'll be back the last week of July. I'd love to spend more time with you before the RA training week."

"Yeah, I'd like that too." Katie paused by the door before letting herself out. Next to the door was a beautifully framed plaque hung at eye level. The words made no sense to her.

He aha te mea nui?
He tangata! He tangata! He tangata!

"What language is that?" she asked.

"Maori. I bought that in New Zealand. It's an ancient riddle of the indigenous people. The first line is a question, 'What is the greatest thing?' The second line is the answer. 'It is people! It is people! It is people!' "

"That's so cool. I love that. I couldn't agree more."

Katie left Julia's apartment floating. "Now that's the kind of woman I want to become," she said to herself.

The only hesitancy that shadowed her declaration was that Julia was single. Katie didn't know if Julia had been married, or if she had not had the time to pursue or be pursued romantically while skipping across creation. For so many years Katie's unspoken focus had been on finding a guy to love and a guy who loved her for who she was. She hadn't contemplated that she might invest the first few decades of her young adult years in other ways. Julia had given Katie much to think about.

On Sunday night Katie and Rick went to their favorite Mexican restaurant for dinner. Katie couldn't stop talking about Julia and their conversation at her apartment. Rick listened all the way in the car and kept listening after they were seated.

When their iced teas arrived, Rick interrupted Katie and said he wanted to offer a toast. "Here's to you, Katie." He lifted his glass of iced tea and smiled at her. "Here's to the end of all your finals, the completion of your junior year, and the start of summer —"

"If you say summer school, I might have to toss this iced tea in your face," Katie teased.

"I was going to say, here's to the start of

summer *vacation,* and to a new job in the fall that provides you with room and board and a new friend."

Their red plastic tumblers gave a dull *twap* as they clinked together.

One thing Katie had discovered being around Rick and his family for the past half a year was that they were big on celebrations. Going out to eat usually included a moment when they paused to offer a toast for something they were thankful about. Katie drank up the tradition, so to speak, and wanted to continue the pattern in her life.

"Oh, and I have other news we can celebrate," she added. "My major dilemma is solved."

"Did you meet with your advisor Friday?" Rick asked. "You said at work that you were going to try to set up an appointment."

"No, I'm going in on Tuesday. But I've decided to switch to sociology. I looked up all the information, and it makes so much sense. The good part is that it looks as if most of my classes will transfer."

"Katie," Rick said, raising his cup again to celebrate her decision. "That's great news."

"I know. I have a major, Rick, not a major dilemma. Just a major. Do you have any idea what a huge relief that is?"

"I know it's been weighing you down for a long time."

"It has."

"This is really good news, Katie."

"I know. And I'll tell you some other news. Just as an F.Y.I., I'm ordering the chimichanga burrito," Katie said. "The *gordito* size."

Rick grinned and looked at his menu, shaking his head.

"What? Are you smiling because that's what you were going to order too? Or are you smiling because you still can't believe how much I can eat?"

"I'm smiling because you're going to be alone in your efforts. I'm not even going to try to compete with you on that one."

"Do you think I can't eat all of it?"

"Oh, I don't doubt that you'll eat all of it. I just know I'm going to hear about it for the next two days. You'll say, 'Rick, I can't believe you didn't stop me!' So for the record, I'm telling you now: Stop. There. Now order whatever you want. This is our celebration dinner."

Katie ordered the *gordito*-sized chimichanga burrito. And she ate all of it.

Then she and Rick took Max for a walk around Rick's apartment complex. They practically had to pull the huge, old dog around by the leash. Max definitely wasn't interested in learning new tricks.

Katie would have opted for something fun to do afterwards like bowling or going to a movie, but she hit a wall. Yes, she knew the truth: the burrito was what stopped her. However, her reasoning to Rick was that she was at the end of her energy after kicking out all week for finals. She told him all she wanted to do was crash and try to catch up on her sleep, so Rick took her back to the very empty dorm.

"What time do your summer school classes start tomorrow?"

Katie groaned. "Do we have to talk about summer school already? Can't I at least sleep off the remains of last semester?"

"Don't you mean the remains of your burrito?"

Katie ignored Rick's comment.

"Call me tomorrow when you get up," he said. Then with a grin he added, "That is, if you feel like you can reach your phone by then."

Katie was too wiped out to even give him a smirk. All she wanted was her bed. And maybe a couple of antacid tablets.

9

As Katie tromped across campus to her art appreciation class at eleven on Monday morning, she still felt full from the burrito.

Note to self: A celebration is only a real celebration when you still feel happy about it the next morning.

Katie's phone chimed, letting her know she had missed a call. She checked and saw that she had missed three calls. Two from Rick that morning, but he hadn't left a message.

It's just as well. He would have asked how I was feeling, and it would have been impossible to lie about my state of fullness.

Katie then listened to the message left by the third caller and perked up. It was Christy. She and Todd were back from their honeymoon.

Katie waited until class was over and she was back in her dorm room before calling Christy.

"Hello? Is this *the* Mrs. Spencer?" Katie quipped.

"It is indeed," Christy said. "How are you?"

"Better."

"Were you sick?"

"No, not really. But I've made a vow never again to eat any burrito that is the size of a small ferret."

"Oh, you went to Casa de Pedro without me!"

"Rick took me yesterday. Hey, are you going to be home for the next hour? I could swing by on my way to work."

"Sure, come over. It'll just be me. Todd isn't home. I'm trying to organize our wedding gifts. We opened all of them last night, and I can barely walk through the maze of boxes."

"I'll bring a machete to help blaze a trail."

"Just bring extra trash bags if you have any. We have an explosion of gift-wrap. Oh, and I bought a little something for you in Hawaii."

"You didn't have to get me anything! You were on your honeymoon, you know."

Christy giggled with a sweet softness. "Yes, I know. But you haven't seen what we bought you so you don't have to thank me yet."

"I hope it's not one of those grass skirts with the coconut top."

Christy went silent on her end. Katie hopped up from the edge of her bed and paced the floor, backpedaling her comment as quickly as she could. "Because, you know, if it is one of those hula skirts, I've always wanted one, but I'm pretty sure they have them here at the Bargain Barn, and I would guess the price would be much better at Bargain Barn than in Hawaii. And besides, since it's always been my dream to have one of those hula girl outfits, well, I don't know if I ever told you this, but I was kind of hoping I could wait and get one when I actually had the chance to go to Hawaii myself. Someday. That way I could buy the complete set, you know? The silk flower lei and the hibiscus for behind the ear and —"

"Katie, you can stop now."

"Thank you. I was running out of breath." Katie rummaged in her closet for a more comfortable pair of shoes to wear to work.

"I have to tell you the story about why we bought the hula skirt."

"Go ahead. I'm going to put you on speaker so I can get ready for work."

"Todd and I saw them in Lahaina at the grocery store, of all places, and I said, 'You know who needs one of these?' and Todd said, 'Katie,' and so we bought it because we both thought of you immediately. We thought it might come in handy next year for all your wild RA-hosted events."

Katie stopped mid-shoe and froze in place. "How did you know about the RA position?"

"Doug told Todd."

"And how did Doug know?"

"From Rick, I would guess."

"This kills me." Katie hopped on one foot to put on her other shoe without unlacing it all the way. "I wanted it to be a big surprise when I told you."

"Just like I thought the grass skirt would be a big surprise for you."

"Oh, well."

"Yes, oh, well. Katie, I think our lives are just too well connected to leave room for many surprises."

"And let's hope it always stays that way. I really missed you, Christy. You should know that it was a challenge for me to make the RA decision without you here to discuss every angle and option."

"You could have called me, you know."

"You were on your honeymoon, remember?"

"Yes, I remember." Christy giggled again

with the same sweetness. "Oh, Katie, it was so —"

"Wait!" Katie interrupted her and reached for the cell phone. Taking the call off speaker, she said, "The direction I think you're heading with this conversation is way too important for us to have it over the phone. I'm coming over right now. See you in a few minutes."

Katie checked the clock on the desk. If she left right now, she would have about forty minutes with Christy before she had to leave for work.

Picking up the pace, Katie hustled out to Baby Hummer. The first thing she saw was a yellow piece of paper under her windshield wiper.

"No! Don't even tell me!" She jumped out and snatched the paper.

"No!" she hollered to the air. "Come on, you guys! It's only the first day of summer school. Give me a chance at least to get to student services and buy my stupid summer parking pass before you fine me the $25!"

Continuing her tirade, she started up the engine of Baby Hummer and gave the gas pedal an extra vavoom. Just ahead on the narrow campus road she spotted a campus security guard in one of the university's puttering golf carts.

"Not so fast, buddy!" Katie laid on her horn, and the guy pulled over. He jumped out of the golf cart as if he were ready to spring into action for an emergency. He spotted Katie getting out of Baby Hummer in a fury, and his expression eased up.

It was Goatee Guy from the wedding reception. He clearly recognized Katie and appeared pleased to see her.

For Katie, the feeling was not mutual.

Waving the yellow slip in the air, she said, "A little grace here, if you don't mind. It's only the first day of classes."

"Is that your Thing?" He still was grinning.

"Yes, that's my vintage, classic, 1978 Volkswagen Thing, and yes, she is a beaut. Now about this ticket. Don't you think this is a bit premature? The day is barely half over. If today is the deadline, which I'm not sure it is, then I still have half a day to renew my parking pass."

"The cutoff was noon today. But sure, go ahead. Take the ticket over to Student Services."

Katie took her vigor down a notch. "Okay. So, you're saying they'll cancel the ticket if I go over there now?"

"Can't say for sure, but you could try."

"How about if I pay for my pass tomorrow morning? First thing. As soon as the offices open. I'll be there with the money in my hot little hand."

Goatee Guy tilted his head and listened as if everything Katie was saying mattered. "You can try paying tomorrow if you want, but you would be better off settling it today. I was told to start ticketing all unregistered student vehicles after twelve o'clock."

"Let me guess." Katie punched both her fists into her hips and gave him an exasperated squint. "Today is your first day on the job."

The noncommittal expression on his face gave away the answer.

"Come on, one more day. That's all I'm asking."

He seemed unaffected. "I'm not the one to make those decisions."

Katie snorted. She meant just to make a huffing sort of sound, but an unflattering snort was what came out.

"Fine," she declared, trying to restore whatever dignity she could manage. "It's your job, right? And you've gotta do your job no matter how you rank in the Mr. Congeniality Contest, right?"

"The Mr. what?"

"Mr. Congeniality," she repeated as a driver in a car behind Baby Hummer honked. Katie turned to see that she had left her door open, making it impossible for the vehicle to pull around her.

"It means . . . oh, never mind." Katie jumped in her car and drove off toward the Student Services office. She looked one more time in her rearview mirror and saw that Goatee Guy still was staring at her, watching her go.

"Take a picture. It lasts longer, buddy."

Katie hit number two on her cell phone, Christy's speed-dial number. Their reunion would have to wait until after work. She wasn't happy about that. Nor was she happy about the detour she had to take to Student Services.

Zooming down the hill away from campus half an hour later, Katie thought, *I am such a fraud! Here I make all these noble statements about how I love people, want to work with people, and study how to solve problems in humanity, and then I make a scene with some guy I don't even know. What is my problem?*

Then, because she didn't have an answer for her question, Katie turned up the music on her car radio and peeled into her parking space at the Dove's Nest fifteen minutes late. She entered through the back door. Rick looked up as if he was going to say something. His expression wasn't good.

Before he could speak, Katie hijacked the conversation. "I know, I know, don't say anything. I have a legitimate reason for being late. Several legitimate reasons, as a matter of fact, starting with a parking ticket that still makes me want to scream."

Rick looked surprised. He paused before saying, "I'm sure all your reasons are legit, Katie. They always are."

"Always?" she echoed. Her irritable edge escalated. She was ready to pick a fight right here, right now. "Always, Rick? Did you say always?"

Rick's jaw clenched. "Katie . . ." he glanced over the top of her head. She was aware that another employee had come within hearing distance of them. She knew how adamant Rick was about keeping the conversations at work limited to business topics and to save all their personal discussions for later.

At that moment Katie could stop blaming the burrito for her irritability. She didn't need to check a calendar to figure out why all her emotions were right on the surface.

Aware that the other employee was still behind them waiting for Rick's attention, Katie scrambled to backpedal yet another time that day. No way was she going to spend the rest of her shift with unresolved tension with Rick.

"Hey, just erase that comment, okay? I'm a little edgy today. Okay, not a little. A lot. I'm very edgy. I shouldn't have spouted off like that."

Impulsively, she put her arms around Rick's torso, pressed her cheek to his chest, and gave him a hug. "Sorry."

The slightly stunned and not-so-happy look on Rick's face told Katie she had made a poor decision. Again. Katie didn't understand why a little hug should be such a big deal. Everyone who worked there knew they were almost a couple. Why couldn't she give him a quick hug? Would her actions shock Carlos? Certainly not.

Rick looked over Katie's head again at the waiting employee. "Did you need something?"

Katie turned to see not Carlos but Carley. Carley wearing a Dove's Nest apron.

"Sorry to bother you guys." Carley's airy voice flitted in their direction like a dragonfly. "Carlos wanted me to tell you, Rick, that ants are under the sink again."

Rick bristled. He moved past Katie and Carley, looking as if he were on his way to punch a wall.

Katie stared at the new employee. "So,

Carley, when did you start working here?"

"Today. Rick was so nice when I came in and applied last week. This is so perfect. If I didn't get this job I would have had to move back to Texas for the summer, and I really didn't want to do that. Rick is the best, isn't he?"

"Yeah, I've pretty much always thought that."

"Always," Carley repeated with a calculating grin. "You said 'always' again. That must be your word today." She turned and walked away.

Now Katie wanted to punch something. She retreated to the restroom and tried the cool-paper-towel-on-the-back-of-the-neck trick. It calmed her down a few notches. Returning to duty, she tied on a clean apron and spent the rest of her shift trying very hard to keep her mouth shut. More importantly, she tried even harder to keep her mind shut. She didn't need to give space to the hurtful feelings that Carley's appearance had ignited. What she needed to do was calm way down.

She had picked up on Rick's choice of the word "always" because of a big argument they had had many months ago. Katie had picked the fight. A huge one. To her surprise, Rick was up to the challenge. He met her verbal blow for verbal blow. In many ways that argument was a breakthrough for them. They saw they could both be at their lowest point, take it out on each other, and still come away wanting the relationship to continue.

Katie couldn't even remember now what the argument was about. But she did remember that afterwards they had agreed not to throw assumptions at each other or to throw the words "always" or "never" into their disagreements. That Carley had thrown the word back at Katie was too much to swallow.

Rick must have hired Carley for a good reason. Katie needed to trust him and believe that his rationale was logical and solid.

That's the real problem right there, isn't it? You keep waiting for a reason not to trust Rick and his decisions. Katie expelled that thought as quickly as she could. Her thoughts, as well as her emotions, were out of whack.

As the afternoon continued, Rick was too busy managing the ant problem to pay attention to Katie as she and Carlos prepared sandwiches, pizzas, and a lot of salad-and-sandwich combos. She watched Rick from across the back room and decided that anger wasn't a good look on him. She couldn't remember seeing his face so tight. His dark eyebrows seemed to be slanted permanently inward as if they were ready to slide forward, aimed for a head-on crash on the bridge of his nose. The worst part was the way he wouldn't make eye contact with anyone.

At least it's not just me. I'm not the only one he's shutting out.

Rick had plenty of work-related reasons to be stressed. But Katie's being late and snappy with him shouldn't be enough to send him this far into Grumpsville.

If he's choosing to stay this mad all night just because I was late or because I hugged him and shouldn't have, then maybe he and I have a few other issues we need to resolve.

Nine o'clock came, and Katie clocked out. Instead of leaving, though, she lingered, waiting for a chance to talk with Rick. He was on the phone, and she could tell he was talking with his brother or his dad.

Rick said, "Hang on just a second." Putting down the phone, he looked at Katie and said in his unemotional manager's voice, "Did you need something?"

"Yeah, I think we should talk."

"Okay, I'll talk to you later."

She nodded but didn't add any words to

the end of their conversation. That, she decided, was a good thing. Her mouth was way too unreliable today. Better to leave this day the way it was without any further foibles.

After making her way out to Baby Hummer, Katie kept the window rolled down to air out her frazzled emotions as she drove to Todd and Christy's apartment. She and Rick had a long history of fresh starts. Tomorrow could be one more of those for them. A "mercy morning" she had labeled them a few months ago. Her theory was that if God could mercifully start fresh with us every morning, why couldn't we start fresh with others and ourselves as well?

Significantly calmed by the time she arrived at the apartment complex, Katie made sure she parked in the visitor's section behind the apartments so as not to invite another ticket at the end of the long day.

Rick's apartment was in the same complex, but she knew he wouldn't be home until after ten. Maybe they could talk then instead of waiting until tomorrow. Katie hated waiting. They could air out everything tonight, and the pieces would fall back into place. Their relationship and their communication would be back on the right track.

Heading down the concrete walkway past Rick's apartment, Katie thought of how she and Rick had walked this trail the day before, lugging Max behind them. Their time together on Sunday had been great. Why was today so awful?

Despite all her positive "mercy" and "fresh start" thoughts, Katie felt the edginess return as she stopped on Christy's doorstep and drew in a deep breath. She told all her rattled feelings to cool it as she rang the doorbell.

No one answered.

She rang the doorbell again. When that failed to produce anyone, Katie stood there, chewing on her lower lip, wondering if she should try to call or just leave. She looked down and noticed that the pot of daisies she and Christy had put there two weeks ago was still alive, even though no one had been home to water the little smilers for the past eight days.

Katie made one last attempt to gain entrance; this time she pounded at the door with her fist.

10

Christy's voice answered from the other side of the closed door. "Who is it?"

"The big bad wolf," Katie popped off. "Open up or I'll —"

The door swung open, and Christy said, "You scared me."

"I've been doing that to everybody today. Sorry."

"No, it's just that I'm not used to this apartment yet, and your pounding really echoed."

"I rang the doorbell a couple of times."

"That's one of several things we've discovered doesn't work. I've started a list for the landlord. Come in!"

Katie stepped inside and gave Christy a hello hug, but her gaze was fixed on the abundance of boxes all over the floor. "You weren't kidding about the maze of gifts. Man, I guess it pays to have a big wedding. Look at all this great stuff!"

The last time Katie was in the apartment, she and Christy had tried to find a way to make the space feel homey with Christy and Todd's sparcer-than-sparce assortment of worldly possessions. At that point all Christy and Todd owned was a bookshelf, a bed, and an ultra-funky "couch" Todd had made. He crafted his one-of-a-kind couch out of the backseat of his now defunct VW bus, Gus, and his beloved orange surfboard, Naranja. When Todd gave Christy the gem before they were married, she had tried to find a place to put it in the dorm room. She and Katie called it "Narangus" after the two patron suppliers of the art parts. The chair looked cool, but it was nearly impossible to find a comfortable way to sit on it.

Narangus was still in its prime position by the wall in the living room area, but now it was flanked by standing floor lamps with price tags hanging from their shades. Sitting on Narangus was one of the many gifts still in a box.

"Is that an ice cream maker?" Katie asked.

"Yes, it is. We received two of those. And four blenders and two waffle makers. We registered, but I think the system went down for a day or something because my mom said the lists didn't update to show people what had been purchased."

"You can easily exchange the stuff, can't you?"

Christy nodded. "First I'm trying to take an inventory to see what we have and what we still need."

"It looks like you were serious about needing trash bags for the gift-wrap." Katie stepped over to a stack of folded gift-wrap that came up to her knees. "Or are you saving this to wallpaper your bedroom?"

"We have enough to wallpaper the whole apartment," Christy said. "But the paper needs to go."

Christy shuffled through a stack of plastic bags and handed one of them to Katie. "I was going to wrap this for you out of the abundance of wrapping paper options, but you already know what it is."

Katie opened the bag and pulled out the celebrated grass skirt and coconut top. The set even came with a plastic orange hibiscus. "Now this is classic," Katie said. "I don't think it could be any cheesier. I love it!"

"Try it on."

"Now?"

"You and I are the only ones here. Put it on over your clothes."

Katie fumbled to untangle the ties and to adjust the coconut top. "Please don't tell me anyone in Hawaii actually wears this sort of get-up."

"The hula dancers wear a more sophisticated version at the luaus," Christy said.

"With the coconut top and everything?"

Christy nodded. "If you have the right size coconuts, it's actually more modest than a bikini top."

"I don't think I have the right size coconuts," Katie said. "And that comment doesn't leave this room, by the way."

Christy giggled.

Katie turned around to reveal a big gap in the back where the grass skirt didn't make it all the way around her waist. "Feelin' a bit breezy back there. Is this a Hawaiian hospital gown or something?"

Christy picked up the wrapper. "Oh, no! Katie, I'm so sorry!"

"What?"

"This is a child-sized set. I'm so bummed. I thought Todd picked up the adult size."

"You let Todd pick this out?"

"I was in line buying the groceries."

"Yeah, that would explain a lot. Here's my suggestion. Don't let Todd pick out any clothing for you from here on out."

"I'm so bummed!"

"I'm not. This is hilarious," Katie said. "Besides, the flower is definitely one-size-fits-all." She snatched up the plastic hibiscus and stuck it behind her ear. When she did, the artificial stamen fell out and did a triple flip on its way to the floor.

Katie and Christy both looked at the caterpillar-like piece of plastic. They turned to each other and burst out laughing.

"It's the thought that counts," Katie said. "That you and Todd thought of me makes this gift special."

"You're being pretty gracious," Christy said.

"Yes, I am. And now to demonstrate my graciousness, I will perform for you and you alone a very special dance rarely seen anywhere this side of the islands." Katie wiggled her hips, swished her hands, and shook her head while humming a string of notes that didn't seem to enjoy being strung together.

Christy laughed so hard she had to sit down.

Katie finished with a toe forward bow and looked at her best friend. Christy wiped the giggle-tears out of her eyes.

"That had to be the worst hula ever," Christy said.

"You're mean."

"No, I'm not. I'm being honest. And here's the thing. I really did try, Katie. I tried to find something to bring back for you that would be fun. After that demonstration, I'd say I succeeded."

"You did. You succeeded stupendously. Thanks. Or do I say *'aloha'*?"

"If you're trying to say thank you in Hawaiian, you say *'mahalo.'* " Christy sounded like an expert.

Katie tried to repeat *mahalo,* and Christy smiled.

That's when Katie noticed what Christy was wearing. She had on shorts and one of Todd's standard, navy blue, hooded sweatshirts with the sleeves pushed up. Her skin bore the golden glow of someone who had just spent a week in the tropics. Her long, nutmeg brown hair was pulled up in a clip with the ends doing their own thing in a happy imitation of a palm-fronds-in-the-breeze dance.

The corners of Katie's mouth curled up in a wistful grin.

"What?"

"You're married, Christy."

Christy's glowy skin rose to an even higher level. "I know."

"So, Mrs. Spencer?"

"So?"

"So, do tell all."

Christy gleamed. Her blue-green eyes grew soft around the corners. "Being married is wonderful."

"And . . ."

A demure, knowing smile was the only response Katie received. The woman had a few secrets, and she was keeping them safe and sound in the corner of her heart.

Lowering herself to the open spot on Narangus next to the ice cream maker, Katie adjusted the grass skirt she still was wearing and leaned back. "I'm not asking for the . . . you know . . . intimate details. I just want to know, from your married-woman mouth to my virgin-woman ears, what's it like on the other side? Tell me the purity part of it isn't a hoax. I need to know that what I'm saving for my future husband is worth the wait."

"Oh, it's worth the wait, all right. Definitely." Christy's glowy blush was now enlivened with an expression of wide-eyed wonder and satisfaction. "It is oh-so-worth the wait, Katie. Trust me on this one."

Katie never had seen her friend so vibrant. Vibrant yet tranquil. If innocence rewarded had an expression, Katie was looking at it.

"You look pretty happy, Chris."

"I am deliriously happy." Christy moved the ice cream maker and sat on the other end of Narangus.

Christy's expression was enough to make

Katie believe in her own abstinence decisions all over again. Katie wasn't entirely inexperienced when it came to guys, but she had changed the path she was headed down when she broke up with Michael in high school. Looking at her friend now, Katie felt all her hope renewed that she might one day return from her honeymoon and be as glowy as Christy.

"You know all those thousands and thousands of kisses you've been saving, Katie? Well, you keep saving those kisses. You will be so glad you did. Because there you'll be, on the other side of the longing, and you'll be a married woman, free to break open the bank and . . . well . . ." Christy's expression changed. She now had the look of a woman who wore a veil of confidentiality.

"Well?" Katie prodded. "Finish your sentence."

Christy thought for a moment. "You know what? I think I'll let you finish that sentence for yourself. On your honeymoon."

They sat in silence looking at each other, blinking and gazing and saying nothing.

A small giggle escaped from someplace deep inside of Christy.

"What?"

"I was just thinking of something a woman in Lahaina said to me when Todd and I bought our bedspread. Come here, you have to see our new bedspread. It's a handmade Hawaiian quilt. We used some of our wedding money to buy it. The pattern is breadfruit."

Katie followed Christy through the maze of boxed gifts into the bedroom. On the bed was spread a beautiful quilt in shades of soft turquoise, brown, and cream. The connecting leaf and bulb-shaped pattern made no sense to Katie, but then she had no idea what a breadfruit was.

"This is what the woman said to me." Christy reached for a slip of paper on the dresser and read to Katie in halting words, " *'Nana no a ka 'ulu I paki kepau.'* "

"Easy for you to say," Katie spoofed.

Christy grinned. "It means 'Go for the gummy breadfruit.' "

Katie let out a guffaw. "I think I understood it better in Hawaiian! Did this sage seller of breadfruit bedspreads explain what she meant?"

"Yes, of course. Breadfruit grows on trees in Hawaii the way peaches grow on a tree. Only the breadfruits can get as large and round as a grapefruit, or even as large as a basketball. The Hawaiians can tell the breadfruit is mature and ready to pick when it turns 'gummy.' "

"Gummy," Katie repeated. "Like a gummy bear?"

Christy laughed. "That's exactly what I said when the woman at the quilt store was explaining this to us. She said the older Hawaiian women would tell the young women to look for a man who was 'gummy,' meaning he was mature and ready to be picked. That's when I turned to Todd and told him he was my gummy bear, and I was glad I picked him."

Katie covered her face with her hands.

"I know," Christy said. "That's what Todd did too. But think about it, Katie. It's true. Love ripens. It really does. And when it's ripe, that's how you know it's time to pick. Not before it's ripe."

"Is that what the woman in the shop told you?"

"No, that's just what I think. The woman at the shop said she thought we were a beautiful couple and circled with aloha."

"And she obviously thought you were beautiful enough to buy her bedspread," Katie quipped. "As well as aloha-savvy enough to carry home the secret proverb of the gummy breadfruit."

They laughed together and Christy asked, "Do you want something to drink?"

"Sure."

Katie couldn't help but apply Christy's Hawaiian folklore to her unstable feelings about Rick. If what they felt for each other was love, Katie knew it wasn't ripe yet. As much as she hated to admit it, the best thing they could do was to keep hanging around together like a couple of ungummy breadfruits on a tree.

Katie considered saying all this to Christy, but her friend was so buoyant that Katie wanted to hold back her relationship woes and just bask in the freshness of Christy's ripe and tender love.

"We have juice and bottled water," Christy said as they picked their way back through the living room labyrinth into the tiny kitchen.

"Here's a question," Katie said. "Where are you going to put all those groovy new appliances?"

"I don't know. We didn't think of that when we registered for these handy gadgets. When you have nothing, the opportunity to be given so many new things is appealing. Then when you get all the stuff and have no place to put it, the appreciation dwindles. That's why I'm making a list of everything and trying to decide what we really need. Right now, what we need the most is rent money. Our next payment is due in twelve

days, and neither of us has a paycheck coming for two weeks."

"You're bursting my bubble about how
dreamy you just said married life is."

Christy looked up at Katie from over the
top of the open refrigerator door. "Oh, it's
still dreamy. It's just expensive. Did you say
water or orange juice?"

"I'll have some O.J." Then Katie realized
water would cost less than the orange juice,
and in an effort to help conserve her friends'
resources, she said, "No, make that water
instead."

"Ice?"

"No, this is fine. Thanks."

"So, tell me about the RA job and how all
that happened."

They sat at the two chairs tucked under
the round kitchen table. Katie still was
wearing her hula skirt outfit and made a
comical attempt to maneuver the open part
around to the side so she could cross her
legs.

"You can take that off, you know," Christy
said.

"It's way more fun keeping it on." Katie
told Christy how Julia approached her at
the wedding right after Todd and Christy
drove off in the limo.

"Wait." Katie stopped her story mid-sentence. "Speaking of the limo, before I tell you anything else, you have to tell me about the letters!"

Christy reached across the table and grabbed Katie's wrist. "Oh, Katie, you saved the day. You know that, don't you? I couldn't believe what those guys did. You saved my honeymoon!"

"I'm not sure you should go that far."

"No, seriously, Katie. Did I say thank you already? I don't think I did. Thank you so, so much. You are the best, Katie. Really."

"So, did you give Todd the letters that night?"

"No, I waited until the next evening." She smiled.

"And?"

"It was perfect. The moment was as wonderful as I ever dreamed it would be. We made dinner at the condo and ate by candlelight out on the lanai."

"Lanai? Is that like a patio?" Katie asked.

"Yes. Uncle Bob's condo is on the sixth floor so the lanai is more like a balcony, and it faces the ocean. It was a perfect night. And the perfect location. Todd and I sat on that same lanai on the night of my sixteenth birthday. That night we looked at the lights on the neighboring island of Molokai, and Todd told me that our future was like those lights. We wouldn't know what was out there until we got close enough to see the details. Then we would know what to do and which way to go. That night, when I was sixteen, he said we should just keep moving forward toward what we could see."

Christy sighed contentedly. "There we were, five years later, sitting on that same lanai, and I was watching my true love read my letters to him by candlelight. Katie, it was perfect. Perfect in every way. Todd cried, and I cried, and all the while the lights across the water on Molokai winked back at us. It was as if they knew we would be back, and they waited for us, under the Maui moon."

"You're killin' me! What a romantic, romantic, romantic moment."

"I know. And Katie, if you hadn't come running to the limo with the letters, we would have lost that moment. So, again, thank you. Thanks for being such a wonderful best friend."

Since she hadn't grown up receiving much affirmation, Katie still found it difficult to take a compliment and just receive it. Her usual response was to make a joke or brush it off.

Unable to let the praise simply sit on her, Katie said, "Well, I'm glad you feel that way because I'm going to need a reference for my new job application."

"Do you mean the RA position? I thought you already had the job."

"This is a different job. It's a side job. I'm applying to be a wedding saver. I must be able to leap over large crowds to catch tumbling bouquets as well as chase limousines wearing only one shoe. Just your basic superhero powers. You will vouch for me, won't you?"

"Any time." Christy grinned. "I didn't hear about the missing shoe, though."

"Oh, yeah. The Cinderella look when running from a party adds to the romantic ambience."

"I think you should stick with the RA position. That job will require enough superhuman strength. Tell me more about what happened. You said you talked to Julia at the wedding and then what?"

Katie rolled out the details that led to her decision to take the RA position and included the part about calling her mom.

"What did she say when you told her?" Christy asked.

"Let's see, she said I should have applied for a janitorial position instead. And my Aunt Mabel passed away."

"Oh, Katie, I'm sorry to hear that."

"Me, too, but I didn't even know I had an Aunt Mabel. My mom never had met her either. But you know, if I called home more often, I would know about Mabel and about the bathroom sink."

"What about the bathroom sink?"

"It backed up."

"Oh."

"It's fine now. Thanks for asking. And as far as my being an RA, well, that news just didn't exactly rock her world."

Christy didn't need to say anything. Her sympathetic expression was enough. Katie had tried to keep a lot of her home life disappointments from being topics of conversation with Christy over the years. Nevertheless, Katie knew that Christy understood some of the voids in Katie's heart.

"What about Rick? What did he have to say about your getting the position?" Christy asked.

"He's okay with it. He's been supportive."

"Are you guys still in the floaty place?"

"By that do you mean is our relationship still undefined? Yes. Today was a pretty awful day for both of us, though, so ask me where we are again tomorrow."

"What happened at work?"

Just then the front door of the apartment opened, and Todd entered. He looked more

151

bronzed than Christy, which was expected since Katie was sure Todd had done as much surfing as possible while they were in Maui. His short blond hair had turned lighter in the tropical sunshine.

Todd looked at Christy with a half grin. Then he noticed Katie and tilted his head, taking in the hula costume she still had on over her jeans and T-shirt.

"News flash, Big Kahuna," Katie said. "One size does not fit all."

Todd gave her a chin-up gesture and brushed the topic aside. "Hey, how's Rick doing?"

"Okay. Why?"

Todd looked at her more intently. "Did you see him today?"

"Of course. At work. Why?"

"Did he tell you?"

"Tell me what?"

Todd looked at Christy. "I didn't have time to tell you yet. Rick called me when I was at the church office this afternoon. He came home from work to check on Max, and something was wrong with him."

"With Max or with Rick?" Katie asked.

"Max. He wasn't moving, and he was having a hard time breathing. Rick called and asked me to come over to help him lift Max into the car."

"What was wrong with him?"

Todd shrugged. "Don't know. We took him to the vet and carried him in, but by then it was obvious Max wasn't going to make it."

Katie's jaw went slack.

"Did the vet put Max down?" Christy asked.

"He didn't have to. Max just went on his own. Rick took it pretty hard. His family has had that dog for a long time. The vet said Max was something like ninety years old in dog years. The move from the Escondido house to Rick's place could have been too much for him."

"That's so sad," Christy said. If she said anything else, Katie didn't hear it. She already had jumped out of her chair and was going for where she left her car keys. In a spurt, she blasted out the door, leaving a flying grass skirt behind in her wake.

11

Running through the apartment complex, Katie felt the string on her coconut top snap. Both halves of the coconut flew off in opposite directions and went rolling down the walkway. She didn't stop to pick them up.

Oh, man! How could I have been so insensitive to Rick? He wasn't angry. He was sad about Max. Why didn't he tell me? Or did he try to tell me, but I was too quick to defend myself because I thought he was going to say I was late for work? Why didn't I see that something really was bothering him?

Katie arrived at the Dove's Nest just as Rick was walking to his car. He was the last one to leave the cafe. She jumped out of Baby Hummer and hurried over to him. Rick saw her coming and stood by his car door.

"Todd just told me," Katie said. "About Max, I mean. Rick, I'm so sorry."

Rick nodded but didn't say anything.

Slipping her arms around Rick's middle, Katie gave him the same sort of cuddly hug she had given him earlier that evening in the kitchen of the Dove's Nest. This time Rick responded immediately. He drew her close and rested his cheek on the crown of her head. His chest seemed to shudder involuntarily, as he took in a deep breath and slowly let it out.

Is he crying?

They stood together in the empty parking lot for a lingering stretch of closeness. Rick drew in his breath and straightened up, pulling back from their embrace.

"Rick, I'm sorry I was insensitive."

"Don't worry about it. You didn't know. It seemed like we both were having a rough day."

"You can say that again."

"It seemed like we both were having a rough day," he repeated.

Katie drew back and looked at his expression in the radiance of the parking lot's overhead light. "Was that a joke? Did you just make a joke?"

Rick shrugged, his lips turned up in the first half-grin she had seen all day.

Katie smiled back at him. "Do you want to get something to eat or some coffee or something?"

Instead of answering, Rick looked at her more closely. "What do you have behind your ear?"

Katie reached for the piece of orange plastic. She touched it and decided to leave it right where it was. Brushing her hair back casually, she said, "It's a hibiscus, of course."

"Of course."

"The yellow part in the middle fell out, so that might have impaired your ability to recognize this work of art."

"Should I ask why you have part of a plastic flower behind your ear?"

"It was a gift from an admirer," Katie said with a twinkle in her eye.

"An admirer, huh?" Rick seemed to enjoy the banter as much as Katie.

"Two admirers, actually. Todd and Christy. This is what they brought me from Maui. There were other parts of the hula girl outfit, but I seem to have lost them on my way here."

Rick's grin grew so that even in the dim light Katie could see how much his affection for her was coming out at the moment. "Katie, you . . ."

"What?"

"I don't have a word to describe you. You

amaze me." He paused. "I . . ."

Katie felt her face blush. *Is he about to say that he loves me? Here? Now?*

"Katie, do you have any idea how gorgeous you look right now in this light?" Rick said in a low voice.

What does that mean? Is he talking mushy or does he really mean it? Goofy flower and all, am I really gorgeous to him? Oh, Katie, stop trying to ruin the moment. Just relax!

Rick took her hands in his, lacing his strong fingers between hers.

"Maybe you're right," he said.

"Right about what?"

"Maybe we have been in the slow lane long enough. It could be time for a lane change, like you said."

Katie felt her heart pick up its pace. Her thoughts collided in a swirl. She heard Christy's voice saying, "You won't regret saving all those kisses." At the same time, she heard herself saying, "This is what you've been waiting for!" On top of those voices she heard Carley's voice: "He is your boyfriend, isn't he?"

"Whoa. This is rare," Rick said, letting go of her hands. "What's wrong?"

"Nothing. I'm . . ."

"You're thinking," he said. "Which means you aren't ready."

"I thought I was. Just maybe give me a minute to . . ."

"No, you're not ready to make a decision. If you were ready, we wouldn't be talking right now."

Katie knew what they would be doing instead. They would be sharing a kiss. A long-awaited, lane-changing, entering-the-next-phase-of-their-relationship kiss. Instead, they were hedging toward an argument.

"How do you know?" she asked Rick.

"Whenever you dissect a moment like this down to the last molecule, Katie, I know you haven't made a decision. Your best decisions are your spontaneous ones. I know this because I know you. You're an open book."

"Well, you're an enigma of legendary proportions."

"Where did that come from?"

Katie was regretting what had just popped out of her mouth. Her words had gotten her into so much trouble today. "What I meant is that you're private with your feelings and with what's going on with you."

"I know what an enigma means."

"All I'm saying is that if I'm an open book, you're a locked-up chest." She added, "But a treasure chest," in an effort to make her assessment more flattering.

"I can't believe you're trying to pick a fight."

"You think this is a fight? This isn't a fight."

"Then what is it?"

"It's a nothing," Katie said. "Let's drop it."

"It's something. What are you upset about? You must have something on your mind." His voice no longer carried the buttery warmth that had made her blush a moment ago.

"Okay. Maybe I'm still upset over your not telling me about Max. Or that you didn't tell me you hired Carley to take my place."

Rick leaned back, his chin turned up to the dark sky. "Is that what you want to fight about? You want to fight about my hiring Carley so she wouldn't have to go back to Arizona for the summer?"

"Texas," Katie corrected him.

"Okay, Texas. Fine. So go ahead. Let's fight about it."

"All I'm saying is that I thought it would have been nice if you would have told me you hired her instead of waiting for me to mess things up and hug you in front of her. I mean, I'm sure you had a good reason for hiring her, but —"

"Katie. She didn't want to go back to Texas for the summer because she has a boyfriend here. She wanted to be around him for the summer."

"She does?"

"That's what she told me."

"I didn't know she had a boyfriend. Who is he?"

"I don't know. The standard job application doesn't have a line that says, 'Fill in name of boyfriend here.' "

Katie looked down at her feet. She was beginning to feel cold in the night air. "I think I overreacted. Again. Not the first time I did that today."

"As for your being embarrassed about someone seeing you hug me at work, well you were the one who overstepped the boundary there. So how can you put that back on me?"

"I know. You're right. I apologize for that."

"As long as I'm getting everything out, and you don't want me to hide my feelings from you, I was going to tell you about Max, but I didn't have a chance." Rick's voice rose perceptibly.

"More like you couldn't get a word in edgewise," Katie said.

"Exactly. So now you know. This has been

a pretty intense day, and I can't believe you're not crying right now." His voice went up another octave.

"Should I be crying?"

"Most girls would be crying by now. I'm standing here yelling at you, and you're just taking it."

"So? I'm not like most girls."

"I know you're not. We haven't had a fight in a long time. I forgot how strong you could be sometimes." Rick's tone was mellowing.

"The things you're saying are true, Rick. I can take truth. I just can't take a lot of silence. I go crazy when I don't know what's going on. I make up stuff, and that's when I make myself cry."

Rick let out a huff and ran his fingers through the side of his dark, wavy hair. "I can't believe I'm going to say this, but it feels really good to fight with you."

"It does?"

He drew in a deep breath. "I have to be so polite all day to everyone, but now with you I can . . ."

"What? Be true to who you really are? Be normal?"

"Yeah." Rick nodded. "I can be myself around you, and you don't get mad or cry or tell me where to go."

"I could tell you where to go, if that would make you feel better."

Rick smiled. "You know what, Katie?" His voice lowered, and his eyes fixed on her green eyes. "I'm going to compliment you now, and I want you to just take it. Don't say anything. Just take this. Katie, you are an amazing, one-of-a-kind woman."

"Oh, you just figured that out, did you?"

Rick put his hand over her mouth.

"Shhh. Just listen, okay? Don't smart-talk your way out of this."

Katie nodded.

He smiled and continued with his hand over her mouth. "When I'm with you, I feel like my life is on track. I feel like I can be myself. I feel like you can be yourself around me too. Do you know how rare that is?" Realizing he was keeping her from responding to his question, Rick said, "Just nod."

Katie nodded.

"Here's what I like about you. You're genuine. Your temper doesn't bother me. I kind of appreciate it. Your honesty gives me the freedom to be honest with you. Ours is the best relationship I've ever had with a girl. Do you realize that? You're my friend, my co-worker, and my . . ."

Katie kept quiet even though Rick had

lowered his hand and her lips were free to speak. If he couldn't bring himself to say that she was his "girlfriend" spontaneously, then she wasn't going to try to pry it out of him. She looked down. Maybe they were still "ungummy" in their love. Maybe that's why she had hesitated earlier.

Rick tenderly brushed her hair off her forehead and drew her gaze back up to his chocolate eyes. "Hey, listen, this is what I know is true. You rock my world, Katie. You know that, don't you? You are amazing and beautiful, and if you want me to start calling you my girlfriend, then I think I'm ready to do that."

A pair of happy tears skidded down Katie's cheeks.

Rick smiled. "Oh, so now you cry."

As happy as she was to hear him finally say the word "girlfriend," it brushed over Katie that his words weren't spontaneous.

He placed both his hands under her chin and dabbed each tear with his thumbs. "You are the red-headed woman of my dreams. Katie Weldon, do you want to be my girlfriend?"

Katie looked into Rick's eyes. She had longed for this sort of declaration from him, but now that it had come to her, she didn't know what to do with it. If Rick was right

163

about her truest decisions being her spontaneous ones, then she knew she wasn't ready to make this decision.

"Not yet," she said.

Rick drew back. "Are you serious?"

Katie nodded. "I'm not ready for us to be official."

Now Rick was the one who wasn't speaking.

"Don't get me wrong, Rick. I'm crazy about you too. I'm not going anywhere. I'm just thinking about how safe it is in the slow lane, and how we probably should stay there just a little longer."

"A little longer," he repeated.

"Am I driving you crazy?" Katie asked.

"Always," he said. Then catching himself in light of Katie's reaction when he used the term "always" to her at work, Rick added, "Look, this is crazy. We said we wouldn't rush anything in our relationship, and we haven't. I can wait. You can take down your deflector shields. I'm not going to kiss you. Not now. I want to. I almost did earlier. But I'm not going to. There. Now you know what I'm thinking. Mystery solved. I am no longer an enigma to you. At least not one of legendary proportions."

His final sentence made it clear to Katie that he wasn't too exasperated. Just enough.

It would be good to leave things right where they were and not try to continue this conversation. Especially not in the parking lot.

"Here's the thing, though, Katie. And this is going to be a non-negotiable for me. I don't want to keep having this conversation. I don't want to keep going back and forth. We'll drive each other crazy. I think we should just be what we are now through the rest of the summer, without having to declare any official titles, okay? This is what works."

"Okay. You're right. As nebulous as this is, somehow it does work. At least most of the time. Slow-lane summer. Okay. Fine."

"Fine," Rick repeated.

They stood awkwardly for a moment, neither of them initiating the next gesture. Katie suspected Rick was feeling the same thing she was. As soon as they established they were going to take things slow, Katie wanted to kiss him more than ever. She leaned her head against his shoulder, and Rick wrapped both his arms around her.

"I'll see you tomorrow." He gave her a final squeeze and let go.

Katie got in her car and waved as they parted ways. "Self-control is highly over-rated," she muttered.

The only thing that kept her driving back to her dorm and not turning around and following Rick to his apartment was the echo of her visit with Christy. Yes, Christy had said all the right things, being the ideal candidate for the now-married-but-once-abstinent poster child. But it wasn't Christy's words that ricocheted through Katie's heart at the moment. It was Christy's look. It was the glow. Katie was willing to be exasperated on nights like this, if she knew that all the waiting would one day make her glow like that.

12

As awkward as Katie and Rick's conversation in the parking lot had been, all was well in the land of Katieness. She and Rick were back in their "floaty" place, as Christy called it. And it was okay. It was familiar and stabilizing. Katie even stopped thinking of their rhythm as being a rut. For them, for now, this is what worked.

Katie reminded herself of that truth as her days of summer school and work fell into a steady pattern. She developed an appreciation for days without drama.

Then, on a Friday morning the last week of June, Katie woke to the musical chime on her cell phone indicating she had a text message waiting. Tumbling out of bed, she went over to her desk and picked up her recharging phone. The message was simple.

IT'S A BOY!

Sometime in the night Doug and Tracy's baby Daniel had made his grand entrance into the world. Katie texted back one word: AWESOME!

She laughed aloud and tried to call Doug. When his voice message came on, she said, "Hey! I'm just calling to add my happy hooray for you guys. Call me when you get a chance."

Next she tried Christy's cell phone. Todd answered.

"I talked to Doug about half an hour ago," Todd said. "Trace is doing great, and Daniel is doing even better. They went to the hospital at 10:30 last night, and Daniel was born at 7:30 this morning. I guess that's pretty good for a first baby."

"How much did he weigh?" Katie asked.

"Something like 14–7. Does that sound right?"

Katie laughed. "It was probably more like seven pounds and fourteen ounces."

"Yeah, that could be it. Doug said he has long fingers, so it looks like we're going to have another guitar player in the family."

Todd's comment brought a smile to Katie. Todd's family situation was dicey like Katie's. That he referred to Doug, Tracy, and Daniel as "family" affirmed the sense that Katie had about her Christian friends. While her parents had dropped passively out of her life, Katie's God-Lover friends had filled the gap.

"Are you guys going to the hospital today to see them?" Katie asked.

"We're thinking about it."

"I want to go with you, if you do."

"Sounds good. I'll tell my bride when she gets out of the shower. Why don't the two of you set up a time?"

His bride. How sweet.

Katie made sure she arrived at the Dove's Nest early. She and Christy worked in the same building, but Christy was in the bookstore. They saw each other less than they thought they would each day, spending their working hours about fifty feet away from each other but separated by a pizza oven, a wall, and two shelves of children's books.

On this particular day, Katie and Christy had their lunch breaks scheduled for the same time. Instead of meeting in the break room at the back of the Dove's Nest as they usually did, Katie convinced Christy to slip outside into the warm afternoon and drive three blocks to a small deli. She hoped this would allow them the freedom to talk without interruption.

As Christy ordered a roast beef sandwich for the two of them to split, Katie checked her phone. A smile lit up her face when she saw the waiting message.

"What are you smiling about?" Christy asked, returning to the table with their food.

"Did you check your phone lately?" Katie said. "Look, Doug sent a picture of Daniel. Is he the squishiest baby ever?"

Christy looked at the phone screen. "Oh, look at those cheeks! He is so adorable. I can't wait to meet him face-to-face!"

"I know. We have to figure out when we're going to leave tonight to go to Carlsbad. Todd said you and I are supposed to figure out the details."

Christy still was studying the photo. "Look at that little nose. He is so cute! I think he's going to have Tracy's chin, though. What do you think?"

"No, that's Doug's chin. Definitely Doug's chin."

"Did you ask Rick if he could get away before six tonight?"

Katie nodded. "He said he could leave anytime."

"Then let's meet at our apartment around five and go from there."

At 5:45 that evening Katie, Rick, Christy, and Todd climbed into Todd and Christy's Volvo. They were together for the first time since the wedding.

This is golden, Katie thought as they

rumbled down the freeway eating fast-food tacos. *I love being "us."*

They arrived at the hospital in Carlsbad with only half an hour left of visiting hours. As they entered the room, they saw Doug standing beside the bed with a tiny bundle cradled in his arms. Katie never would forget the image of baby Daniel receiving one of his first "Doug hugs" from his awesome daddy.

Tracy looked up. Her heart-shaped face was weary but radiant. "I'm so glad you guys came. Perfect timing. Did you see my parents? They were just leaving."

"I didn't see them," Todd said. "How are you doin', Trace?"

"Good. Better."

Doug's smile looked as if it were about to sprout wings and fly across the room to greet them. He turned to give the gang a better view of his son.

"Ohh!" Christy and Katie said in unison.

"He's so tiny," Katie said. "The picture on the phone made his cheeks look so chubby. But he's so tiny!"

"Seven pounds, fourteen ounces," Tracy said. "That didn't feel so tiny when he was making his grand entrance."

"I guess you were right, Katie," Todd said. "I thought he was fourteen pounds and

171

seven ounces."

Tracy made a face. "I can't even imagine!"

"He is absolutely perfect." Christy stretched out her arms. "May I hold him? Please, oh, please?"

"Of course," Doug said and then addressed Daniel with "Are you ready to meet your Auntie Christy?"

Christy received the precious cargo into her arms. She looked like a natural, holding Daniel effortlessly and smiling at him.

"Hello, Little Wonder. You beautiful baby, you." Christy's voice was soft and cooing without sounding gooey. Katie wondered if the year Christy spent working at the orphanage in Switzerland had ripened her heart to little ones in a way that Katie had never experienced. Todd seemed to admire his wife's tenderness as well.

Rick, in an uncharacteristic and yet perfectly natural gesture, stepped closer to Katie and put his arm around her shoulder. Katie felt warmed from the toes up.

"He's amazing." Christy looked up at Doug and Tracy. "I'm so happy for you guys."

"Thanks. We're still in awe," Tracy said.

"I cut the umbilical cord," Doug said proudly.

Katie put up her hand to stop him from

saying anything else, and Rick removed his arm from her shoulders. "Sufficient info, right there," Katie said. "I'm not ready for any word pictures you were thinking of sharing with us."

They laughed, and Daniel gave a little shiver of a start from the burst of sound.

"Oh, sorry," Christy whispered and placed a sweet kiss on the top of Daniel's head. "He smells so brand new and fresh!" She kissed his little bald head again.

"He's not a new car," Katie said.

"I know."

"He's a new soul," Todd said. "A new life."

"Do you want to hold him?" Christy asked Katie.

"I'm good," Katie said.

"Are you sure?" Doug asked.

"Yeah, I'm sure. Don't get me wrong. I love him. I think he's adorable. I'm not rejecting my little nephew baby. It's just that he's so little. I haven't brushed up on my newborn-handling skills lately and . . ."

"It's okay, Katie. You'll have plenty of chances to hold him later," Tracy said. "And don't worry. I understand what you're saying."

"We'll put a little meat on his bones," Doug said. "Then he won't be so intimidating."

"I don't want to give him back," Christy said. "But the woman at the front desk made it sound as if they're really strict on the visiting hours."

"They are. Here, I'll take him," Tracy said.

Doug assisted in the transfer as if he had everything under control. "Thanks again for coming, you guys."

"One more thing before we go." Todd stepped closer to the hospital bed. He placed his large hand on tiny Daniel's forehead and spoke with gentle authority. "May the Lord bless you and keep you, young Daniel. May the Lord make his face shine upon you and give you his peace. And may you always love Jesus first, above all else."

"Amen," Rick and Doug said in unison.

Katie, Tracy, and Christy exchanged tearful smiles. The joy they shared in that moment came from a sisterhood of full hearts.

Three weeks later, Katie dreamed she was at the beach around a campfire with Christy, Todd, Rick, and the rest of the gang. Her heart was full in her dream as well. They were singing, laughing, and roasting marshmallows.

Her dream was interrupted when she sensed Rick gently pressing his hand on her shoulder. Katie opened her eyes. He was standing over her. She had fallen asleep at work on her lunch break.

"You all right?" He pulled up a chair beside her at the lunch table. They were the only two people in the room.

She nodded and checked the sides of her mouth to make sure she hadn't been drooling. "Just tired. I stayed up until three o'clock last night writing a twelve-page paper. It took me forever."

"Your art history paper?"

She nodded.

"Did you get it done?"

Katie nodded again and yawned. "Ask me anything about the Pre-Raphaelite Movement, and I will dazzle and amaze you."

"No need." He subtly placed his hand over hers and gave her what could be considered a brotherly pat if anyone were watching. "You already dazzle and amaze me."

Katie smiled at him. "You're not going to quiz me?"

"If you really want me to, I will. But how about if I do the quizzing Friday night?"

"What's Friday night?"

"We're going to the beach with Todd and Christy, remember?"

"Oh, yeah, I more than remember. I was

175

just dreaming about it."

"You're ready for a break, aren't you?"

"More than you can imagine."

"Good. I can get away from here around four on Friday. Do you want to drive down with Todd and Christy or by ourselves?"

"Either way is fine with me." Katie stood up and accidentally bumped into Rick.

He grabbed her elbow and teasingly said, "Watch where you're going, Weldon."

"You watch where you're standing, Doyle." She gave him a playful nudge.

They smiled at each other, as Katie slid past him with a saucy flip of her chin. It was difficult to come across beguiling in a café apron and wearing a hairnet, but somehow, at the moment, it was working for Katie, and she knew it.

Rick gave her a dark-eyed, you-are-the-red-haired-woman-of-my-dreams look that sent Katie into orbit.

Yup, I would say the two of us are getting more and more "gummy" by the day, Rick Doyle. The more we hang around on this tree together, the gummier we get.

The question Katie didn't want to ask was, "What's going to happen when I start the RA job, and we're not hanging out on the same tree every day? How gummy will we get then?"

The rest of the day and the remainder of the week rolled along at its normal, quick pace, and then Thursday hit with a surprise. As Rick later recounted to Katie, Carley called him that morning half an hour before her shift started. She told him she had a new job at Casa de Pedro and was done working at the Dove's Nest.

Katie couldn't believe how understanding Rick was. One of the other employees said Carley was having boyfriend troubles, and apparently her boyfriend worked at the Mexican restaurant, so that prompted her sudden job change.

Even though Katie wouldn't say she was glad Carley no longer worked at the Dove's Nest, she was relieved. The two of them never had hit it off as co-workers, and it seemed to Katie that Carley flirted with Rick whenever she talked to him.

At the same time, Katie had to sympathize a little with Carley wanting to work where her boyfriend did; Katie understood those benefits firsthand. The only odd thing was that, in the weeks Carley had worked at the Dove's Nest, her boyfriend never had come in to see her. At least not while Katie was working, which was just about every day. Now her hours were bumped up since Rick and Carlos were on the spot, trying to cover

Carley's shifts until they could hire someone else.

Katie was supposed to have Friday afternoon off. She had planned to use the free time to do the essential catch-ups like laundry and email before preparing for their evening at the beach. Instead, she took Carley's hours, and she and Rick had to reschedule their beach date with Christy and Todd for the following Friday.

"I'm so bummed," Katie told Christy while Christy was getting ready to leave work. "Not about working more overtime. That's okay with Rick and me. Missing out on the beach date depresses me."

"It'll work out for another time," Christy said.

"I can tell you one thing I decided about an hour ago."

"What's that?" Christy asked.

"A customer came in talking about how he just had returned from Italy, and I decided the smartest thing I ever did was to blow all my savings and go to Europe last summer with you and Todd. No way could we have gone this summer. I'll never regret that we made the trip when we did."

"Me either," Christy said. "Even though right now the memory of hiking in the Alps and picking wildflowers with you seems like something we did a lifetime ago."

"A lifetime and a half."

They sighed together.

"Growing old and being responsible really stinks," Katie said.

Christy laughed. "What are we going to be saying when we're thirty?"

"Or forty?" Katie asked.

Neither of them projected further than that. It seemed impossible to imagine what life would be like that far in the future. All Katie knew was that she was only going to be young once. She didn't want to miss out on any adventures because she was being responsible and working all the time.

13

A week later, when Katie and the gang were supposed to go to the beach, Rick had to postpone their plans. His older brother, Josh, was in town to make plans for opening another café like the Dove's Nest in Arizona where he lived. Friday evening was the only time he could meet with Rick.

The beach party was postponed one more week. However, when it finally did happen, all four of them agreed the timing worked out the best. For her part, Katie was relieved because she just had finished summer school.

Todd and Christy had a full tank of gas in their car, so they offered to drive. Rick was in a great mood because he finally had found a roommate that looked like a good match.

"Where did you find the roommate?" Katie asked, as she and Rick were leaving work and driving back to the apartment complex where they planned to meet Todd and Christy.

"He's a guy Todd knows. He's able to cover first and last months' rent, which is going to make my life easier than you can imagine."

"When does he move in?"

"In a couple of weeks. I'm telling you, Babe, it's going to be so nice to finally put some money in the bank."

"Babe?" Katie echoed.

"Yeah, Babe. That works. Don't you think?"

"Ahh, no."

"No Babe, huh?"

"No. Definitely a big, huge no on the Babe. Did you miss the movie that goes with that one?"

"What movie?"

" 'That'll do, pig'?"

"You lost me at hello," Rick said.

Katie rolled her eyes. "It's 'You *had* me at hello,' not 'lost' me. 'Had' me."

Her cell phone rang. "If that's Christy . . ." She answered before the second ring. "If you're going to tell us that you're canceling this time, one of you better be mortally wounded!"

"Katie?" A pause was followed by, "Katie, it's Nicole."

"Oh, Nicole! Sorry, I should have looked at the number. I thought you were somebody else."

"That's a relief."

"Disregard what you just heard." Katie switched ears and tried to sound upbeat. "So, how are you? Did you have a good summer?"

"Pretty good. It went fast. How was yours?"

"Two words," Katie said. "Summer school. And the lesson well learned from those two words is that never again in my life do I want to put those two words together because the school part pretty much cancels out the summer part."

"But you're done, right?"

"Yes. And to celebrate, we're on our way to the beach this afternoon."

"I hope you have a great time. I won't keep you. I just wanted to let you know that I got the okay today."

"The okay for what?"

"We can move into our rooms in Crown Hall North any time after noon tomorrow."

"Tomorrow? I thought we couldn't get in until next week."

"I did too. That's why I thought I should call you in case you hadn't seen the email yet. They said all the repairs were done, and we could move in. My guess is that they fixed up Crown Hall first this year, which is fine with me. I'm going to drive down from Santa Barbara tomorrow to move my stuff out of storage and into my room."

Katie hung up and stared at Rick. "I'm going to scream."

"Why?"

"This summer is over before it even started."

"New job jitters?" he asked.

"No, I'm not nervous about the job. I'm mourning the loss of any sort of summer break."

"We have our break right now. We'll just have to make sure this beach night is memorable enough to make up for all the times we wanted to go this summer and didn't."

Rick's words held a lot of promise for Katie. Maybe even more promise than he intended to place on them.

Christy, Todd, Rick, and Katie arrived at the beach in Carlsbad a little after five. They set up camp in a spot that by Katie's estimation wasn't the best choice. But the seaweed-strewn cove was close to Doug and Tracy's house, and the plan was that, if baby Daniel was doing okay, Doug and Tracy would come down to the beach to join the others for a while. This was the designated spot.

The beach was crowded, and the sand still hot after being under the intense scrutiny of the sun all afternoon. The sky was clear, and the waves were calm. Voices of children splashing in the water echoed off the boulders that formed a backdrop to the spot where they settled. They were fairly sheltered from the wind, and the late afternoon warmth hung in the air.

Rick's cell phone rang, and he started a complicated conversation with his brother.

"Do you want to go in the water with us, Katie?" Todd asked.

She glanced at Rick. He was pretty involved in his phone call.

"Sure." She peeled down to her bathing suit and gave Rick a little wave as Todd, Christy, and she left Rick with the duty of watching their stuff while he talked to his brother. Katie had that uncomfortable yet sort of flattering feeling that Rick was watching her as she walked through the sand.

The contrast between their hot footsteps in the heated-up sand and the cool foaming waves at the water's edge was shocking to Katie's bare feet.

Todd walked straight in and dove under

the water. He came up on the other side of a wave, shaking his head in Katie and Christy's direction so the water beads flew toward them.

"Eee!" Christy protested, putting up her hands to block the spray. "It's so cold!"

Katie thought the cold felt pretty good and strode through the water toward the waves. Todd headed back their way. His mischievous grin was classic. Katie knew what would follow.

"Don't you even think about it, Todd Spencer!" Christy backed away from her husband in the ankle-deep water.

Todd grabbed Christy around the waist and seemingly effortlessly carried his bride over the "threshold" of what this surfer boy likely considered to be his true home — the ocean. Todd took five or six high steps to reach the spot where the waves were breaking. Christy let out a gleeful protest at first, but then she put her hands around Todd's neck and smiled at him like he was the man of her dreams.

The two young lovers went under the wave together and came up shimmering and laughing. Katie seemed forgotten as Todd and Christy locked in a deep kiss and ducked under the next wave before it had a chance to break over them.

"Yeah, okay, that's cool," Katie muttered while standing alone in the water that now rose up to her waist. "I'll just hang out here while you two go be a married couple."

Katie watched them as they splashed, laughed, and clung to each other as naturally as if they had been one heart for a long time. They were so in love. Everything seemed still to be fresh and new, as if they were the only two lovers who had ever discovered the bliss of the ocean on a summer afternoon.

"You two are the gummiest breadfruit this side of Maui. I think I'll leave you alone with your beloved ocean." Katie walked down the beach a short distance before deciding to dive under the waves. She kept looking back at their spot on the sand, hoping Rick would finish his phone call and join her. She didn't expect their frolicking in the water to be as playful or romantic as Todd and Christy's, of course, but any attention at this point would be great.

The cool ocean water and the early evening breeze set Katie's teeth chattering. She returned to the shoreline and shook the salt water from her hair.

Todd and Christy had taken off for a romantic stroll along the shoreline. Doug and Tracy had arrived and were in the middle of unpacking enough paraphernalia to survive on a deserted island for a month. For such a little guy, Daniel sure appeared to have a whole lot of needs. Rick was helping to set up the umbrella and seemed oblivious to Katie strutting through the sand.

Tracy set up a collapsible travel crib and positioned it in the umbrella's shade. She opened her folding beach chair and placed it next to the portable nursery. Her final touch was pulling a cloth burp towel from the diaper bag and draping it over her shoulder as if the cloth with fuzzy lambs and daisies were part of her beach-day ensemble.

"Is it like this every time you go somewhere?" Katie wrapped herself up in her warm beach towel.

Tracy looked slightly irritated by the question. "This is the first time we've taken Daniel to the beach. We didn't know what we would need."

Doug stood with his hands on his hips, looking out at the ocean.

"Go ahead," Tracy said. "I know you're dying to get in the water. I have everything I need here."

"If you're going in, Doug, I'll go with

you," Rick said. "You coming back in, Katie?"

"Maybe. As soon as I warm up."

"Trace, if you want me to come back, just wave, okay?" Doug peeled off his shirt and hustled down to the waves with Rick. Sleeping Daniel seemed to know he had just lost his doting papa's attention and broke into a loud wail.

"Whoa!" Katie said. "The little guy has a pair of lungs."

Tracy unstrapped him from the car seat carrier and cuddled him on her shoulder, patting his back and talking to him softly. It was endearing to see Tracy utilizing her nurturing skills. But it also seemed odd.

Katie's favorite times at the beach with this gang had been spent around an open fire pit with a cuisine of hot dogs and marshmallows. This time Rick had marinated steaks for everyone and brought two large gourmet salads from work. Todd had carried down to the sand a hefty-sized camp stove and left his guitar at home because they didn't have room in the car.

What's happening to us? Instead of surfboards and guitars, these guys are bringing collapsible baby beds, diaper bags, and an old people's beach umbrella to our cookout. When did everyone become so practical and responsible?

Katie settled in next to Tracy as she said hello and good-bye to summer in the same breath. She felt as if a new page had turned in the book of her life. She and her friends were all in different chapters now. Chapters with titles such as "First Comes Love," "Then Comes Marriage," "Then Comes the Baby in the Baby Carriage."

Todd and Christy were obviously at the "marriage" chapter while Doug and Tracy were starting the "baby carriage" chapter. She wondered if she and Rick were about to turn the page to the "first comes love" chapter. They had floated through the summer without a single Define-the-Relationship conversation. Now that they were at another crossroads, Katie was feeling that nudging of anticipation she had experienced right after Todd and Christy's wedding. She wanted to know what was next.

Rick, however, didn't seem to think it was time to reevaluate their relationship. That became evident to Katie when the two of them walked along the shoreline after Rick returned from the water.

He reached for her hand and gave it a squeeze. "I was just thinking how great it is that we're still in the slow lane."

"Why is that?" Katie asked.

"I hope you don't take this the wrong way, but being in the slow lane with our relationship has allowed me the chance to be in the fast lane with this potential business deal with Josh. I'm so glad you're a patient woman, Katie. I have a feeling I'm going to be really busy the next few months. But then, you will be too. We're in such a good place right now."

Katie nodded. Rick was starting his own new chapter in life. She didn't know exactly what chapter she was starting next. All she knew for sure was that one very definitive chapter ended that evening on the beach with the gang.

Five days later, Katie began the official training for her new resident assistant position, and everything in her life shifted once again.

She set her alarm and hunted everywhere for the RA manual she was supposed to have read during the summer. Today was the first time she had picked it up out of the box where she had deposited it when she first received it nine weeks ago.

Her intentions all along had been to sit down right when the summer term ended and go after the reading project all at once. She had it all planned out — she would set aside several hours with a pitcher of iced herbal tea and a sharp pencil so she could be on top of everything before the first meeting. That ideal study time never happened. She worked at the Dove's Nest right up until closing last night, and now hoped she could somehow fly under the radar at the meeting.

Julia had invited Katie to come to her apartment two days earlier, but Katie couldn't squeeze that in either. She hadn't even managed to fit in time to visit with Nicole because, as soon as Nicole moved into the dorm, she had to go back to Santa Barbara for her father's birthday party.

Without any preparation relationally or study-wise, Katie showed up for the first day of RA training on an August scorcher of a morning. The designated meeting place in the grassy shade behind the library was a good spot. At least the location gave the promise that things were going to be casual.

Craig provided donuts and beverages. Julia brought the blankets for them to sit on. The two of them seemed like an unusual pair to lead together, but somehow the combination of their temperaments and leadership styles worked. Both of them were well respected by the other RAs, Katie could tell.

Glancing around at the group as everyone started in on the donuts, Katie wondered if the others had read the manual. She was acutely aware that she was the only new woman on staff; the other two new RAs were guys. All the others assembled on the grass had served the year before in the same dorms and on the same floors. That five of them had returned for a second year said a lot about their previous experiences. It also meant that five of eight already had spent a year growing close to each other.

Her donut finished and water bottle drained, Katie sat silently waiting for the meeting to begin. Everyone else was caught up in circles of conversations while she sat alone. At that moment, she wondered if she was really up for this challenge.

The thing was, she knew she couldn't go back to the way things had been at the Dove's Nest after making her grand departure last night. This was it. This was the next step forward. She thought of the trip to the beach on Friday night and how her long-time, everyday friends were busy pushing strollers and spending their free evenings kissing, cuddling, and returning wedding gifts. Rick was working into the role of an even more amped-up businessman.

If this group, which now was spread out

in front of her on the blankets, was going to be her new everyday people, Katie would have to figure out ways to fit in.

Craig officially opened the meeting with prayer and then said, "Here we are, Crown Hall team. I think we have a great year ahead. We'll be spending a lot of time together; so as some of you know, this group may end up feeling like your family in terms of support and encouragement. I hope that's what happens. Now, my first question for all of you is, did you read through the manual?"

The rest of the group nodded and made smug sounds like a bunch of Honor Society students.

"Has anyone not read through it yet?"

Katie hesitated. She wasn't a good liar. Her hand rose before she could stop it.

"Okay." Craig gave her a nod. "Anyone else?"

The others stared at Katie as if she were insane. Either insane for not doing the required reading or insane for admitting she didn't. Either way, they were cool, and she wasn't.

Note to self: Sit on your hands at the next meeting.

Julia leaned over and whispered "You'll be fine, Katie. If there's anything you're not clear on after the meeting, just let me know, and I can go over it with you."

Katie smiled her appreciation.

"Let's jump in," Craig said. "I'm sure you'll be able to pick up what you need as we go along, Katie. As most of you know, every year we have a different theme verse. This year the verse is from Philippians 2. You'll see it printed on the manual's first page. I used the version found in *The Message*. This is a paraphrase, of course, but I think it expresses the idea of what the apostle Paul was saying."

" 'If you've gotten anything at all out of following Christ, if his love has made any difference in your life, if being in a community of the Spirit means anything to you, if you have a heart, if you care — then do me a favor: Agree with each other, love each other, be deep-spirited friends. Don't push your way to the front; don't sweet-talk your way to the top. Put yourself aside, and help others get ahead. Don't be obsessed with getting your own advantage. Forget yourselves long enough to lend a helping hand.' "

Craig looked up. "That about sums up the objective of what a resident assistant is. You're going to have incredible opportunities this year to serve, and my desire is to see you enter that place of service agreeing with each other, loving each other, and becoming deep-spirited friends."

Katie looked around at the others and hoped those words would come true.

14

"I love that phrase, 'deep-spirited friends,' " said Nicole.

"I do too," Talitha agreed. She was the tallest of the four female RAs and had high cheekbones and a long neck that gave her an elegant profile. "I think deep-spirited friends is a great description."

"Yeah," Katie said and then added spontaneously, "It's like being Peculiar Treasures."

Everyone turned to look at her.

For a second she thought they hadn't heard her correctly so she repeated the phrase. "You know, like in the Old Testament. Exodus, I think. God calls his people his 'Peculiar Treasures.' "

When no one blinked in recognition of the term, Katie attempted to explain. "It's what my best friend and I used to call each other. Actually, we still call each other that. I mean, not every day and not always aloud but, you know, it's just . . . it's another way of saying that we're God Lovers."

The group continued to stare at her.

"God Lovers. Believers. You know, Christians." Katie halted her fumbling.

Craig gave Katie a smile. To Katie it seemed the sort of smile one gives a playful kitten tangled in its ball of yarn.

"Okay." Craig slowly nodded his head. "Good. Thanks for adding that, Katie."

No one else had anything further to say about the theme verse, so Craig brought their attention back to the binder.

Another note to self: Keep your beak shut!

Craig skimmed over the beginning section, spent an hour on various dorm procedures, monitored a debate over how many floor events they should plan that year, and went through the checklist of details to be covered on the weekend when students moved into the dorms.

Katie kept her ears open and her mouth shut.

Craig moved on to how to handle counseling situations. Some of the topics were what to do if a student showed evidence of an eating disorder or signs of contemplating suicide. Katie took notes in the margins, writing as fast as she could. This is where the training got intense. She hoped she wouldn't need to use any of the steps outlined for the specific problems. But if she did end up counseling girls who had these serious problems, she wanted to be prepared.

As soon as they finished that section, the meeting broke for lunch at the cafeteria. Katie walked over with Julia, and Julia said, "I'd never heard that term before. What was it? Peculiar Treasures?"

Katie nodded.

"I like it a lot. I'm glad you added that to the conversation. You're going to be a good addition to this group, Katie."

Katie gave Julia a skeptical look.

"Blending people together takes a little time," Julia said. "That's one thing we'll have lots of this semester — time together."

They entered the cafeteria, and Katie noticed that the staff was minimal. This was the short break between the summer sessions and the fall term, and limited food service was available to people who worked on campus. The salad bar was stocked, pepperoni pizzas waited under a heat lamp, and the frozen yogurt machine was purring with a stainless steel gut full of low-fat strawberry yogurt.

A contest soon began to see who could fill his or her yogurt dish the highest before the soft pink stuff sloshed over the sides. Katie thought she was in the running, but one of the more studious guys, Jordan, managed to add one more swirl to his towering dish of frozen yogurt than Katie could.

"So close." Katie sat back down next to Nicole.

"We didn't warn you that we're a rather competitive bunch," Nicole said.

That was a good thing for Katie. She did competitive pretty well. As a matter of fact, all they had to do was head on down to the softball diamond, and she would show them what a little competition looked like on a hot August afternoon.

Katie brought up the topic to the group but once again was met by curious stares. She backed off, realizing it had been months since she had swung a bat. If she was going to fit in with this group, it was going to be on their terms and their turf, not hers.

Carrying her tray to the designated cleanup area, Katie noticed Goatee Guy coming the other direction. He was wearing his campus security uniform and looked tan, which she guessed was a result of riding around in his golf cart all summer.

"Hey," he called out, recognizing Katie even though she tried to turn her head away from him.

"Hey, what?"

"Hey, whatever happened with your parking ticket?" He was next to her now, and the cell phone sitting on his tray was vibrating and hopping around on the plastic.

"I paid it. Old news. Your phone is ringing."

"Thanks."

"Any time." Katie cut ahead of him and placed her tray on the intake slot. She heard him say "Hello?" and kept walking.

Why does that guy bug me so much? He makes me uneasy. It's like he's trying to get to know me, but I see no reason he should want to.

Instead of returning to the grassy area, Craig directed the group to a conference room in the cool and quiet campus library. Seated around a large table like a gathering of executives about to find out who was going to be fired, the Crown Hall RAs began a different sort of training. Craig told each of them they would be asked two questions. The first question was from a random list. The next question would come from one of the people in the group.

Talitha was the first to answer. In three minutes the group learned that she wanted to be a ballerina when she was growing up in Philadelphia and that her ancestors on her father's side came from Somalia.

Katie was next. Her first question was, "What is your favorite trait that you inherited from your mother?"

Katie had no answer. She blinked and waited for a reply to fly through the air to land on her lips.

"Just one," Craig said, as if she were sorting through the endless possibilities. "A single trait you inherited from your mother that you would consider your favorite."

"I guess I'd have to say my nose because my dad's nose is really wide, and I'm glad my nose is more like my mom's."

No one responded.

"I actually was looking for something more internal," Craig said. "A trait, attribute, or characteristic is more along the lines of what I was going for. You know, like being a good listener or being generous. Something like that."

Katie shrugged, unable to give Craig the kind of answer he was looking for. This was one of the problems Katie had encountered when choosing to go to a Christian college. The classes were great. The instructors were stellar. The quality of her education was excellent on both academic and spiritual levels. But during moments like this, when a "Sunday school" answer was expected, Katie didn't know any Sunday school answers. She could almost tell just by looking at the others that they had grown up in Christian families. They probably had teddy-bear tea parties with their mothers when they were little and received purity rings from their fathers when they were in high school. Their care packages from home probably came every week with cute little love notes and sugar cookies with pink frosting.

At this moment it seemed the rest of the group was catching on to the "peculiar" part of Katie's Peculiar Treasure expression.

Talitha asked a different question. "How about this, Katie. Did your parents have a nickname for you when you were growing up?"

"Yes."

"What was it?" she asked.

Katie quickly covered the near-break in her façade. "That's three questions. Didn't Craig say we only had to answer two questions? The answer to my second question was 'yes.'"

The laughter that rippled around the table was the kind Katie loved to extract from people, especially when she was caught off-guard in new situations. If people who didn't know her labeled her as funny, they were less likely to expect her to divulge any of the serious parts of her life. Katie liked it that way.

Always get them to laugh before you walk away; that's what they'll remember. That was Katie's unwritten motto.

Besides, how could she tell these potential new friends that the nickname she grew up hearing from her parents was "Our Little Miss Take"?

No, none of them would understand what it was like to be unwanted. Katie had explained it to Rick last winter as growing up feeling tolerated as a child, ignored as a teen, and now set aside as a nearly forgotten nuisance. She told him that all she ever wanted was to belong.

Rick had surprised her with his reply. Part of her had hoped he would say something like, "I want you, Katie. You belong to me now. I'll take care of you." He didn't say that. But his answer was the best one, really. "You belong to Christ, Katie."

Katie drew in that truth and held it like a fully executed adoption form. It didn't make her feel different. It certainly didn't make her feel warm and special the way she knew she would have felt if Rick had said, "I want you. You belong to me."

But it was truth. And truth, the kind of truth that has the power to set free, sometimes comes with no emotion. Like an anchor, it simply holds fast. Katie's identity storm was subsiding. Even today, while the winds and waves of insecurity kicked up, the truth of Rick's words stayed fixed in Katie's heart. They came back to her now as she put aside the "Our Little Miss Take" nickname and heard Rick's strong voice in the back of her mind. *You belong to Christ.*

Katie wondered if the old nickname her parents had given her was the reason she was leery of Rick's nicknaming her. She didn't want to be labeled as anything other than herself. Her college-woman self. Katie. Just Katie.

She knew that if last winter Rick had said, "You belong to me," she would be a different person than she was now. She wouldn't have had the freedom Rick opened to her to establish her own identity. Katie knew she would have attached herself to Rick and gone wherever the winds and waves took his life.

"All right. Let's go on to the next question," Craig said. "You're up, Nicole."

Nicole's question from Craig was, "If you hadn't come to Rancho Corona, what do you think you would have done instead?"

Nicole thought a minute. "I think I would have gone to Australia to live with my sister for a year."

Her answer produced lots of fake accents and chatter about kangaroos and koala bears.

"Okay," Craig broke up the down-under discussion. "The next question for Nicole needs to come from one of you."

The exercise continued around the circle. Lots of information about each RA was shared. Katie realized she wasn't the only one with a bumpy childhood. The honesty of the others helped her to relax and to feel as if maybe, just maybe, she could fit in with this group. If she had been the last one in the circle, she knew she would have been more open with her responses.

Craig concluded their session with a summary of why he had them do the exercise. "I want all of you to learn to listen to each other as well as learn how to answer honestly. Boundaries need to be honored, and I think all of you did a pretty good job in that area. We are a team, and we need to learn how to work together as a cohesive unit. Learn to ask the right questions of each other, and more importantly, learn to listen to the answer."

The training session continued without a break until after 6:30. Craig managed to make it through nearly all the remaining sections in the binder, including security procedures and health procedures. The final subject that perked up the returning RAs was the mention of the two-day retreat all the RAs would embark on the next morning.

Before the group broke for dinner, Craig passed out two large black trash bags to each person and made one final statement that didn't make sense to Katie. Instead of interrupting the flow of the meeting, Katie waited until they were on their way to dinner.

She took Nicole aside to ask, "What did Craig mean when he said we should only pack what we can fit in the trash bags? Did he mean we're going to put our luggage into the trash bags?"

"No, the trash bags are your luggage. You're supposed to pack the bare necessities, and those items fit into one trash bag. That includes your sleeping bag."

"Don't you mean it has to fit into two trash bags?"

"No, only one. The bags have to be doubled for strength." Nicole smiled.

Packing light wasn't a problem for Katie. She didn't mind being a minimalist. What bothered her was that she didn't know where they were going for the retreat. None of the students knew. That made packing a challenge.

As Katie and Nicole walked into the cafeteria behind the rest of their group, they sniffed the air, turned to each other, and said in tandem, "Fish sticks."

"And french fries, no doubt," Katie added.

"I don't think I ever ate a fish stick in my life before coming to college," Nicole said.

"Oh, all the taste sensations of freezer-burned food that you missed during your childhood."

"No, I experienced the taste sensations from freezer food. My mom used to make frozen chicken potpies all the time. Not the fancy potpies with the name-brand labels. She would stock up on the generic store brand and cook them for us on a cookie sheet that would get caked with the overflow goo when the potpies exploded, which they always did. Guess who washed the dishes and tried to scrape off the burnt chicken potpie goo?"

"Okay, you win," Katie said. "Your child-hood least favorable food is worse than mine. And to be honest, I actually like the fish sticks they serve here. As long as they have french fries too. If you put both in your mouth at the same time, I think the french fries cancel out the fish taste."

"I'll try that. I usually cover the fish sticks with ranch dressing. That works too."

Katie's phone was vibrating so she took a peek at the text message that had come in. It was from Rick. MOVIE? 7:15.

She texted back, STILL IN MTG.

As Katie and Nicole picked up their trays and started through the line, Rick came back with, 9:20?

"Do we have anything after dinner?" Katie asked Nicole.

"I'm sure we have something, but I don't know what. Last year we just hung out to get to know each other more as a team."

Katie texted back, CAN'T.

Rick's response came before she had made her way to the ranch dressing. STILL? AT 9?

SORRY. CAN'T TONITE.

Katie paused and looked at the table where the rest of the RAs were waiting for her. This wouldn't be a good time to duck out. She sent a message back to Rick that she would call him later. She hoped he would understand. She was working. She had a new job. This was it. The hours of RA training weren't neatly defined like the hours at the Dove's Nest.

Rick would understand. He wasn't her anchor. This was the next chapter of their relationship, and it was going to be different from the previous ones.

15

By the time Katie returned to her dorm room on Monday night, it was after eleven. She had her two black trash bags that Craig had passed out to each of the RAs as well as some papers she had to fill out before they left for the staff training retreat in the morning.

What she didn't have was a settled feeling about what lay ahead. Katie usually gave the appearance of someone who enjoyed living spontaneously, in the moment. She did love the idea of new adventures and taking new steps of faith. However, when it came down to the moment of risk, she often found herself anxious and full of doubts. These were the times she seemed to come face-to-face with her truest self. The Katie who didn't always have a quick comeback or a funny facial expression. That was the Katie reflected now in the full-length mirror on the back of her dorm room door.

"What are you trying to prove?" the unveiled Katie asked herself. "Why did you take this RA position? You don't know how to counsel anyone. Truth be told, you're probably the one who needs counseling. When you try to lead, do you honestly think anyone is going to follow you?"

The clear-eyed Katie in the mirror didn't answer.

"Is it too late to back out? Can I go back to the Dove's Nest and just be with Rick every day? Is it possible for my life to flip back to what it's been the past seven months?"

Katie walked away from the mirror. She could hear the unveiled Katie reply, "For the past seven months you've been looking for something more. Remember how restless you've been? This is what the Lord has placed in front of you. Take it and be thankful."

Katie smiled. The last line she just heard from her psyche was from a video she had watched several months ago, back when she actually had enough time in her life to do such things. The film opened with a scene in an orphanage in which all the quivering children lined up for their spoonful of castor oil. The cranky orphanage matron gave each child the evil eye before thrusting the medicine into his mouth. To each of them she said, "Take it! Take it and be thankful!"

Katie smiled because she knew in her heart of hearts that this opportunity of serving as an RA wasn't a distasteful spoonful of castor oil. This was a gift. She was thankful. She had taken the position willingly and with gladness.

With her hands on her hips, she spoke aloud into the room. "All of you insecurities and doubts have to go now. Go to the place Jesus sends you. You're not welcome here. Get out."

Her words surprised her. *Where did that come from?*

All she knew was that the room seemed more spacious. Her thoughts felt lighter.

Another note to self: Be bold when the lies come at you. You belong to Christ, Katie. Follow close after him.

An image came to Katie of a bunch of lies and doubts nipping at her heels. The image was like a cartoon sketch of a bunch of slimy green slugs with razor-sharp teeth inching along behind her and snapping their jaws. Yet, when she drew close to the Lord and started to walk in step with him, the slimy slugs shrieked and crawled in the opposite direction. Lies perish when they get close to truth.

In keeping with the freshness that laced her deep breaths, Katie decided to make her bed. She wasn't, by nature, a bed-maker. The past two nights since she had moved into this room at Crown Hall, Katie had slept in her sleeping bag on top of the bed because that was the simple, fast, and convenient thing to do. Now that she needed to pack her sleeping bag for the RA training retreat, she wanted to really move in and get situated in her new surroundings.

Going to the corner of her room, Katie opened the top box that teetered on a stack of four lopsided containers. The bottom box was beginning to cave in. Setting to work, Katie released her belongings from their cardboard prisons and found her sheets and favorite Little Mermaid pillowcase that she had bought last year at the Bargain Barn. Scooping up a bag of dirty clothes, Katie tromped down the empty hallway to the laundry room, stuffing her sheets and clothes into two of the washing machines.

While her clothes washed, Katie placed her belongings into the dresser drawers with plenty of room to spare. Total move-in time, approximately twenty-eight minutes. She thought of how it took almost that same amount of time to simply plant and raise the beach umbrella for Tracy and Doug when they went to the beach with baby Daniel. She never would have guessed the two of them would have turned into a traveling circus with all their baby gear. They were even talking about buying a bigger car and moving into a larger house.

She then thought of Christy and Todd, who had run out of closet space for all their gifts and gadgets. Their apartment still contained some stacked-up boxes of wedding gifts. They were trying to decide if they should keep or exchange some of the items. Their married life was full of "domestic stuff," as Todd called it.

A few weeks ago Christy had convinced Katie to go "returning" with her after work one evening. Katie's response had been, "Sure. I still have a gift certificate from your aunt that I need to use for something. I could do a little shopping."

"No, no, no. Returning is different than shopping," Christy explained. "You have to answer questions, fill out forms, and try to decide right then and there if you want to look around for something to use your store credit. Returning uses a different sort of mental energy than shopping, and I'm sick of going by myself. Todd has only gone returning with me twice. I'm at the point where I can only stand going to one store per trip."

Katie felt like a pack mule on the returning excursion, carrying into the store a boxed blender, boxed toaster, and two boxed waffle irons. Christy carried in a bedspread in a plastic wrapper that came with a handle. With her other arm she balanced a coffee maker and a throw pillow with a palm tree on it. To the woman at the register she said, "These are duplicates." True to Christy's description of the process, she was required to fill out several forms and was then invited to "look around for something else."

"No thanks," Christy had said as she tucked the gift card into her wallet behind three gift cards to other department stores.

Katie spotted a dorm-sized refrigerator on their way out the door. She bought it and had it hauled out to Christy's Volvo on a dolly.

As Katie now broke down the four cardboard boxes in her room, she compared her quota of "domestic stuff" to what Christy and Todd had to manage. She decided she liked the simple blessing of living trimmed down to the basics. She wasn't ready for toasters and blenders and having to take an umbrella to the beach. But the mini-fridge was sure a nice treat.

As soon as her clean sheets were fresh from the dryer, Katie smoothed them over her new bed. For her, in the quiet of this midnight moment, this gesture was a small act of worship. Her spurt of nesting was her way of saying she was willing to "take it and be thankful." Whatever came next, Katie was ready to take it. And without a doubt, she was grateful.

With the bed made, her clothes hung in the closet, and her drawers organized, Katie packed the essentials as listed on the retreat "To Bring" list. Her sleeping bag and everything else she was taking fit easily into the doubled-up trash bags.

Then, because it seemed celebratory, Katie took a steamy and fragrant shower before climbing into her clean, fabric-softener-laced sheets. Checking the clock on her cell phone, she noticed another message from Rick. CALL TONITE.

She was about to press #1 for Rick's speed-dial number. Then she stopped and reconnected the phone to the charger. It was 1:15 in the morning. Even if Rick still was up, she didn't want to try to summarize this long day in a choppy conversation. She knew he might be upset that she hadn't called earlier, but she had a long list of legitimate reasons.

Katie decided she would call him in the morning, when both of them were fresh. A new "mercy morning" was the time to talk with him.

Lying in the clean softness of her room, Katie realized sweetness accompanies solitude when a heart is surrendered and ready for what's next. She didn't know that she was entirely ready for what was next, but she was willing.

I wonder if being willing is just as good in God's eyes as being ready. Especially since it's kind of difficult to be ready when you don't even know where you're going in the morning!

Katie dreamed that night of floating on a raft in turquoise waters. On her small air mattress of a raft all her belongings surrounded her. Somehow, the balance on the raft was just right. She wasn't afraid of being toppled over by all the "domestic stuff." Kicking back, with her elbows bent behind her head, Katie dreamed of floating contentedly for what seemed like two minutes before her alarm went off at 6:30, forcing her out of bed and out of her dream.

Groaning and mumbling all the way down the hall to the large shared bathroom, Katie shuffled in and found Nicole leaning toward the mirror, feathering the ends of her lashes with a mascara wand.

"Morning!" Nicole greeted her.

"Hummh."

"Not a morning person, I see."

"Baffumph."

Nicole smiled. "Are you all packed?"

"Mmmhmm."

"Good. Why don't you stop by my room when you're ready, and we can go together to the fountain for the sign in? I know you probably remember Craig saying this yesterday, but be sure to wear really comfortable walking shoes. Last year it was hot the morning we left, and a bunch of us wore flip-flops. The bus let us out on the road before we reached the conference center, and we had to walk more than a mile on gravel. My feet were a mess."

Katie was ready in record time. As she headed down the hall for Nicole's room, Nicole came out of the bathroom with her makeup bag. Katie was wearing jeans, a tank top, her Rancho Corona sweatshirt tied around her waist, and her most comfortable pair of athletic shoes.

"How can you look so cute so fast?" Nicole asked. "That took you, like, four minutes."

"I've decided I'm a minimalist," Katie said. "I unpacked my room last night and realized all my worldly possessions can fit in my car with room for a friend in the front seat. Some married friends of mine just had a baby, and they took more stuff with them to the beach for one afternoon than all the stuff I own. So, last night, I decided I like being a minimalist."

"You're going to be a good influence on me," Nicole said with a grin. "You haven't seen my room yet, have you?"

"Not since I helped carry in a few boxes on Saturday."

"Promise you won't mock me."

"Why would I mock you?"

"Because of this." Nicole opened the door to her room, and Katie's jaw went slack. The room looked like something out of a decorator's magazine. Nicole's bed had a dust ruffle, matching bedspread in yellows and blues, half a dozen throw pillows lined up perfectly, matching striped curtains over the window, a plush rug in the center of the room, a cushy chair in the opposite corner with a matching blue cushion in the center of the poofy-looking nest. Half a dozen framed pictures were balanced perfectly on the walls.

Katie dropped her garbage bag.

"I know. Shocking, isn't it? I was up until after midnight the past three nights. I'm way too focused on making my surroundings pretty. It's a sickness."

Katie turned to Nicole, and in a voice sharper than she meant to use, she said, "Don't you ever say this is a sickness."

Nicole pulled back.

"Your room is beautiful." Katie redirected her thinking to a more positive approach. "That's what I was trying to say. What you did with your room is amazing. Don't dis on your art. It's a talent, Nicole, not a sickness. You took a bunch of space and nothingness, and you made art. You made beauty."

Nicole's eyes teared up. She gave Katie a big hug. "Thank you."

"For what?"

"Thank you for saying that. Thank you for making me feel as if maybe it's okay that I love to make my room pretty."

"It's the truth," Katie said. In her imagination she could almost see a pack of slimy slugs running from the truth she had just spoken into Nicole's room.

Nicole nodded slowly. "Yes, it is the truth. What did you call it? My art? You're right. I'm just like my mom; this is how I express myself. Thank you, Katie."

"You're welcome. I hope your creativity rubs off on me this year. I'm a minimalist, and my mother is barely an enough-ist. Or maybe she's more of a why bother-ist."

Nicole laughed, but Katie didn't. "It's true," Katie said.

"Come on, we have to take our minimalist retreat stuff down to the fountain."

As they slung their trash bags over their shoulders like Santa Clauses, Katie said, "So tell me what to expect."

"It's hard to say. You know that last year we went to a conference center in the mountains and stayed in cabins. I heard rumors we might be going there again."

"Why do they keep the location a secret?"

"I think it's to put everyone on the same level at the start. No one knows what to expect, and since we can only take what's on the list, we're all sort of even."

Several dozen students were gathered at the fountain area when Katie and Nicole arrived. More seemed to be coming from all directions. Katie found it strange to watch so many people walk around campus with big, black garbage bags.

"How many RAs are there?" Katie asked Nicole.

"Last year the total was thirty-six, eight from each dorm."

"We only have four dorms. That would be a total of thirty-two."

"You forgot Brower Hall. That's where the other four are."

"Oh, yeah. How could I forget Brower Hall? That's where I lived last semester. Before that I lived in Sophie Hall."

Sophie Hall was the newest, most impressive of the dorms. The hall's entry was designed to look like the lobby of a classy hotel. In the center of the building was an open patio complete with what Katie called "the jungle." Tall palm trees, lots of leafy plants, and a walkway with benches made the patio a favorite spot for couples to go for their heart-to-heart conversations.

Katie preferred the fountain area at the center of campus. The way the sunlight continually changed the look of the water against the blue tiles made her feel as if this was the place where life and hope sprang up in the middle of the surrounding buildings. It offered her a little bit of happiness every time she passed by or stopped to put her feet in the cool water.

She also decided she preferred Crown Hall to the other dorms on campus. The rooms were a little smaller than in Sophie Hall and Brower Hall, but Crown offered larger windows. She also liked the lobby in Crown better than Sophie. It was straightforward. The sliding glass doors opened to a large area with couches, a pool table, and coffee tables made of heavy wood that could take whatever students placed on them — feet, laptops, books, or board games. To Katie, Crown Hall's lobby felt like the bonus room of the home she always wished she had grown up in. The only bonus room cliché missing was a stuffed moose head on the wall. Or maybe a stuffed marlin with a long, pointy nose.

The other feature Katie loved about Crown Hall was the "secret nest" on the roof. The stairway led up to a door that opened to a flat area on the roof. The wall railing around the nest was tall enough that a person could sit at the patio table or stretch out in one of the three lounge chairs in the compact area, and no one would know anyone was up there. Katie already had plans to utilize the hideaway for a place to breathe or take a quiet nap.

"Here." Nicole handed Katie a roll of duct tape and a permanent marker. "You need to write your name on the tape and then put it on the side of your bag."

Katie obliged, adding a smiley face after her name.

"You should add your last name," Nicole said. "There's another RA named Katie in Sophie Hall."

"You're kidding." Katie looked around. "Do you know who she is? Is she here?"

"I haven't seen her yet."

Katie didn't know any other Katies at Rancho. Her name wasn't particularly popular, and she didn't have to share it often. In this small group, she didn't like being one of two Katies. She knew it was ridiculous, but her uniqueness suddenly felt diluted.

"I'll introduce you when I see her," Nicole said.

Katie wrote "Weldon" on another piece of duct tape and added it right after the smiley face. If she couldn't be the only Katie onboard, at least she could be the only one with a smiley face for a middle initial.

Their bags were tossed into the back of a rented trailer. Greg and two of the other resident directors stood on the edge of the fountain and called out directions to the crew. They were told to pick up their breakfast from the tables under the tarp and then to board the chartered bus waiting for them across from the soccer field. Katie and Nicole each grabbed an apple, a banana nut muffin, and a bottle of water, and stepped onto the bus.

"That's her." Nicole nudged Katie and nodded toward a girl with short dark hair and cute sunglasses. Katie recognized her because she used to check people in at the on-campus workout room. The other Katie had a quiet temperament and kept to herself. In an odd way, knowing that the other Katie didn't have red hair or resemble her in any particular way was comforting.

Once everyone was on the bus, one of the leaders passed out T-shirts that had the Rancho Corona University logo on the back. Each dorm had a different color, and the dorm name appeared on the right sleeve. The RAs from Sophie Hall were handed white T-shirts, and Brower Hall RAs were given blue T-shirts. Next came Crown Hall; Nicole was happy when their T-shirts turned out to be chocolate brown.

Katie caught her shirt when it was tossed to her and thought, *Cocoa brown, just like Rick's eyes.*

A sudden uh-oh feeling covered her like a net. She hadn't called Rick back. He didn't know she was leaving today for the staff training retreat. If Katie had read her training manual ahead of time, she would have known the details about the day and could have told Rick.

Katie pulled her phone out of her backpack and tried to call. She got his voice message and decided not to leave a message since people around her would hear what she said. Also, she wasn't sure what to say.

Opting instead to send a text message, Katie typed out that she was off-campus for the next three days for training. Pressing "send" on her phone, Katie knew why the uh-oh feeling was so intense. This was the first time today she had even thought of Rick or remembered that she should tell him what she was doing.

Gazing out the window as the bus lumbered down the freeway, Katie asked herself, *So what does that say about my commitment to Rick? If I cared about him as much as I think I do, would I forget about him for big chunks of time? Maybe we're not getting gummier. Maybe we're getting floatier, and we're floating away from each other.*

16

After an hour during the bus ride of group speculation about their destination, one fact was obvious. They were heading west, toward the ocean, and not east toward the mountains. Katie liked the idea of a beach retreat. Not everyone shared her interest. It seemed those who had heard about the mountain location last year had locked into that idea and were disappointed, even though they didn't know where they actually were going.

All of them were surprised when the bus pulled off the freeway in Long Beach and headed to a harbor-side parking area where the sign read, "Parking for Catalina Island Ferry."

A wild buzz ran through the group. Almost all the RAs had slipped the various colored T-shirts on over whatever they were wearing, adding to the general feeling that a race was about to start. One of the girls behind

Katie and Nicole said, "I love Catalina! I'm so glad we're going there! My family used to rent the same cottage every summer when I was in grade school. I haven't been back to the island for almost ten years. This is going to be great. I know all the good places to swim."

The off-loading of the bus took a lot less time than the boarding at Rancho had taken. Katie helped to form a brigade line as they passed the bags from the trailer to the waiting ferry. Tourists as well as island residents boarded the huge sea craft, and all of them took a long look at the small army of Rancho students that must have appeared to be preparing for an invasion.

"Let's go up on the top of the ship," Katie suggested to Nicole. She didn't want to be stuck on a bench seat on the inside cabin when the view would be so much better in the open air on top.

Talitha joined them. The midmorning sunshine reflecting off the ocean seemed twice as bright as it had been in the parking area. The three Crown Hall women flipped on their sunglasses and headed for the last available seating at the front of the top deck.

"I'm telling you," Talitha said, "the RDs really outdid themselves in planning this. I've always wanted to go to Catalina Island.

I heard it's really laid-back, and that everything is pretty much the same as it's been since the fifties or something like that. Vintage California. This is so great! I'm going to swim every chance we get."

Katie's cell phone rang as the ferry was leaving the harbor for the hour's jaunt to Catalina. She saw the ID on the screen and stepped away from the rest of the group as she answered. "Rick, hi. Sorry I didn't call back last night. Did you get my text?"

"Yes. I'm really missing you, Katie. It's killing me that you're not here at work. Where are you?"

Katie looked out at the California coastline. The most visible landmark, the *Queen Mary,* a huge steamer permanently docked in Long Beach Harbor, was shrinking in the distance. "You're not going to believe this. I'm on a ferry on my way to Catalina. I wish you were here."

"I thought you were in staff training for the next three days."

"I am. This is our staff retreat. We're going to Catalina. It was a big surprise for everyone."

Rick's end of the line was silent.

"Are you still there?"

"I'm still here."

"I thought maybe I lost the signal because

we're heading away from the shore. If the signal does cut out, I'll call you back when I can. We're supposed to be gone until Friday, but I don't know if we're going to be on Catalina the whole time. The training location is a secret."

"Another secret?"

"Yeah, we don't know if we're going to be on the island, on a boat, or what. It's crazy." She cupped her hand around the mouthpiece to protect it from the interference of the ocean breeze that suddenly kicked up and made a loud crackle over her cell phone. "I should tell you why I didn't call back last night. We had training on campus all day as well as last night. Then I had to pack for this retreat, and we had to report in at seven this morning. We didn't know where we were going until we saw the signs about Catalina. . . ." Katie kept going, blabbering on, making good use of her try-always-to-be-entertaining defense mechanism.

"So, by the time I pulled all my stuff together last night, it was after one, and I knew I could still call, but if you were asleep, I didn't want to wake you, so . . ."

She paused and realized the line was dead. "Hello? Rick?"

The message on the screen of her cell

phone read, "Signal faded." She didn't know at what point the call had dropped and how much Rick had heard of her explanation. Not that it mattered. Rick could have heard all of what she said or none of it, and still the "signal" between the two of them would be "faded." This was the worst thing for her: to feel emotionally disconnected from the people who were supposed to be the ones who mattered most.

Katie went back and sat next to her friends on the prow of the upper deck. An RA from Brower Hall joined them. She was the only blue T-shirt in with their five brown ones. It was funny how putting on a colored shirt set up an unspoken boundary.

Katie set her chin toward the open ocean and drew in the brisk sea air. The Brower Hall RA looked over at Katie and said, "Hey, I met a guy who knows you last night. Carley told him I was an RA too. He asked if we were still in our training session, which we thought was funny because we were at the movies. But then he said your group was still in training, and we told him you must be with Crown Hall because they're the overachievers."

The other Crown Hall RAs had responses to her "overachiever" comment.

Katie interrupted them. "Who was the guy

you saw?"

"His name was Rick. He was sitting in front of us."

"At the movies?"

The girl nodded.

Rick went to the movies without me. That felt strange.

"Carley said he was her old boss too. He seemed really nice."

"Carley?"

"She was with Rick last night at the movies."

That bit of news went down Katie's throat like a jalapeno pepper. "Who else was there?"

"Just the two of them. Rick asked if we had seen you yesterday because I guess he tried to call you a couple of times."

Katie nodded, still keeping her expression fixed. Trying to change the subject, she asked, "Anyone know where the restroom is on this thing?"

"The 'head,' " the other RA said. "On a boat they call it the head."

Katie didn't care what it was called. She wasn't going there anyway. She was just looking for an easy out so she could walk away from this conversation. As soon as she was out of view, she dialed Rick's number and waited for the phone to connect. Eleven attempts all produced the same response: "Signal faded."

Katie drew in a deep breath and felt the brisk air from the open ocean chill her lungs. She tapped out a text message to Rick and tried to send it. Whenever it went through, at least Rick would know she was thinking of him that morning and missing him too. The most important thing for Katie to remember at the moment was that she had no reason not to trust Rick.

Carley she wasn't so sure about.

"Hi there." Julia came up to Katie and leaned against the railing, looking out to sea. "Gorgeous day, isn't it?"

"Yeah."

Julia turned and gave Katie a long look. "Everything okay?"

With a sigh Katie asked, "How much do you want to hear?"

"Everything. Or at least as much as you want to tell me."

Katie looked at Julia. Here on the deck, in the open air with the reflection of the water on her face, Julia looked like a reflecting pool. When Katie looked into the calm blue of Julia's eyes, she felt as if she could see herself looking back.

"This could get lengthy," Katie said.

"I'm not going anywhere for the next, oh,

forty minutes or so," Julia said.

"Okay, well, there's this guy . . ."

"Yes?" Julia smiled as if she had heard a few stories before that started with the same opening line.

"His name is Rick, and I just found out he went to the movies last night with someone I don't get along with that well. I can't explain why I don't like her. I just don't. So I don't know what's going on with him. He called me last night and asked me to go to the movies, but I couldn't. Part of me thinks he probably tried to set up a group trip to the movies, but in the end Carley was the only one who could go."

Katie stopped herself. "Oops. I wasn't going to say her name."

Julia gave a slow blink with a "keep going" sort of gesture.

"I guess I should tell you how Rick and I got to be where we are today." Settling into a corner out of the breeze, Katie explained how she and Rick first met in junior high and how she had a crush on him even then. She moved on through high school and how she was the school mascot, Katie the Kelley High Cougar, and Rick was the popular quarterback for their winning football team.

"He didn't really pay attention to me back in high school. All the girls were after him.

Then Christy moved to Escondido. Christy is my best friend and has been for years."

"I know Christy," Julia said. "She was in the one elective class I taught last year on intercultural studies."

"That's right. You were at her wedding. She and I met at a sleepover when we were sophomores. We toilet papered Rick's house. He took one look at the elusive Christy, and the guy was smitten. That's a really long story.

"For my part of the soap opera," Katie continued, "aside from a few odd blips in high school, Rick didn't notice me until last fall. By that, I mean he didn't notice me as a potential girlfriend. He's changed a lot since high school, and I guess I've changed too."

Katie unpacked for Julia the extended version of Rick's high school crush on Christy, his wild college years, and the two kisses he stole from Katie in the middle of all that, starting with their first kiss at the Rose Parade on New Year's in Pasadena.

"The Rose Parade is actually a sweet memory in a strange way," Katie said. "A bunch of us were camping out on the street waiting for the parade the next morning. It was midnight. Everyone was kissing. I was there. Rick was there. He kissed me. End of details.

"The second time we kissed was a few months later. It was late at night outside Rick's apartment in San Diego. Christy was inside watching, but I didn't know that at the time. Rick didn't 'give' me a kiss that time. He definitely took one from me.

"Of course, I tend to be competitive, so not to be outdone, I took a kiss right back from him. It was all strange and awkward without any meaning. We spent the next day at the San Diego Zoo, and Rick pretty much ignored me. It was all a bunch of high school stuff."

"But it still hurts," Julia said. "And it stays with you a long time."

"Exactly." Katie went on to tell Julia about the letter Rick sent her a year ago and how he had apologized for the way he had treated her. "I forgave him after reading the letter. I didn't think I'd ever see him again.

"Then last fall I was at the Dove's Nest the night Todd proposed to Christy, and Rick was there. I hadn't seen him in a long time, and we started to hang out. Since then, we've been . . ."

Katie realized she was stuck and not sure how to continue.

Julia waited for her to find the right

descriptive phrase.

"We're not exactly dating. Not officially. We do stuff together. But we're not boyfriend and girlfriend. But up until last week we saw each other just about every day because we worked together."

Julia nodded her understanding.

"In so many ways our relationship has been amazing, wonderful, and just right. But now I'm flipping out because I don't know what's going on. And the thing is, I shouldn't be worried. I mean, Rick has proved over and over that I can trust him. We agreed to take our relationship as slow as can be. And believe me, it's been going about as fast as an old lady driving with a flat tire in the slow lane. I mean, if Rick wants to hang out with other people, that shouldn't bother me. I could hang out with other people if I wanted to. We're just floaty, you know? We're not committed."

"You sound pretty connected," Julia said, "what with seeing each other every day for so many months and being romantically interested in each other. May I ask a question?"

"Sure."

"Are you and Rick involved with each other physically?"

Katie shook her head. Julia looked surprised. Pleasantly surprised.

"I mean, we have a few hugs and snuggle moments here and there, but we haven't kissed yet. Or, I guess I should say, we haven't kissed since high school." Katie sighed. "When I hear myself talk, the way Rick and I relate sounds so bizarre. I don't know any couple that has a relationship like ours."

"That's part of the Peculiar Treasure theme in your life, isn't it? You're unique, Katie, and so is your relationship with your almost-boyfriend. I think you're doing well."

"You do? Really?"

"Yes, really. It sounds like the two of you have chosen to take your time and to let your friendship become your foundation. That's wise."

"It can also be boring."

Julia laughed.

"I told Rick at the beginning of the summer that we were in a rut, and he said ruts can be good. So if ruts are good and you're saying our relationship is good, then I guess I don't need to freak out about the movies. Even if he did take Carley on a date or something, it's not my place to make demands on his social life."

"Is it the sort of relationship in which the two of you don't feel peace about moving forward yet you don't see a reason to pull apart and go your separate ways?"

Katie thought a moment before nodding. "Sort of. This RA position has become a natural kind of parting for us. Rick actually was ready to ask me to be his girlfriend earlier in the summer."

"And you weren't ready?"

Katie nodded. "I thought I was. I told him I wanted to move out of the slow lane. Then, when he was ready to talk about it, I closed up. I didn't want to take that next step. I don't know why exactly."

"Did it have anything to do with your not trusting him?"

Katie looked surprised at Julia's question. She quickly spouted, "I trust Rick."

"Okay."

Katie gazed out at the ocean and thought about her comment. "Well, I guess I mostly trust him. I just realized you and I wouldn't be having this talk about his going to the movies with Carley if I trusted him completely."

Julia grinned.

"Are you going to tell me to work on my 'hot on God's heels' theology so I'll be close enough to the Lord to hear what he's trying to tell me about Rick?"

"Sounds like I don't need to tell you that

one again. You already have that lesson down."

"Are you going to give me any advice?"

Julia crunched up her freckled nose. "I don't think so. It sounds like you've already given yourself a lot of solid advice. With such a long-term relationship as this one, you need to give yourself time and that's what you're doing. Good for you. But I would like to hear the updates on how things go for you guys."

"Okay. Thanks for listening. It helps to just get everything out."

"Anytime."

Katie and Julia rejoined the others from the Crown Hall group. Katie was surprised to realize that she felt the situation with Rick was sort of resolved after talking it over with Julia.

The power of one understanding woman who opens her ears and her heart to another woman should never be underestimated.

Katie loved having Julia in her life. Especially now.

The ferry slowed as it approached Catalina. Ahead of them, the crescent-shaped bay of Avalon Harbor came into view. Katie stood beside Nicole at the railing, drinking in the quaint view of the small buildings that dotted Avalon's landing. She remembered how Rick had said on the phone earlier that he missed her. She couldn't remember his ever saying anything like that to her before, at least not in the tone of voice he had used this time. That memory convinced her things would be okay with Rick once she returned home.

17

As soon as the huge ferry docked at Avalon, the Rancho Corona teams shifted into high gear, gathering their belongings and congregating in the parking lot where two compact, chartered buses waited for them.

Craig gave directions, and the RAs boarded the buses, holding their trash bags on their laps. The buses rambled up the hill away from the bay. The views expanded as they continued on through the arid landscape. Catalina, despite being an island, couldn't claim inland bodies of water as one of its plentiful natural resources.

"Okay, listen up," Craig said to the group, as the bus slowed down. "If you have a cell phone, pull it out and hold it up."

He waited while nearly every person on the bus went for his or her phone.

"Here's the first rule. No calls in or out. No texting. No podcasts. Some of you will see that your service doesn't work here. The rest of you will either have to turn off your phones or, on your honor, leave them off. If you need a little intervention on this, hand over your phone to Julia, and she'll return it at the end of the training."

Phones clicked off everywhere and were put away.

"Next, we need all of you to leave your trash bags in the bus but take your backpacks and anything else you carried on with you. When you exit, gather by dorms and we'll give directions from there."

They shuffled off the bus, and Katie gathered with the rest of the brown T-shirted RAs. The view from the top of the island was astounding. The Long Beach Harbor, which they had departed from, no longer was visible because of the smog and costal haze. All they could see was the unfurled Pacific Ocean shimmering in the early afternoon sunlight.

"It looks like a field of stars," Nicole said.

"A field of stars?" one of the guys echoed.

"You know, like this is where all the falling stars land when they drop out of the heavens. It's a corral for fallen stars. This is where you can come to view them in the daytime."

Katie smiled. Nicole was definitely an artist. Katie liked being around artistic people, mostly because she always hoped their lyrical fascination with life would rub off on her.

"Okay." Craig walked up to their group. "Gather closer, you guys. We're hiking into camp, and this is where the trail begins." He nodded toward the road that turned from paved to dirt and gravel. "Whatever you have chosen to bring with you in your backpacks, you will need to carry with you the rest of the way."

"How far is it?" Jordan asked.

"Not far." Craig grinned.

A few of the people in their group groaned at the mystery of being sent off on a hike but not knowing how far they were going. Katie didn't groan. She was ready to stretch her legs. All summer she spent most of her days on her feet at the Dove's Nest. Sitting a lot wasn't something she was used to.

"We have some boxes over there with bags of trail mix, some cheese sticks, and bottles of water. As I'm sure you've noticed by the surroundings, this is an arid island, and we're going to be in the sun for nearly the entire hike. Everyone receives two bottles of water. I'd advise you to take small sips as you go so you stay hydrated. Everyone ready?"

They picked up their lunch items and hit

the trail behind the white T-shirted group from Sophie Hall. Dust rose as the sounds of the happy campers ahead of them floated in the air. One of the girls behind them was saying how disappointed she was that the camp wasn't located near the water. This journey over the ridge of Catalina and down the backside wasn't the experience she had expected.

Katie had the opposite response. This was one of her happiest sort of dreams, and she loved the adventure. Falling into step beside Nicole, she said, "I'm glad you gave me the reminder about the comfortable hiking shoes."

"I know," Nicole said. "I saw one girl wearing platform sandals. I feel for her already. She is going to be miserable. I love that we'll see a side of Catalina not a lot of people experience."

"I've been hoping all summer to get out and do something; this is my idea of a good time."

"Did you grow up camping with your family?" Nicole asked.

"No. I wished we had. I only went to summer camp once, but that week changed my life. I think that's partly why I get so excited about camping. Any sort of camping."

"If you like camping so much, why did

you only go to summer camp once?"

"My family didn't exactly take summer vacations to Yellowstone. The only way I could go camping was with friends. My family didn't go to church either, so when I was invited to go with some friends to a church summer camp, it was a big deal. My parents agreed I could attend because they wanted to go to Las Vegas without me. Sending me to camp provided a free week for them."

Nicole looked as if she didn't know how to respond.

Katie decided to keep going. "When I think about it, I guess it ended up being a 'free' week for me, too. Church camp at Hume Lake was where my heart got freed up."

"Do you mean that's where you came to Christ? At Hume Lake?" Nicole asked.

"Yeah, except it was more like Christ came to me because I didn't even know I could come to him."

Nicole gave Katie a surprised look.

Katie tried to explain. "That week at church camp was the first time I ever heard that God wanted me. That was pretty huge, you know? I can't imagine where I would be or who I would be if I hadn't taken God's dare that week."

"His dare?" Nicole's expression made it clear she still was puzzled by Katie's odd choice of words. Katie thought she should shut her beak before another quirky peep came out. Then she decided she might as well lay it all out since she and Nicole were going to be doing life together for the next school year. So what if Katie didn't know all the correct Christian terms for everything? She knew what had happened in her life. If Nicole was going to know Katie at the core of who she was, this was the starting place.

"I know I'm not saying all this the right way," Katie said as she and Nicole kept up their steady hiking stride on the gravel road. "For me, trusting God was sort of like a dare. If everything the speaker at camp said was true, which I now know it was, then to me, it seemed like a dare."

"I don't know what you mean by a dare," Nicole said.

"God was holding out this free gift of forgiveness, eternal life, and entrance to his kingdom. All I had to do was believe and receive it. Like a gift. That's what captivated me. I mean, that is a really bad deal on his part. It was as if he was saying, 'Go ahead, Katie. I dare you to see if I'm real. Trust me. You won't know unless you reach out and take what I'm offering. That's the only way you'll believe me when I say I love you.' So I took God up on the dare."

Nicole kept walking, her eyes hidden from Katie behind her sunglasses. "You know what I'm beginning to appreciate about you, Katie?"

"I'm going to guess it's not the perspiration rolling down my arms right now."

Nicole laughed. "What I appreciate about you is your freshness and honesty. You say things I would never think of saying, and you say them in a way that makes me think."

"Think or shrink? As in shrink back in regret when you realize I'm the one you're stuck with for the year."

"Katie, don't say that!" Nicole gave Katie a firm expression without adding her signature smile. "You know how you told me this morning not to dis on my art of decorating my room? Well, I'm telling you, don't dis on your personality. You're one of a kind. You're a work of art. You really are. You make life seem real and not an act."

Katie didn't know what to say.

Nicole smiled. "So, what I was saying before you so rudely tried to belittle my comment, is that you make me think about familiar truth in new ways. My childhood was probably the opposite of yours. Did you know my dad is a pastor?"

"No."

"He's been a pastor at the same church in Santa Barbara for more than twenty years. I've heard the gospel a thousand times. My whole life. I went to a Christian school, and now I'm at a Christian college. In a lot of ways I've gone numb or immune or something. But you! You infuse all your conversations about God with a rush of freshness. Being around you is like being by a waterfall. You're refreshing. All the spray from your freefall wakes me up."

Now Katie really didn't know what to say.

"Like yesterday." Nicole picked up the pace with her feet and her conversation. "When you used the term 'Peculiar Treasures,' I didn't know what to do with that. I mean, I grew up being told I was a princess in God's kingdom. My job is to be his sweet and loving daughter. That's a lot different from being 'odd' or 'peculiar.' Especially when you tie the word 'peculiar' with 'treasure.' "

"I hope I didn't mess with your theology," Katie said. "I just never really fell into the princess category."

"Oh, yes, you do!" Nicole said. "Every woman who is a follower of Christ is a daughter of the King, and that makes her a princess. But what you said about being Peculiar Treasures makes so much more sense for where we are now. We're living in a broken world. We're unusual when we're compared with most people. I'm not saying this clearly, the way you did, but I get it. We're valuable. That's the 'treasure' part. But let's face it; we're peculiar. I love it."

" 'Peculiar Treasure' honestly is a term from the Old Testament. I didn't make it up."

"When we reach camp, I want you to show me where it is. Did you bring your Bible?"

"Of course. It was on the list." Katie didn't know exactly where the Peculiar Treasure verse was. She hoped she had underlined it so it would jump off the page when she went hunting for it.

"Katie, I want you to know that I meant what I just said. I love your fresh take on life and God, and I'm so glad we get to be RAs together this year. You have no idea how glad."

"I'm glad too," Katie said.

Nicole's welcoming comments helped more than Katie at first realized because, when they stopped to rest about halfway through the hike, Katie started to slide back into the margins again. The RAs that had been together the previous year had an inside joke about something Jordan had done on the hike into camp last time. Even Craig was joking and laughing with them, which was great, of course. But it kept going on, and Katie was lost. If the sweetness of Nicole's welcoming words weren't in her heart, she would have felt more left out.

Katie realized in that moment the challenge she and Nicole had ahead of them for the coming year on their floor. If half the women were returning to Crown Hall North, half of the women would have formed cliques, developed inside jokes, and established preferred routines. And so they should. That was the fun of being in community. Yet the newbies could have many moments like she was experiencing now, when they felt marginalized simply because they were new.

Katie stepped away from the other team members as they enjoyed their joking-around time. She pulled her bottle of sunscreen from her backpack and reapplied some to her nose, arms, and back of her neck. If she could have put it on her hair, she would have. The midday sun felt so strong, she was sure that rubbing two strands together would start a fire.

Craig announced they needed to get back

on the trail. One of the other groups already had gone ahead. Competitive Crown Hall picked up the pace.

The trail narrowed through an arid and rocky place. The stones they kicked from the trail took off skittering down a frighteningly steep cliff.

"Take it slow," Craig called out. "Keep to the inside. Single file."

"I feel like we're the children of Israel walking through the Red Sea on dry land," Nicole said.

"I'd prefer to think of us as the children of Israel when they crossed through the *Jordan* River." That comment came from Jordan, as he emphasized his favorite word in the sentence.

"Well, Jordan," Craig said, "if you want to go with that crossing on dry ground, then we'll have to take twelve stones and pile them up where we camp tonight as a memorial. You want to pick your boulder and start carrying it?"

"I prefer sticking with the retelling rather than the re-enacting of the Old Testament accounts," Jordan said.

"Good choice," Craig said.

They passed through the narrow, stony patch and turned a bend where all of them stopped like a freeway of bumper-to-bumper vehicles.

"Buffalo?" Talitha asked. "Am I looking at a herd of buffalo?"

"They're huge," Nicole said. "They're not going to stampede us, are they?"

"Don't think so. Just keep to the trail," Craig said. "They probably won't bother us, if we don't bother them."

Katie's water from both bottles was gone, but she really was ready for a cool sip. The air was as dry and hot as the trail, only now the unpleasant scent of livestock accompanied the swarming flies.

"How much farther do you think it will be?" Talitha asked. "I feel like we've already gone ten miles."

"The trail is much more strenuous than last year," Nicole agreed.

"Craig?" Talitha called out. Her voice roused one of the buffalo that snorted and raised its head to look at them.

Craig motioned for her to keep her voice down and keep walking, slow and steady.

Katie recalled a western movie in which cavalrymen put their ear to the ground to hear the thundering of hooves. They wouldn't have to listen here to try to locate a herd. The buffalo were within plain sight and easy charging distance.

The team stayed close together and

walked the next quarter of a mile without anyone talking. Katie noted that, in the presence of potential danger, the silence and closeness of their group brought a certain sense of security and protection.

Along with everyone else, Katie was glad when they stopped again for a rest. All she wished was that she hadn't been so quick to guzzle her water supply early in the trek.

Jordan pulled out his bottle of water and took a drink. Katie watched him but tried to think about something other than water.

"You want some?" Jordan asked.

"Am I that obvious?"

"Go ahead."

He handed her the bottle, and she took a couple of thimbles full. It was enough to settle the dust in her throat.

"I have gum, if you want some," Jordan said.

Katie took him up on the offer and thanked him again. It was a considerate thing for Jordan to do, and she knew she would remember his kindness.

The last portion of the hike was the most tiring, but they had partial shade, and that made a tremendous difference. The Crown Hall group passed the waning team that had taken the lead earlier, and Craig and Jordan were the first two hikers to enter the campground. Katie and Nicole were right behind them, followed by the rest of the Crown Hall RAs.

Julia and some of the other staff, who had taken the vehicles into camp, were at work organizing the food at an outdoor grill area flanked by eight solid picnic tables. Two other leaders were putting up the last of a dozen large tents.

Removing her backpack, Katie offered to help Julia.

"Do you see the plastic water containers over there?" Julia asked. "When the others come into camp, could you direct them to fill up their water bottles from that container?"

Katie filled one of her empty bottles, took a long drink, and then positioned herself as the water monitor. She fell into the rhythm of the camping pace and stayed in the groove for the next few days.

True to the same organizational bent of the earlier RA training, the retreat ran on an efficient schedule that allowed for occasional adjustments, such as their first night around the campfire. The plan was for singing, sharing, and roasting marshmallows. Accomplishing those objectives was more complicated than it probably had seemed during the planning stages. The marshmallows were toasted, and a few songs sung, but the hikers were too wiped out to take turns telling their stories to the group.

Before some of the propped-up campers fell asleep on their friends' shoulders, one of the leaders from Sophie Hall gave instructions for the morning. "We're going to fast tomorrow until dinnertime. If any of you have medical reasons for not participating, let me know. We'll wake everyone at six and maintain a discipline of silence until six in the evening. You'll spend the day alone with God in whatever location suits you. Take your water with you along with your Bible and notebook. Spread out, but not too far from camp. Find your listening place and take advantage of the alone time with God. As the returning RAs will tell you, the year ahead will hold very few opportunities like this. I've asked Nicole to say a little about what she liked about this part of the retreat last year."

Nicole stood. "I used the time last year to read through most of the Psalms and journal about the verses that stood out to me. During the year I would open my journal and discover that one of the verses I'd written down was exactly what I needed at that point during the semester. It was as if the Lord had prepared me at the retreat for the year by having me pick out just the right verses that I needed for the journey."

Craig spoke up about how there was no right or wrong way to use the day. "Just be available," he said. "This is time for you and the Lord. All you have to do is listen."

18

Katie had mixed feelings about the agenda for the day. The thought of spending the day reading, writing, and listening didn't appeal to her, especially on the heels of summer school. At the same time, she liked the idea of being alone with God and concentrating on him. She couldn't think of a time in her life when she had dedicated a day to such concentration.

Katie was up before six o'clock because one of the girls stepped out of her tent, and the zipper sound combined with the early morning light on Katie's face woke her. Still wearing the layers of clothes she had put on the day before at this time, Katie took her backpack with Bible, journal, and water bottle and stepped out of the tent. The day already was bright from the unblocked sunlight filling the eastern sky.

Julia was up and sitting at one of the picnic tables.

"Morning," Katie called over to her.

Julia turned to Katie and quickly put her finger in front of her lips to silence the rabble-rouser.

Katie slapped her hand over her mouth. She was dying to whisper "sorry," but that would only break the discipline of silence all over again.

I can't believe the first thing I did is talk! I hope no one else heard me. I better move away from camp as quickly as I can.

She bent over to lace up her shoes and then left the camp in search of her "listening spot," as Craig had called it.

By midmorning the strong sun overhead was bearing down on Katie's selected spot. She had set up camp on a smooth boulder where she could gaze at the ocean in the distance. The rock had been cold when she began her vigil four hours earlier. Now the stone felt hot enough to fry bacon, which was sounding pretty good at that point to Katie, as her stomach grumbled over missing breakfast.

She set out to find a new hangout spot and hopefully to forget about food. Following the trail back toward camp, Katie passed eight RAs, each sequestered in a corner of nature. Most of them were in partial shade, which she knew would be at a premium as the day ripened.

Katie wondered how this soul journey was going for the rest of them. Her first few hours felt unproductive. Not that she exactly knew what it was she was supposed to produce, but she hadn't had any big spiritual breakthroughs or insightful revelations. The first hour or so she had spent thinking, praying, and studying the scenery. Then she stretched out on the warming rock and took a nap. Her nap was disrupted by a flock of brightly colored birds that seemed to be caught up in a group argument in the bushes below her.

In an effort to accomplish something, Katie wrote a few paragraphs in her journal, trying to express her feelings. Journaling wasn't her area of expertise. Some of her friends, like Christy, were energized by writing out their thoughts and feelings. That's why the letters Christy had written over the years to her future husband had been so important to her.

As Katie scouted around for a new listening spot, she fought a sense of failure. She didn't know how to do the monastery gig out in the wilds. Talking to God wasn't the problem; listening definitely was.

Wandering off the main path, Katie found a clump of bushes. She checked to make sure she was visible from the trail, which was one of the requirements for any location chosen. On close inspection, Katie found that the bramble grew up in an arched shape, leaving a natural cave inside the thicket that was large enough for her to crawl into and benefit from the lattice of sporadic shade.

With her backpack as a pillow, Katie curled up and dozed off into another nap. When she woke in her bramble cave, she was aware that someone was staring at her. She looked down at her feet and froze.

Inches from her shoes was a fox, crouched and unblinking. Their eyes met. As soon as Katie moved, the fox darted away, with its reddish orange coat blazing a trail away from her. She had never seen a fox before. She couldn't remember being that close to untamed wildlife before either. Her heart was pounding.

Uncurling from her open cavern, Katie stood up and stretched, looking in all directions. She had no idea how long she had been asleep, but it felt good. The burst of adrenaline the fox had triggered brought her blood and her breath to the surface. She felt better than she had in a long time, rested and well exercised from the hike the day before.

Drinking the remainder of water in her first bottle, Katie stretched again and wondered what she should do now. She reached for her backpack and realized it weighed so much because of her Bible, which so far today had gone unopened.

Katie walked a little ways and thought that, even though the only word she had uttered all day was "morning" to Julia, she still was doing a lot of talking in her head. It would be good to listen to God. The only way she knew to do that was to read the Bible.

Finding a third hangout, a patch of cleared dirt under a eucalyptus, Katie sat down and leaned against the tree's narrow trunk. With the pungent, green-spice scent of the tree floating around her, she opened her Bible and went looking for the Peculiar Treasure verse. That seemed a good place to start.

She found several snippets of verses she had underlined over the years. In an effort to listen to what God had to say instead of being the one doing all the talking, Katie listed the underlined verses in her journal the way Nicole had suggested. Within an hour or so, she found that all the phrases she had been drawn to were like pearls. The phrases were strung together on the page of her journal where they formed a beautiful "necklace."

Katie noticed that hope formed a repetitious pattern in the verses. In each phrase she felt as if God was showing her his heart for her and reminding her of who he was. Having a fresh reminder of God and his love gave Katie hope.

Across the top of her journal page she wrote: "God loves me. He said so." Then she read through the excerpts she had listed.

"I lavish my love on those who love me" (Exodus 20:6a).

"I have chosen you and will not throw you away" (Isaiah 41:9b).

"I have ransomed you. I have called you by name. You are mine" (Isaiah 43:1b).

"You are precious to me. You are honored, and I love you" (Isaiah 43:4b).

"I will be faithful to you and make you mine, and you will finally know me as LORD" (Hosea 2:20).

Katie knew each verse contained deeper truths than the phrases and snippets she had chosen reflected. She had been at Bible college long enough to know the hazards of taking part of a verse out of context. Yet the clarity of God's heart for his creation was what Katie heard in the string of pearls as she read them. She was his daughter, his princess, his Peculiar Treasure. He held

Katie in his heart. In the spicy silence under the eucalyptus tree, God was reminding Katie of who he was. She felt his truth go deep inside, almost as if he had whispered his promises into her ear.

Katie never had experienced this sort of affirmation from God before. But then, she couldn't remember the last time she had shut up and sat long enough to listen.

Flipping her Bible's pages back to Exodus 19, where she had seen one of the references to Peculiar Treasures, Katie noticed another verse across the page in Exodus 20. "Build altars in the places where I remind you who I am, and I will come and bless you there."

She thought of Craig's comment the day before about the children of Israel carrying stones out of the Jordan River to build a monument. Twelve stones for the twelve tribes of Israel.

Then, because her heart felt so full and because she wanted to remember this moment, Katie scouted around for twelve small stones. She arranged them on top of each other as best she could, there under the eucalyptus tree.

Setting aside self-conscious feelings and reminding herself that no one but God was watching, she lifted her hands to heaven and prayed aloud with a solemn contentment filling her heart. "Father God, today in this place you reminded me of who you are. You reminded me that you took me out of a place of abandonment and delivered me from a desert of a childhood. You brought me into a place of hope, friendship, and love simply because you chose to lavish your love on me. I place these little stones here today because I want to remember who you are. And I don't want to forget the truth you showed me today. The truth that . . ." Katie could barely finish speaking the final three words. ". . . you love me."

19

Sun-kissed from Catalina, Katie entered the Dove's Nest on Saturday morning eager to surprise Rick. She sashayed up to the register, but the surprise, it seemed, was on her. Carley was behind the counter wearing a Dove's Nest apron.

"Carley, when did you start working here again?"

"A few days ago. Rick was really great to let me come back and take your place."

Carley's choice of words, "take your place," hit the mark to which they seemed to be aimed — in Katie's spirit.

Andrea came out from the back and seemed happy to see Katie. "We heard a little about your retreat from some of the guys that came in last night," she said. "It sounded like a great trip."

"It was," Katie responded.

Carley said, "I heard you guys didn't get to shower the entire time. I don't think I could have done it — all that hiking and no showers."

"I loved it," Katie said firmly.

"We heard that when you hiked out yesterday you and some others went swimming in the ocean with all your clothes on," Carley said. "Is that true?"

Katie nodded.

"Good for you," Andrea said.

"That was better than the alternative," Katie said. She was one of the spontaneous leapers who had decided not to wait in line to use the changing room at the public beach. Barefoot, in her jeans and tank top, Katie had taken the plunge in the bay. Then, after a refreshing swim, she rinsed off under the outdoor shower. The line for the changing room was gone by that time, and she contentedly put on the crumpled but still clean clothes in the bottom of her garbage bags. The extra trash bag worked out great for her soaked jeans. The dip was one of her favorite parts of the trip.

"I still say I never could do a trip like that." Carley's airy voice rose an octave for emphasis. "It was like you guys had to go through boot camp."

"So," Katie said, looking at Andrea and trying to get back to the reason she was standing at the counter. "Could you go in the back and let Rick know I'm here?" She didn't feel right going into the back area the way she had when she worked there.

"Rick isn't here," Carley answered.

"He's not?"

"No, he's with his brother," Andrea said.

Katie tried not to appear surprised. "Oh, right. Okay."

"Didn't he tell you?" Carley asked.

"My phone has been off. I'll catch him later." Katie smiled at Andrea and turned quickly, eager to exit.

"Bye!" Carley called after her. "You'll catch me later too. I'm in 204."

Katie had no idea what that meant, but she didn't want to stand there one more minute. She took off for the bookstore side of the building to find Christy. If ever she needed her best friend, it was now.

Christy was assisting a customer when she spotted Katie. She gave Katie a wave and a smile.

While waiting for Christy, Katie calmed down. She tried to shake off the Carley encounter and think of something else. Out of the corner of her eye, Katie saw Christy motioning for her to come over to the register. She stepped up to the counter, and Christy said, "I heard you saw a fox."

"Why does everyone know my life?"

"One of the guys from your group was in last night. I don't remember his name. He was talking about the buffalo or bison or whatever they were, and then he said you saw a fox."

"I did. It was pretty cool. We also saw either a sea lion or a dolphin on the ferry ride back. It was some sort of big, dark, swimming creature."

Christy looked beyond Katie and said, "Excuse me just a minute."

Katie stepped aside as Christy helped a woman who had come in to pick up a book she had ordered.

"It's been really busy all morning," Christy said as soon as the woman left. "How long will you be here? I can take my lunch break in about two hours."

"I can't wait that long. I have to get back. Nicole and I have a lot of planning to do for our hall, and I have a list of supplies to pick up at Bargain Barn. All our welcome packages and wall decorations have to be ready by Thursday. Our goal is to make Crown North the most desirable hall on campus. But, Chris, I really need to talk with you soon."

"What's your schedule tonight?" Christy asked. "Do you have time to come over around seven?"

"Maybe. I'm trying to figure out what Rick is doing. I don't know what's going on with him. I haven't seen him in almost a week. I'm hoping he and I can connect tonight."

"I thought Rick was with Josh in Arizona."

"Arizona?"

"You didn't know that, did you?"

Katie shook her head. "I'm way out of the loop on everything. I didn't know Carley was hired back. I feel as if I'm stepping in as an alien from another planet. Nothing feels normal."

"It's still normal, Katie. Don't worry. Rick went to Arizona with Josh yesterday. He came over to ask Todd to pick up his mail."

"Didn't his new roommate move in yet?"

"I guess he hasn't. I don't know. All I know is that Rick told us he was leaving messages on your phone, but you were out of range or something."

"It's worse than that. I left my phone on the whole time I was gone. The battery died. Now something's wrong because it won't charge. I can't listen to any of my messages. The phone store is my first stop after I leave here."

"Do you think you might be able to come over tonight, then?" Christy asked.

Katie nodded. "Is 7:30 okay?"

"Perfect." Christy's nutmeg brown hair was pulled back, and she was wearing a button-down, royal blue blouse with a crisply pressed collar. Her blue-green eyes stood out. Katie remembered how Rick used to call Christy "Killer Eyes." If he were here today, he undoubtedly would pull that nickname out of the past.

"May I borrow your cell phone?" Katie asked.

"Sure."

"I want to call Rick before he forgets who I am."

"You know what? Just keep my phone the rest of the day and bring it over to the apartment tonight. If anyone calls for me, you can let the voice mail pick it up."

"Great. Thanks, Chris. That helps a lot. I'll see you tonight." Katie dashed out to Baby Hummer, punching in Rick's cell phone number. She got his voice mail.

"Hey, it's me. My phone is having a personal crisis. I'm on my way to buy a new battery for it now. Call me back on Christy's phone. I'm hoping my phone will be recovered within the hour and that you're having a great time with your brother. Arizona, huh? So, you'll have to tell me all about it. And I'll tell you all about Catalina when —"

The voice mail recording cut her off and announced she had exceeded the limit for a message.

"Okay, fine." Katie put Christy's cell phone in her cup holder. She was almost to the phone store when the phone rang. Assuming Rick was calling back, she answered with, "Hey, how are you? I miss you something awful."

"Katie?"

"Todd? Sorry. I thought you were Rick!"

"That's okay. I miss you something awful too."

"Very funny. My phone is dead, so I borrowed Christy's for the afternoon. She's at work. But then you probably knew that."

"Yeah. So, how was Catalina? Rick said you went over there for your training retreat."

"Catalina was amazing. We should all go camping there sometime. I loved it. It's pretty rugged, and the campground where we stayed was remote; so we had to hike in, but I loved it."

"Did you stay at the one on Mt. Orizaba?"

"Yeah. Have you been there?"

"No. I checked it out one time for a youth retreat."

"Well, if you ever decide to take a group over there, I'd love to go back."

"Okay, cool."

"I'll see you tonight," Katie said. "I'm coming over around 7:30."

"Cool again. Is Rick back from Arizona?"

"No. At least, not that I know. I just left him a message."

"It's wild how everything happened so fast with the building in Arizona. If anyone can get a business going from the ground up, it's Rick."

"Yup. Rick, Rick, he's our man. If he can't do it, no one can."

"Was that a cheer or something from your high school days?" Todd asked.

"Yup, again." Katie was pulling into a parking space in front of the phone store and signed off saying, "I have to go, Todd. I'll see you tonight."

Katie got out of the car but stopped in her tracks before entering the store. *Did Todd just say Rick was going to get the Arizona café running from the ground up? How can Rick do that unless he moves to Arizona?*

Katie tried Rick's number again. Voice mail answered again. Katie was about to leave a message along the lines of, "What's this I hear about your moving to Arizona?" But she hung up without saying anything. It had been a wild week. A lot had happened to both of them. She hadn't told Rick she was going to Catalina, so she hardly was in a position to jump all over him for not telling her about Arizona. He probably had left a bunch of messages on her phone. Once her battery was fixed she could listen to her voice mail, and then she would know what was going on.

Unfortunately, Katie's phone had bigger problems than a battery replacement. The salesman, who Katie noted couldn't have been more than eighteen years old yet acted as if he had invented the Internet, was adamant that she purchase a new phone. Yes, her phone was old. Yes, she hadn't taken very good care of it, especially while it bumped around in the bottom of her backpack during the retreat. And, yes, she knew that even the least expensive new phone would have twice the power and options of her defunct unit.

In spite of all those "yeses," Katie said no and walked out in a huff without making a purchase. She couldn't believe a new phone was her only option. She hated feeling pressured to make decisions that involved withdrawing a significant chunk of her limited funds. At moments like these Katie hated being what she called "alone in the world." She was an adult, true, which meant she was responsible for her own decisions and for covering her expenses. But she hated not having anyone to turn to in moments like this.

Rick had supportive parents, and Christy had her wealthy Aunt Marti and Uncle Bob as well as her parents. Katie knew it would be pointless to call her mom and tell her she needed a new cell phone. Her mother would likely say, "Why do you need one of those gadgets anyway? Don't they give you phones in your room?"

Katie's attitude improved when she entered the Bargain Barn and looked through the bins of random items to fulfill the shopping list she and Nicole had come up with. Katie loved this crazy warehouse. She always found what she needed — and lots of things she didn't need. The prices were rock bottom, and besides, she was shopping with money from the Crown Hall account this time. Craig had given her more than enough petty cash for the decorating items they needed.

As Katie loaded her Bargain Barn plunder into the back of Baby Hummer, Christy's cell phone rang. This time it was Rick.

"Katie." His voice sounded golden. "I can't believe I finally got ahold of you."

"Rick, I miss you something crazy! I just

found out you're in Arizona. What's happening? I haven't been able to pick up any of your messages."

"I miss you, Katie," he said slowly, as if they had all the time in the world to talk.

"I miss you too." She leaned against the side of her dirty car and turned her face up to the midmorning sun. Closing her eyes, she realized this was the first time in her busy week she had stopped to think about how much she actually did miss him.

"I don't think you and I have gone this long without seeing each other since last fall," he said.

"I know. I didn't mean for it to turn out this way."

"Neither did I. This Arizona trip happened pretty fast. Some property opened up here in Tempe. My brother and Dad flew over a few days ago to have a look, and then they brought me here yesterday. We're probably going to buy the building. The location is fantastic, and another buyer is lined up right behind us so we can't afford to hesitate."

"Wow."

"I know. Unexpected, but definitely, as you would say, a God thing."

"And how is it all going to work?" Katie asked cautiously.

"Do you mean will I have to move here?"

"Yeah, that's what I mean. I didn't want to say the words aloud."

"I don't know. We haven't gotten that far. Carlos can run things at the Dove's Nest without me. They need me here . . ."

"Rick?"

"Yes?"

"Can we talk about this when you come back? Face-to-face? I'd rather have this conversation when we're in the same room."

"Okay."

There was a pause. Katie switched the phone to her other ear. "So, when are you coming back?"

"I don't know. Maybe tomorrow. Maybe in two or three days."

"Wow."

"You said that already." Rick's voice sounded deep, and if Katie wasn't mistaken, he seemed sad.

A tear rolled down her cheek right there in the Bargain Barn parking lot. Katie didn't think it would be helpful to tell Rick she didn't want him to move to Arizona. He might say something flippant the way she often was or repeat back to her one of her lines such as, "Learn to live with disappointment."

Instead of saying what she felt, Katie

decided to guard her heart. The conversation lasted only a few more minutes before Rick said he had to go. He hung up without their discussing Carley's being back at work or the odd incident of Rick and Carley's trip to the movies together a week ago.

Katie wasn't sure the detailed answer to either of those questions would change how she felt. If she and Rick had been face-to-face, she might have decided to pick a decent fight over the Carley stuff. But why? None of that seemed to matter. She was content to shake it off. All the questioning and uncertainties had melted right along with her heart when she heard Rick's voice and the way he said he missed her.

The way I feel right now is a good gauge to measure how I really feel about Rick, right? Things have been so up and down with him. I need to see him. We need to have another DTR.

Thinking about what she would say to him the next time he called, Katie realized she hadn't told Rick her phone was beyond resuscitation. The next time he called, would she still have Christy's phone?

That was it. She needed a phone. Her phone. Today.

Getting into the driver's seat and revving up the engine, Katie drove directly to the phone store, stomped inside, and bought the best phone she could afford. She didn't want to miss Rick's next phone call.

20

Rick's tour of duty in Arizona lasted until Thursday, the day before the new students were to start moving into the dorm. In the four days he was away, Katie and Nicole had gone all out preparing their hall. The two of them spent hours pouring their creative energy into the decorations.

With Nicole's creativity and Katie's tenacity, they were an unstoppable machine. The theme they had agreed on for their floor was Peculiar Treasures. Katie couldn't have been happier. Nicole was effusive whenever she told anyone about it.

Nicole had an artist friend prepare a banner that went over the double doors opening to their floor. Both Katie and Nicole loved the font and colors the creative artist used. What they liked even more was the thought that every time anyone entered or exited their hall all year long, that person would pass beneath the Peculiar Treasures banner.

For each of the women on the floor, Katie and Nicole prepared a small treasure chest, one of Katie's fabulous finds at the funky Bargain Barn. Nicole and Katie filled the treasure chests with gold foil coins that had chocolate doubloons inside the circular wrapping. Another Bargain Barn special.

Katie taste-tested the chocolate coins and made a face. "They're edible but not exactly fresh."

"Maybe the women will consider them as decoration only. They're too perfect not to use with our treasure theme," Nicole said.

"We'll just tell them the taste puts the 'peculiar' into the phrase 'Peculiar Treasures.' "

In the midst of their creative efforts, Katie came up with an idea that Nicole hesitated over. Katie wanted to put up a picture wall like The Kissing Wall from last year, only Katie wanted to title this one "The Peculiar Treasures Wall." Her idea was to put up all the Bible verses they could find in which God expressed his affection for his children and called them by a loving name.

Nicole said some of the women would protest not having The Kissing Wall, but Katie convinced her that The Peculiar

Treasures Wall went with their theme. Nicole finally agreed.

Then Katie had to convince Nicole that the banner verse, which would appear directly under the "Peculiar Treasures" header, should be a phrase from Exodus 19:5 in the King James Version: "Ye shall be a peculiar treasure unto me above all people."

Nicole wasn't sure about sticking with King James to keep the word "peculiar" in the verse. New translations used terms such as "special treasure" or "treasured possession."

"I really want to stick with 'peculiar,' " Katie said. "For one thing, Christy's grandmother was the one who told Christy that we were Peculiar Treasures, and I'm sure she only read the King James Version her whole life. None of these other paraphrases and translations was available way back when Christy's grandmother was growing up. To me, it's like a blessing, a legacy. I like the 'ye' and the 'shall.' Besides, we can put the same verse in the other versions on the wall too. Saying the same thing a variety of ways will only give a fuller picture of how God views us."

Nicole agreed again, and they set to work filling in the wall space with a variety of verses. In between the quotes, they left room for pictures. The plan was to take a photo of each woman the day she moved into the dorm and to put her photo up on the wall next to one of the verses.

While Katie and Nicole were deep in their creative burrow, Rick remained in Arizona. He called several times each day, and a couple of times they talked for more than an hour. Katie felt as if they were getting back into a rhythm. A different rhythm than being in the same space for hours every day, but they were connected, and she was content.

She loved teasing Rick that, every time he called, somewhere in the conversation he would say, "It's so hot here."

The night before Rick came home, Katie saw his number on her dandy new cell phone screen and answered with, "Is this my regularly scheduled Arizona weather report?"

"What?" Rick asked.

"Let me guess. It's hot there, right?"

Rick laughed. "You got it. I don't know how people live here, Katie. I go from the air-conditioned car to the air-conditioned building, but in between I'm walking on melting asphalt. The temperature readout on the bank across the street from me right now says it's 103. It's 8:30 at night!"

"Yes, but it's a dry heat, right?"

"Don't start with that. Dry heat is still heat. I've never drunk so much water in my life. It evaporates out of the bottle before I can drink it."

"I, for one, am thrilled that you don't like it there."

"Why do you say that?"

"Because if you don't like it in Tempe, that means you'll try to come home as quickly as you can, and that makes me happy."

"Then you'll be happy to know my flight leaves here at 8:30 tomorrow morning. I left my car at the airport in San Diego; so by the time I drive home, I'm thinking we could go out to lunch someplace pretty wonderful to make up for our being apart for two weeks."

"Ohh!"

"Is that a happy-good oh or an I've-got-to-work oh?"

"The latter. Tomorrow at noon is when the students start to move in. I'm going to be on duty for like forty-eight hours while Nicole and I help everyone settle into their rooms."

"Forty-eight hours? That puts us at lunch on Sunday. Should I make a reservation somewhere or wait to see if it's a true forty-eight hours or more of a projected forty-eight hours?"

"Better wait on the reservation. But don't wait on coming by the dorm. You know where Crown Hall is, don't you? You can come by while everyone is moving in and at least give me a big k—" Katie almost, almost, almost said "kiss," but she salvaged the moment by trying to turn the work into "hug." It came out "kug."

"A big kug, huh?"

"Yes, a big kug." Katie smiled.

"Are you smiling?" he asked.

"How did you know?"

"I can hear your smile over the phone, Katie Dear."

"Katie *Dear?* Ew."

"Don't bother to comment on that one. I'll toss it out right now."

"Good choice, Rick Dear."

"Don't mess with me, Katie," he said with a playful laugh.

"You started it, Rick Dear."

"I'm warning you!"

"What? Warning me about what, Rick Dear? What are you going to do? Come home and what? Try to haul me out to the dumpster again?"

Rick didn't answer immediately.

"I can hear you smiling," she said.

"Hold that thought," Rick said. "I have to take this other call. I'll see you tomorrow."

"Can't wait."

Nicole didn't say a word about Katie's conversation. She simply pulled out a pair of sunglasses and put them on even though they were sitting on the floor inside Nicole's dorm room.

"What are you doing?" Katie asked.

"It's a little bright in here," Nicole said. "Someone, who shall remain unnamed, is radiating a whole lot of sunbeams of lo-o-o-ve."

Katie cracked up. She and Nicole were getting along great. Rick would be home soon, and the two of them could pick up where they had left off. Life was sweet.

The next morning Nicole and Katie were ready for what Katie called the arrival of the happy campers. The two of them had taken off the night before at 8:30 and hit a discount clothing store that closed at 9:00. In twenty minutes both of them found new tops to wear for their first official day as Crown Hall North RAs.

Neither of them needed a new top, but the thrill of the hunt, on the clock, and the subsequent success was an exercise that jollied up both of them after so many days of staying on task with their hall preparations.

Sitting at the front table in their new tops, with the list of their fifty-two residents, Katie and Nicole came alive with the challenges before them. The first challenge was an inordinately nervous pair of grandparents who were at the beginning of the line with their granddaughter.

"This is Emily. Her parents are on the mission field in Mozambique. Both her parents came here to Rancho Corona. She's on a scholarship. She has all her papers completed." The grandfather leaned closer. "This is very difficult for us. She's only been with us for five days, and we're not sure she's ready for this."

Katie looked over at the young woman with feathery blond hair and large glasses who hung back, her shoulder tucked up against her grandmother's arm. Katie walked over to Emily, opened her arms, and said, "I'm so glad you're here. Welcome, Emily. I'm Katie."

Emily shyly received Katie's hug and blinked back a few tears.

Katie leaned closer and whispered to her, "You're going to be amazed at what God is going to do in your life this year. You're in the right place. I'm so glad you're on our floor."

The grandmother pulled out a tissue and dabbed her eyes and nose while Katie reached for the bedraggled piece of luggage beside Emily. "Come on, I'll show you to your new home. This way."

Katie caught Nicole's eye as she slid through the double doors under the Peculiar Treasures banner and headed down the hall. In training that week they had been instructed to stay at the desk while checking in each student. The students were supposed to manage their own luggage. Apparently in years past the RAs had turned into baggage handlers and had overstressed their backs while carrying heavy boxes and suitcases during the move-in days.

When Katie exchanged glances with Nicole, they both communicated that Emily would be the exception to the rule.

Katie looked over her shoulder and saw that Emily's grandfather hadn't come with them. "He can join us," she said.

"But it's the women's dorm," the grandmother said.

"Yes, but the floors are open during move-in. Don't you think he would like to come with us?"

Emily went back a few steps and timidly motioned for her grandfather to enter the hallway with them. "It's okay," she said.

"She's not used to anything in the West," the grandmother confided in Katie. "She's been in Mozambique all her life. This is such a big step."

"We have your phone number in the file, I'm sure." Katie lowered her voice so Emily and her grandfather couldn't hear. "How about if I call you in a few days to let you know how Emily's doing?"

"Oh, would you?"

Katie nodded and smiled. A big lump had been forming in her throat from the moment she had first looked into the eyes of this caring set of grandparents. Katie couldn't imagine what it would be like to have relatives so involved in her life that they would hand deliver her to college with such concern and tenderness. Being loved was a power that couldn't be tamed. Katie was sure of it. She knew these grandparents wouldn't rest until they knew their beloved granddaughter was doing just fine.

"Here's your new hangout," Katie said brightly, working to bring a lighthearted feel to this tearful moment. "Room 204, and your roommate is going to be . . ." Katie looked at the handmade nametags on the door and read the name: "Carlene Fischer."

That's when Katie made a connection that had eluded her during their room prep sessions. Carlene was Carley. That's why Carley had said she would be seeing a lot of Katie because she was in "204." Katie had missed the connection earlier. No one called Carley "Carlene."

"Actually, no." Katie not so subtly pulled the name card off the door.

"What's wrong?" the grandfather asked.

"This is the right room for Emily. Yes, here, 204. Welcome to your room. Don't worry. I just made a little mistake on the nametag for the door, and I need to check on what happened." Katie tried to sound easygoing. "So I'll let the three of you start moving Emily in, and I'll be at the front desk if you need anything else."

"She will have a roommate, won't she?" the grandmother asked.

"Oh, yes, definitely. Emily has a great roommate. I'll just get that settled and, um . . . yeah, you can start moving in."

Katie hurried back to the desk where Nicole was swamped with a line of five families, eager to assist in making their freshman daughter's first moment on the college campus a good experience.

Nicole was handing over some papers to the next young woman and explaining that she hadn't completed one of the forms necessary to have her car on campus. Nicole's sweet temperament mixed with her experience from having done this last year allowed Katie a moment to study the list of residents and try to make a last-minute change in roommates for Emily. In her heart of hearts, Katie couldn't see Carley with Emily.

Why isn't Carley in Brower Hall again? I had no idea she selected Crown Hall. Why would she do that? She's a senior. Emily can't be more than eighteen, if that. Carley will consume this little butterfly girl.

"Katie, could you start the paperwork with the next student?" Nicole asked.

"In one minute." Katie flashed a smile at the waiting student, who was chewing gum and standing next to a perturbed-looking mother.

Katie leaned closer to Nicole and whispered "I have to change Emily's roommate to another room."

"Now? Katie, the assignments are settled."

"I know. Please, trust me on this, Nicole."

The two women looked at each other, and Katie knew Nicole was going to back down and let Katie go with her gut. Their training time together had accomplished what both of them needed in a moment like this. Confidence.

"Okay," Nicole whispered back. "Just be

as quick as you can about it."

At 11:30 that morning Carley arrived ready to check in. "I don't understand," she said to Nicole. "The papers I received a few weeks ago said I was in room 204."

"I know. And I'm sorry for the confusion," Nicole said. "Your actual room is 238."

"How could that be? I requested a room close to the front door and away from the bathroom. Room 238 is right next to the showers. I don't understand why the room assignment was changed."

Nicole looked down at the papers. Katie couldn't stand to see Nicole take the grief from Carley so she spoke up. "I changed the room, Carley."

"You did? Why?"

"I had to make a roommate adjustment."

"What do you mean a roommate adjustment? My roommate is Marissa Stockbridge. Don't tell me you put us in different rooms. The only reason I'm in Crown Hall is because of Marissa."

Nicole and Katie looked at each other and then down at their papers. "We didn't have you listed with Marissa," Katie said.

"How did this get so messed up?" What made Carley's legitimate complaints an even bigger problem was what Katie saw listed on the papers in front of her.

"Carley, I need to tell you that Marissa already has checked in, and she's in room 259 with Kim Choy."

"What? This is a mess! Why did you put Marissa with Kim?"

Katie glanced at the form again. Marissa and Kim had requested each other. According to the paperwork in front of Katie, Carley hadn't been a requested roommate. That's why she had ended up with Emily, who also hadn't specified a roommate.

"We didn't —"

Nicole interrupted Katie and calmly said, "We can figure this out. Do you mind waiting for a little while so we can put all the pieces back together?" The line behind Carley had grown, and the patience of the waiting freshmen women was shortening.

"No, I can't wait. I have to go to work." She shot a glare at Katie. "My boss is coming back today, and I can't be late."

Katie felt her jaw clench. She was about to say a few choice words to Carley and ask her to stop causing a scene, but then, if Katie said anything, she knew she would be the one causing the scene.

Rubbing the back of her neck and looking off to the side, Katie saw something that caused her to stop breathing. Heading her direction was a tall, incredibly good-looking guy with dark, wavy hair. He was wearing sunglasses and a freshly pressed shirt. Katie would know that determined stride anywhere.

"Rick," she whispered.

21

This, her first Rick sighting in two weeks, set Katie's heart pounding in a way she never had felt it race before. She sprang from her chair and hurried to meet him halfway, greeting him with a huge hug and a happy squeal.

Rick let out a low rumble of a laugh and lifted his sunglasses. "Good to see you too, Sunshine," he murmured. "How was that for a kug?"

Katie laughed. "The kug was great. But tell me you didn't bring that perky little nickname back with you from Arizona."

"You like it?"

She reached up to rub the back of her hand across his bristly jaw line. "I think you can definitely send the 'Sunshine' back to Arizona, Cactus Boy."

"Cactus Boy, huh?"

"Yeah. That wasn't the look you were going for?"

"No. I had an early plane to catch."

"It's so good to see you, scruff and all."

"You too, unscruffed and all." Rick looked over the top of Katie's head and said, "It looks like you guys are pretty busy here. I better let you get back at it. Call me when you can, okay? I'm on my way to work now."

"Okay. I'll see you later." She took a closer look at his bristly face. "It's a pretty good look on you, you know, Mr. Lumberjack."

"Lumberjack is definitely not the look I was aspiring for."

"How about Undercover Secret Agent?"

"Better." Rick leaned close and whispered in Katie's ear. "You, by the way, look absolutely gorgeous."

He turned to go, but as he did, Carley called out, "Rick, wait! You have to help me. Everything is a mess."

Rick looked at Carley and glanced back at Katie. She tried to tell him with her eyes that he really didn't need to get tangled up in this. But Rick Doyle's hero complex took over, and he strode past Katie to hear Carley's problem.

The only good thing about Rick taking an interest in Carley's room problem was that he pulled her to the side, away from the lineup of listening ears. Katie and Nicole were able to meet the next young woman and check her in with no complications.

They processed the paperwork for three more women in line before Rick stepped over to the table. "I'm going now, Katie. Carley said she needed to make some phone calls and come back and register after work today. I guess she has a friend in another dorm she might switch with or something." He ended his sentence with a softening expression around the eyes, and Katie felt herself blush remembering how he had said earlier that she looked gorgeous.

"Thanks for helping her. We'll figure everything out," Katie said.

"I know you will." Rick reached over and gave her forearm a squeeze. Then he smiled a classic, Rick Doyle, most-charming-man-alive smile just for her.

Katie couldn't believe how being around him after their time apart was unraveling her emotions.

Rickster, what are you doing to me?

Nicole and Katie checked in the rest of the women in line without any snags and after half an hour had some free time. Nicole leaned back in the folding chair. "Mama mia!"

"No kidding," Katie said. "What an on-slaught."

"I wasn't saying 'mama mia' about the

people checking in. I was making reference to you and your boyfriend."

"He's not my boyfriend. I explained it to you before. We're still floating. No commitment. Just 'almost.' " Katie could feel her face flush.

Nicole smiled broadly and shook her head. "I don't think you're going to convince anyone of that. Least of all yourself. Katie, I'm thinking you two better have another DTR pretty soon. You are the most in love 'almost' couple I've ever seen."

"In love!" The phrase jumped out of Katie's mouth like a caged bird finding the door left ajar. She was glad no one was around at the moment to hear their conversation.

"Katie, you guys were smoldering."

"Smoldering? Oh, come on."

Nicole nodded, seeming to enjoy this moment a whole lot more than Katie was. "I'm telling you, Katie, if I had a coat hanger and a couple of marshmallows near you two a few minutes ago, we'd be having s'mores right now."

Katie laughed off Nicole's comments. She thought back to how she had used the "L" word when she was telling Christy how she felt about Rick when the two of them started hanging out last fall. But that was at the beginning of all this, and she had been talking to Christy; Katie could exaggerate all she wanted with Christy.

Now that she and Rick were so many months into their relationship, Katie didn't want to exaggerate anything. She wanted all decisions and promises to be clear and not subject to wavering, just as they had been proceeding the past few months.

Another group of students arrived. Katie put her Rick thoughts away.

Some of the women who had checked in earlier were coming back to the table with questions and problems. Two of them had keys that didn't work on their door, so Katie had to send them to Student Services.

One young woman brought all her clothes in a literal wardrobe. The beautiful, large piece of furniture was offloaded from a trailer in the parking lot and navigated up to the front door on a dolly. The dolly lost one of its wheels right in front of the main double doors where dozens of students were trying to bring in their boxes. Placing a call to campus maintenance, Katie went down to the front to help redirect traffic.

One of the wobbly green campus golf carts pulled up and a guy in a cap came toward Katie with a tool chest.

"Thanks for coming so quickly," she said.

The campus maintenance employee looked up at her from under his cap and broke into a wide smile. It was Goatee Guy. Katie had almost forgotten about him.

"I was wondering when I would see you again," he said. "How's your summer been?"

"Fine, thanks," Katie answered curtly. She couldn't believe he was trying to start a conversation. "You may have noticed we have a traffic jam going on here. Would you mind if we skipped the chat?"

He looked at Katie more closely. "Sure. But I have to tell you something."

"Can you tell me later?"

"No, I don't think so. I waited to run into you again, and I told myself when I saw you I would tell you this."

"Okay," Katie said impatiently.

"You should know that you are unforgettable. That's my problem and not yours at this point, but I thought you should know."

He turned and left Katie looking right and left to see if anyone had heard what he had said.

What? What was that? What am I supposed to do with a declaration like that? Is it my new top or what? This is crazy!

Shaking off the awkward encounter with Goatee Guy, Katie hurried back to the desk where Nicole was once again busy with

300

women waiting to check in. No other break in the workflow arrived until almost four o'clock.

Nicole went in search of something for them to drink while Katie tried to figure out the Carley room problem. So far, forty-three of their fifty-two women had checked in. Unfortunately, Katie wasn't acquainted with any of the remaining check-ins, so she didn't know if any of them would be a good match for Emily.

Why did I start this? Craig told us in training not to make more work for ourselves by rearranging anything at registration. Maybe it was God's idea all along for Carley and Emily to be roommates. What if I'm the one messing things up?

Katie thought it odd that Carley had selected Crown Hall and hadn't told Katie about her decision except for her encrypted statement about being in 204. Even though Carley was someone Katie didn't exactly want to be around, Carley was assigned to their floor. She was one of the women Katie was supposed to be "assisting" as a resident assistant.

I really need you to give me some direction here, God. Do you want Carley and Emily in the same room? Because if you do, I'll back off.

Katie didn't feel any peace about backing off. She didn't have confidence that the two women should be together in 204. If anything, she felt more determined to find a different roommate for Emily after she prayed.

Julia came by a few minutes later and apologized for not checking in earlier to see how Katie and Nicole were doing. Apparently the freshman floor had experienced challenges all day, and Julia had been the problem solver.

Since no one else was around at the moment, Katie told Julia about Katie's decision to do a last-minute roommate swap. Julia seemed to read between the lines the declarations Katie wasn't making. She had just enough background from the conversation Katie had had with her on the Catalina ferry to fill in some of the missing pieces.

"What are your thoughts on this at the moment?" Julia asked.

"I prayed about it," Katie said. "And I don't exactly have peace about backing off in my quest for a different roommate. I know we're not supposed to listen to our feelings for stuff like this, but that's all I have at the moment."

"Who says you're not supposed to listen to your feelings?" Julia asked. " 'Listen,' of course, is the key word. Listen to your feelings. Don't be dominated by them."

Katie nodded and tried to figure out how in the world not to let her strong feelings dominate her. Before she had any clue as to what that might look like, the next student arrived carrying a guitar case in one hand and a cell phone in the other.

Lowering the cell phone, she said "Hey, there. How y'all doin'? I'm Emilee Monroe."

"I'm Katie. This is Julia. Welcome to Crown Hall."

"We're really glad you're here," Julia said.

"Shoot! You're gonna make me cry!" said Emilee.

"Cry?"

"You have no idea how sweet those words sound to me. I've been waiting a long time to be here. This is like a dream come true."

"I felt the same way when I came here," Katie said.

"So you know what a privilege this is."

Katie nodded. She looked down at her list and put a check next to the name Emilee Monroe from Alabaster, Alabama. Without verifying her original room assignment, Katie made an on-the-spot decision. "You're in room 204."

"Is that right? Because I think the papers

I received listed me as being in a different room. Here, hang on. Jared? I'm gonna have to call you back. I'm checking into my room now. I know. Yeah, you too. Say hi to Mom for me."

"Did you request a specific roommate?" Katie asked after Emilee closed her phone.

"No. Are you kiddin' me? I don't know anyone here."

"Then you're definitely in room 204," Julia said.

"We had to do some adjusting with the assignments," Katie explained. "I hope you understand. Your letter might list a different room, but you're in 204."

"Shoot! You could put me in a dugout on the baseball field for all I care. I'm just over the moon about bein' here. Plus, I don't mind tellin' you that I prayed a lot about my roommate, and I'm sure she's going to be just great."

"She is." Katie grinned wide. "There is one small detail I should tell you about your roommate, though."

"What? Does she snore? 'Cuz I brought earplugs just in case. Course, I packed them originally thinking my roommate would want some earplugs as soon as she heard me on the guitar."

"You'll have to find out from her about

the snoring and music preferences, but at least you won't have a hard time remembering her name because it's Emily."

"No kiddin'!"

"She's checked in already so she might still be in your room."

"This is great. Thanks so much." Emilee extended her hand to shake Katie's and then Julia's. She was the first student to thank Katie with such a gesture of appreciation.

"This is gonna be a great year," Emilee said as she stepped under the Peculiar Treasures banner. Her curly blond hair was pulled up in a high ponytail that bobbed like a bunch of dandelions in the fist of a toddler.

"Yes," Katie said softly. "It is going to be a great year with women like you on this floor, Miss Emilee Monroe from Alabaster, Alabama."

Julia placed a hand on Katie's shoulder. "Sometimes listening to those feelings is the best way to go."

The rest of the move-ins fell into place like puzzle pieces. Nicole solved the Carley conundrum by putting her in room 203, across the hall from Emily and Emilee, and pairing her with Sierra's old roommate, Vicki. Sierra was still in Brazil, and all Vicki had requested on her signup form was that she be in the same room she and Sierra were in last year.

When Vicki checked in close to 5:30, she was in a great mood and gave Katie a hard time about the melted shoes last spring. Vicki pointed to her feet and said, "These are the shoes you bought to replace my melted ones, and guess what? I like these much better!"

Katie hoped Vicki would have the same happy feelings about the roommate Katie had "replaced" for her. She explained that Carley probably was going to be Vicki's roommate, but they hadn't heard back from Carley if she was switching to a different dorm.

"Okay," Vicki said without hesitancy. "I don't know her that well, but that's okay because I was hoping to be matched with someone new. Sierra and I went to high school together, and even though it was great being roommates last year, I wanted a chance to branch out and connect in new circles."

Nicole and Katie exchanged quick glances.

"Thanks for being so flexible," Nicole said.

When Carley returned and verified that she was, in her words, "stuck" at Crown Hall, she was at least happy to hear that she was rooming with Vicki.

"Well." Katie closed her folder after the last girl had checked in. "We provided everyone a bed without bloodshed. I think it's going to be a good year."

"It's going to be a *great* year," Nicole said.

Now all Katie wanted was the chance to sit down and have a long reconnecting conversation with Rick.

She had to wait.

Between Rick's demands at work and her demands at school, four days passed before the two of them finally connected. Rick brought lunch for Katie, and the two of them met by the fountain in the center of campus.

Instead of biting into her roast beef sandwich, Katie started the conversation with, "Before we talk about anything else we have to have an argument."

"An argument? About what?"

"It doesn't have to be an argument, but it could be, so I'm just warning you."

"Okay, so what's the problem? You don't like roast beef?"

"It's not the sandwich. It's Carley."

"She didn't make the sandwich. Carlos did."

"Rick, it's not the sandwich or who made the sandwich." She put aside the food to gain his full attention. "A couple of weeks ago I heard you went to the movies with Carley."

"That's right. You and I never had a chance to talk about that, did we?"

"No. It wasn't my favorite piece of news. I heard about it on the ferry on the way to Catalina."

Rick looked intently at Katie. "I'm sorry. That whole night was odd. Carley said she was meeting her boyfriend at the theater and asked if you and I wanted to join them. That's why I kept texting you. Todd said he and Christy might come too, so I went to the theater thinking it would be a group. Turned out it was just Carley, and she already had bought tickets. I should have paid her for the ticket and gone home." He shrugged. "It was a big nothing. The movie, the whole thing."

"Okay, that's what I thought it might have been. A group plan gone awry. That's all. End of argument."

"That was easy."

Katie took a bite of her sandwich, her appetite returning. "Mmm. Carlos remembered the mustard. It's perfect."

"He said he knew how you liked your sandwiches."

"Do you like mustard on your roast beef?"

Katie asked.

"Not particularly." Rick held up his sandwich. "I went with turkey and avocado."

Katie tilted her head. "Does it ever baffle you that we're so different?"

"No, different is good. Maybe it's time you made peace with the notion that opposites attract because if I haven't made it perfectly clear, I'm very attracted to you, Katie Girl."

She smiled. The nickname "Katie Girl" didn't bother her too much. Maybe it was because Rick put it at the end of such a delicious sentence. A young woman could build an entire dream castle on such a line.

Rick reached over and touched the corner of Katie's lip. She thought it was a heart-melting tender expression until he showed her his finger and the smudge of mustard he had removed for her.

Katie reached into the bag for a napkin. What her hand touched wasn't soft napkin paper but stiff paper. "What's this?"

Rick made a funny grin. "It's my surprise."

Katie pulled out two tickets for a baseball game in San Diego. "Rick!" She wrapped her arms around his neck and gave him a squeeze, nestling her nose into the aftershave-scented curve of his neck.

"I thought you might be ready for a little

social event. Just the two of us. I know how much you like baseball and hot dogs."

"With mustard," Katie added.

"With mustard," Rick repeated.

"This is great! How fun! I can't wait."

"Me too. I thought I'd quit work early Friday, and we could drive down along the coast. Put on some good music. Take our time."

Katie froze.

Rick read everything he needed to know in her expression. "Friday night is a problem for you."

"Oh, Rick, I can't believe this. It's our All Hall Back-to-School Event. Nicole and I are in charge of the whole thing. Every pair of floormates takes one of the four major events of the year, and this is the one Nicole and I picked. We thought we would go first to get it over with. Rick, I'm so bummed."

"Me too." He took the tickets back from her and put them in his pocket. "I should have asked you first, but then it wouldn't have been a surprise."

"I love that you tried to surprise me."

"Good," he said. "At least that part worked."

"Could the two of us try to do something on Saturday?" Katie tried to sound hopeful and not as demolished as she felt.

"Sure, we can figure something out." The tone in Rick's voice made it clear he was disappointed his surprise hadn't worked.

"It feels like it's been weeks — months — since we've done anything together," Katie said.

"I know. This isn't working as smoothly as it's supposed to, is it?"

"Do you mean my RA position?"

"It's not just your position," Rick said. "It's my job, this Arizona project, and your class schedule. It's everything at once. We'll do something on Saturday, and that's what matters at this point, right?"

"Right. Saturday. What do you want to do?"

"We could have dinner at the new Thai place in Temecula."

"Sounds good. Does that mean you're going to wear a tie?"

"I could," he said, apparently not noticing her play on words. "I'm not sure it's that formal of a place, but —"

Katie laughed. "That was a joke, Doyle. Thai restaurant? Tie? Get it?"

"Oh, got it."

Katie took another bite of her sandwich with a smug grin on her face. She didn't see the splash of water Rick scooped up and

sent her direction, but she definitely felt its
effect.

22

Some women keep albums with photos of their favorite moments. Katie's best moments were stored in her heart. She always liked the verse about Christ's mother keeping all her memories of her Son treasured in her heart.

Katie knew what it felt like to treasure a moment in her heart. And that's where she kept her memory of the picnic lunch she and Rick had by the fountain. The snapshot memories included an action sequence of the all-out water fight that followed Rick's initial splash.

Her reflexes were fast, but on that particular day, Rick's were faster. Within three and a half minutes, both of them were soaked. Rick was laughing hard, but Katie laughed harder. The injustice of it all, Rick said, was that Katie could go back to her room and change while he had to dry out on his drive down the hill back to work.

What made the moment most memorable wasn't only the sequence of memories Katie held in her heart but also the way she felt as Rick walked away. She knew what it was like to treasure a memory and to treasure a person in her heart.

Katie didn't have a chance to talk to Rick for two more days. She barely had time to give thought to anything other than all the RA responsibilities that kept coming in waves. Aside from the expected dorm problems, such as students getting locked out of their rooms and a broken showerhead, Katie and Nicole hadn't finished The Peculiar Treasures Wall.

During check-in, Katie and Nicole had forgotten to take photos of all the girls to put on the wall next to the verses they had compiled. The challenge now was finding all the girls to take their pictures.

On Thursday afternoon Nicole and Katie made the rounds with a camera in hand. In nearly every room, Katie and Nicole ended up engaged in long conversations. That was great for getting to know everyone better and for building a sense of community. It wasn't so great for finishing the project as well as jumpstarting their class work. Not to mention all the details they needed to finish for the All Hall Event Friday night.

Katie and Nicole took some great shots of Emily and Emilee. The two new roommates were getting along as fabulously as Katie had hoped. They had rearranged their beds so they were both up against the window. On Emily's wall above her desk was a stunning piece of woven fabric in a brown and rust African motif. On Emilee's wall was a lineup of framed photos of her family, friends, fans, as well as one slobbery close-up of her big dog. No one would wonder which side of the room belonged to Emily from Africa and which side belonged to Emilee from Alabama.

When Katie and Nicole moved on down the hall, Katie told Nicole to go ahead. "I just remembered a call I have to make. I'll catch up with you, okay?"

"Don't worry about it," Nicole said. "I only have four more to go."

Katie went to the RA office and pulled out Emily's file. The lobby was so noisy she went up to the rooftop hideaway where she had the perch to herself. Pressing in the number of Emily's grandparents, Katie spoke with both of them and gave a radiant report on how well Emily had connected with her roommate and how she was settling in nicely.

"We want you to know," Emily's grandfather said, "my wife and I set aside time every morning after breakfast to pray. We have added you to our prayer list, Katie. We will be praying for you every day."

"Thank you." Katie didn't know what else to say. She had never been told something like that before. She knew her friends prayed for her — at least they said they did, whenever she asked them to. But no father figure had ever taken it upon himself to pray for her regularly.

"My wife and I want you to know how much we appreciate what you're doing there for our granddaughter. Her parents are very appreciative as well. You made Emily's entrance into college just about as first-rate as it could be."

Katie felt encouraged after that phone conversation, which was a good thing because at 10:15 that night a red-faced Nicole came to Katie's door. "We have a situation. The women in 229 have a guy in their room. It's past open hours, and their door is closed."

Katie sprang from her desk where she had been printing out the photos of the girls on the floor to finish The Peculiar Treasures Wall. "Do you have the master key?"

Nicole held it up. "Right here. We need to do this together. Remember from training, we need to be firm and specific, but we're not supposed to take on the police role."

Katie nodded. Part of their training during the week of meetings and dorm prep after the Catalina retreat had been role-playing problem situations. Each RA was put in a dorm room with another RA who role-played a predicament.

Katie's assignment had been to deal with a student who was depressed and homesick. After Katie moved past her initial response, which was to roll her eyes and to want to say, "Oh, come on, grow up," she was given a little extra time to think through the situation and ended up receiving a strong evaluation. The reviewers said she was sympathetic without being weak and gave the homesick student specific direction and opportunity to take steps out of her depression.

Katie didn't think she would have scored as well if she had to respond to a role-played suicidal scenario or the one she and Nicole were about to attend to in room 229.

Nicole knocked on the door. Katie checked the names on the door tag she and Nicole had made a few days earlier. "Sabrina and Tasha," Katie repeated, trying to remember if she had met them yet.

"It's Nicole and Katie." Nicole knocked a

second time. "We need you to open the door."

They could hear low voices and shuffling inside. One of the voices was definitely a male.

"Sabrina, Tasha, we know you're in there. We've heard you have a guy in the room. May we please speak with you?" Nicole said.

The doorknob clicked and turned, and the door opened.

The two roommates stood beside each other, looking cool and calm. Katie remembered them. She also remembered this room. Sabrina was the one with the large wardrobe that had been a problem moving in.

Nicole glanced around the room. Katie checked behind the door.

"Hi," Nicole said, ever the softhearted woman. "We were told you had a guy in here, and I'm sure both of you are familiar with the policy for Crown Hall."

They nodded.

"So, is that correct? Do you have a guy in here?"

"Do you see a guy in here?" Sabrina asked with a snip in her tone.

"There was a guy in here earlier." Tasha looked at Sabrina and then back at Katie and Nicole. "We didn't do anything wrong.

318

He was here during open hours."

"When did he leave?" Nicole's voice was still light and friendly.

The girls looked at each other and shrugged.

"Okay." Nicole brushed back her hair. "Well, I just need to remind both of you of the school policy and to say that it's not a good idea to go against the rules established here at Rancho. The rules are for your protection."

"Except the rules are ridiculous," Sabrina said. "I mean, we're in college. Why should someone tell us who can come into our room and when that person has to leave? I mean, come on, trust us a little. We're not in middle school."

"I know," Nicole said. "Very few colleges have the sort of restrictions that are in effect here at Rancho. But that's part of what makes us Rancho. Until those rules change, part of my job is to be an advocate of them."

Katie took a step closer to the women. "What Nicole is saying is that by coming to Rancho you both signed off on the school policies, and that means you wouldn't have a guy in here right now."

"We know."

"Okay." Nicole started to leave the room.

Katie wasn't satisfied to walk out. She had

heard the shuffling and the deep voice. On her way toward the door Katie had an idea. She reached over and gave the wardrobe a resounding thump with her fist.

The three other women jumped, and a male voice let out a "whoa!" from inside the wardrobe.

"You don't have a guy in your room, but you have one hiding in your wardrobe. Is that it?" Katie flung open the wardrobe door, but the guy didn't come out. He was hiding behind the hanging clothes.

"Yo," Katie said, "if you're looking for a path to Narnia, you're not going to find it there, dude."

She could hear him breathing, but he didn't come out.

"Come on." Katie couldn't help but laugh as she stood in front of the open wardrobe. "This is ridiculous." She pulled back the clothes, and there stood a frightened-looking guy trying to exude a tough expression.

He forcefully pressed his way past Katie and said, "It was just a joke. Man, you guys are whacked. Not that it matters because I don't go to school here, so I don't have to go by your stupid rules."

He took off, and Sabrina and Tasha shifted their gaze from each other to Nicole.

"Aren't you going to yell at us or something?" Sabrina asked.

Nicole shook her head. "No, but we do need to let you know that one of the RDs will contact you in a few days to meet with you and talk about this."

Katie followed Nicole down the hall to her room. Once they were behind Nicole's closed door, Katie said, "That was insane. You have so much class, Nicole."

"You have so much smarts," Nicole said with a hint of a nervous laugh. "I was going to get Craig. I never would have thought of pounding on the wardrobe."

"It was obvious. Where else could he be? And what were they doing having an off-campus guy in their room? I wouldn't have been as nice as you were. They totally lied to us."

Nicole picked up her cell phone and dialed campus security. "Hi, this is Nicole from Crown Hall. We had an off-campus male on our floor after hours. Could you have security make sure he finds his way off the grounds?" Nicole went on to give a detailed description of what he looked like and was wearing.

With that security step covered, the two of them found the incident report form and filled it out together. It took them more than an hour. Then they returned to have the girls sign off that the details on the report were accurate.

This time the women opened their door the first time Katie knocked.

"Is that it? All we have to do is sign this?" Sabrina asked. "Aren't you going to call our parents or send us to the dean or anything?"

Nicole shook her head. "It's like I said earlier: You're college students now. You know the guidelines and the rules. You can choose what you want to do with your freedom here. I mean, the truth is, if you prefer going to a college without these restrictions, you have plenty of other schools to choose from. Rancho Corona isn't for everyone. And yes, it may seem like a little Christian bubble sometimes, but that's how things are set up, and that's what has worked at Rancho all these years."

"You know what? We want to apologize," Tasha said.

"Yeah, we talked about it, and we don't want to mess up here. You're right, it's our choice about the rules, and having the guy in our room after hours wasn't a good choice."

Katie stepped across the room and gave both of them a hug. Neither of them seemed to expect the gesture of acceptance.

Tasha's flighty laugh gave away her nervousness. "When you guys called out our names and said you were going to open the door, we thought it was going to be gruesome."

"We don't want you to be afraid of us," Katie said. "We want to develop a great relationship with both of you. A relationship that's based on honesty and respect."

"We really thought you would be mad at us for a long time," Sabrina said.

Nicole shook her head. "What would that accomplish? Katie's right. We're going to be living together for a year. What we want is what's best for both of you."

Afterwards, as Katie and Nicole finished putting the rest of the photos up on the wall well after midnight, Katie thought about how the incident had played out. It occurred to her that as a child her parents used a combination of anger, shame, and threats to keep her in line. She realized now how much could be accomplished with firmness and kindness.

Nicole went back to her room for some more of the approved wall adhesive putty. Katie stood back and took a look at their work. In her hand she had a printout of Isaiah 43:1: "Fear not, for I have redeemed you; I have called you by your name; you are mine." She was trying to decide which photo she should match up with the verse.

Emilee stepped out of the bathroom and waved at Katie with her toothbrush. Instead of returning to her room at the other end of the hall, Emilee shuffled along in her floppy PJs and stood next to Katie.

"I love what y'all did with this wall. The verse you put next to my roommate's photo is perfect for her, with the 'far off lands' part and everything."

The verse was Isaiah 49:1, "Listen to me, all you in far off lands! The LORD called me before my birth; from within the womb he called me by name."

"That is a great verse," Katie agreed. "I think Nicole put that one there."

"Did Nicole put the verse by my picture?"

"I'm not sure."

"Well, I really love it." Emilee reached out and touched the paper as if it were precious. She read aloud, " 'I will give you the treasures of darkness, riches stored in secret places, so that you may know that I am the LORD, the God of Israel, who summons you by name.' "

"That's a good one too," Katie said.

"How did y'all know which verses to put by which pictures?"

"We didn't," Katie said.

"Then how did they end up matched so perfectly?"

Katie smiled and answered Emilee with one of her all-time favorite expressions. "It must have been a God thing."

Katie held up the as-yet-unassigned Isaiah 43 verse.

"You don't have a verse by your photo yet," Emilee noted. "Is that yours, the one in your hand?"

Katie read it again. "I like it," she said. "I like that God has redeemed me and called me by name, but I'm not feeling it's my verse for the year."

"How about if I find a verse for you?" Emilee asked. "You're doing all this for us. Let me do something for you."

"Okay, I'd like that. Thanks, Emilee."

"I'm going by 'Em' these days. My roommate is going by 'Emily,' and I'm goin' with Em. I like it, don't you?"

Katie nodded. "Good night, Em."

"Good night, Miss Katie."

Tucking herself into bed that night well after 2 a.m., Katie felt herself floating away on a dream pillow. In her imagination she was back at the picnic with Rick by the fountain. She fell asleep with a smile.

23

Friday was such a full day that Katie didn't eat until that evening when the fifty pizzas arrived for the All Hall Event, which took place on the soccer field. She was in charge of setting out the food, but as soon as she opened the first box to check on the pizza's size, she knew she better take a slice before she became dizzy.

Katie and Nicole had organized the crowd-breaker games and worked together to start the party. Crown Hall had a total of 208 students, and it looked as if about 150 had come to the event. Craig said it was a good turnout. He helped Nicole by giving directions through a bullhorn for the first mixer game.

While the group got caught up in the successful mixer, Katie set up a logical order for everyone to move through the food line. Like locusts, the students descended and made the pizza disappear.

Katie recruited Em and Emily to help with cleanup along with Jordan and six guys from his floor. Katie didn't stop moving the entire time. At 10:30 the last trash can was cleared off the field, and she looked around.

"What was that?" she muttered to herself.

Julia, who was standing a few feet away, said, "That, Katie Girl, was an immensely successful All Hall Event. Well done."

Katie remembered how Rick had called her "Katie Girl" on registration day and she had kind of liked it. When Julia called her "Katie Girl," she really liked it. With Julia, the name felt like an initiation into a special group. It felt like being a "surfer girl."

"All I know is the whole event was a blur," Katie said.

"Then let me be the first to tell you, it was a good blur," Julia said. "Everyone had a fantastic time and started to get to know each other. You and Nicole did a great job. We had enough of everything, which is rare at these events. Usually we have way too much or too little. This came out just right."

"I feel kind of bad that I didn't spend time talking to anyone," Katie said.

"What do you mean?"

"I know my role as an RA is to connect with all the residents on a personal basis, but I turned into a worker bee and barely talked to anyone or noticed what was going on."

"Being a servant has a lot of different forms," Julia said. "This time around you served your women by being a worker bee. The next All Hall you won't be in charge of the details, and you'll be able to socialize all you want."

Katie shivered in the cool night air. Now that she had stopped running around and was standing on the grassy field, her T-shirt and shorts weren't adequate for the temperature's dip. "Can we walk back to the dorm while we talk?"

"Sure."

"I'm feeling like I can't connect well with each of the women the way I want."

"It's only been a week, Katie."

"I know, but I guess I was thinking of how at summer camp in high school our counselor bonded with each of us in one week. Our whole cabin was really close."

Julia smiled. "How many girls were in the cabin? Eight? Ten?"

Katie crossed her arms across her middle and nodded. "Something like that."

"And you were all in the same cabin," Julia added. "Sleeping in the same space. That makes a difference. At camp, all you had to do that week was be together. This is college. Quite a bit different, as you know. You have three times as many women and these women have classes, jobs, friends. Give yourself time, Katie. Your job is to be available. Remember? You're not their mother. You're not their counselor. You're not their exclusive new best friend. You are an assistant. A servant. Tonight you helped facilitate their connecting with each other, and that's what All Halls are about."

"I guess I thought I was going to be doing more one-to-one sort of . . ."

"Counseling?" Julia finished the sentence for her.

"Yeah, something like that."

"Think of your role as being a listener more than a counselor. Most people can figure out their own challenges and problems once they're given the chance to hear themselves lay out the issue."

Katie thought about how Julia had done that for her more than once. Julia initiated time for them to talk at the beginning of the summer when Katie went to her apartment for tea. She also made it convenient on the Catalina ferry for Katie to talk about what was going on with her and Rick. Julia mostly listened during those times. Yet Katie left each conversation feeling as if she had received wise counsel.

"I'm so glad you're my RD," Katie said as they entered the front door of Crown Hall.

"The feeling is mutual," Julia said. "How's everything going with Rick, by the way?"

"Good. Really good."

"Glad to hear that," Julia said.

The two of them parted ways at the stairwell, and Katie remembered how she would have been with Rick right now in San Diego if she weren't an RA in charge of the All Hall Event.

Wondering if Rick went to the baseball game without her, Katie stepped into her stuffy dorm room and noticed her cell phone blinking in the charger where she had left it. Kicking off her sandals, Katie checked her voice mail. The first was from Christy. She said she was just checking in. She and Todd were on their way to Carlsbad to baby-sit Daniel. Katie could just picture the two of them doting over the little guy.

The next voice mail was from Rick. "Hey, call me as soon as you get in, okay? I need to talk with you."

Katie pressed his speed-dial number and stretched out on her bed.

Rick answered on the first ring. "How did your big event go?"

"Good. Julia said it was a success. It felt like a whole lot of work, and I haven't stopped all day. This is the first time I've sat down since I left my room this morning. I'm just fried. What about you? What did you do tonight? Did you go to the game?"

"No, I gave the tickets to Doug and Tracy."

Katie realized that was why Todd and Christy had gone to Carlsbad to baby-sit. "So what did you do?"

"I flew to Arizona this afternoon. I'm in Tempe now with my brother. We needed to make some final decisions on the new café, and this was a good time for me to get away."

Katie swallowed. She was almost certain next he was going to say was that he wouldn't be back in time for them to do something together Saturday night. Instead of extracting that information from Rick, she asked, "How's the new café coming along?"

"Good. A lot of details. We're meeting with a new contractor in the morning. The previous one didn't work out."

A tense pause lingered between them.

"Listen, Katie —" Rick began.

"It's okay," she said quickly.

"You don't even know what I'm going to say."

"Yes, I do. You were going to say that you

don't know if you'll be back in time for us to go out tomorrow night. And I'm saying, it's okay. We can do something on Sunday evening if you're back by then. Or Monday night. Well, after my 8 to 10 study group. Or whatever. We'll do something next weekend. It's okay, Rick. I understand."

"You sure?"

"Yeah, I'm okay with it. You know I'd tell you if I wasn't."

"I do know that. It's one of the many things I adore about you, Katie. You have no guile."

She laughed. "What does that mean? Doesn't guile have something to do with gallbladders? Are you saying I don't have a reliable gallbladder?"

Rick laughed. It was a good, deep, happy Rick sort of laugh. "I think the gallbladder connection is 'bile,' not 'guile.' When I say you have no guile, I mean you aren't devious. You say what you mean and mean what you say. You don't play head games. I love that about you."

Katie's heart did a little flutter-roo when Rick said the word "love." True, he didn't say he loved Katie. But he did say he loved something she did, or rather didn't do. He loved a character trait of hers.

With a flashback to the first day of staff

332

training, Katie thought of when Craig asked her what favorite characteristic she had inherited from her mother. Now she had an answer. Her mother said things plainly, as they were. Katie did the same. It was a small, fractured gem, but a scrap worth picking up and saving. Katie spoke plainly. Rick loved that about her. She had no guile.

At that moment it seemed possible to Katie that everything in her splintered life might be redeemable. Even the fragments of broken childhood gems had value and were worth holding onto for closer inspection.

For the next hour, Katie and Rick talked about everything and nothing. They were together, even though they were miles apart. They were figuring out how to be "us" in the next season of their relationship.

Despite all the obstacles, it was working. The distance and the interruptions should have fragmented them, but somehow the challenges pressed them closer to each other. Closer at the heart level. As Katie was discovering, that was the part of their relationship that mattered the most.

Two weeks later, the long-awaited date night finally happened. Rick had finished his weekend trips to Arizona for the time being. Katie had fallen into the routine of her classes, and aside from a few ups and downs, everything was going well on the floor for Nicole and Katie at Crown Hall North.

That is, aside from a petition signed by twenty-three women on the floor. They wanted The Kissing Wall back. Apparently it had been a tradition on Crown Hall North for something like twelve years. The initiator of the petition said she had an older cousin or sister or some such relation who helped to start The Kissing Wall, and tradition dictated they should have one again this year.

"Do they want us to take down The Peculiar Treasures Wall?" Katie asked Nicole when the two of them met to look over the petition in Nicole's room.

"No, all of them said they love The Peculiar Treasures Wall. They just want it located at the beginning of the hall where everyone enters so it will help them become familiar with the other women on the floor. They suggested we move The Peculiar Treasures Wall across from my room, since that wall is blank. Then six of them have volunteered to put The Kissing Wall back in its traditional spot at the end of the hall across from your room. What do you think?"

Even though Katie thought it might be a

private torture to look out her door every day and be reminded that everyone on campus was kissing except her, she said, "We can't be the ones to break the tradition."

"That's what I think too," Nicole said.

The wall projects took most of Saturday afternoon to complete. Nicole printed out the same kissing verses she had put on the wall last year. Some of the English majors on the floor added quotations from literature. Other eager Kissing Wall supporters had photos ready to contribute.

In no time The Kissing Wall was up. Katie stood with a dozen other women and admired their handiwork, reading the quotations.

The kiss, together with music, is the one universal language.

Anonymous

For it was not into my ear you whispered, but into my heart.
It was not my heart you kissed, but my soul.

Judy Garland

Say I'm weary, say I'm sad;

Say that health and wealth have missed
  me;
Say I'm growing old, but add —
Jenny kissed me!

Leigh Hunt

A man had given all other bliss,
And all his worldly worth for this,
To waste his whole heart in one kiss,
Upon her perfect lips.

Alfred Lord Tennyson

Her lips on his could tell him better than
  all her stumbling words.

Margaret Mitchell

The sunlight claps the earth,
And the moonbeams kiss the sea:
What are all these kissings worth,
If thou kiss not me?

Percy Bysshe Shelley

The moment eternal — just that and no
  more —
When ecstasy's utmost we clutch at the
  core
While cheeks burn, arms open, eyes shut,
  and lips meet!

Robert Browning

First time he kissed me, he but only kissed
The fingers of this hand wherewith I write;
And, ever since, it grew more clean and
   white.
                    Elizabeth Barrett Browning

Where one drop of blood drains a castle
   of life,
so one kiss can bring it alive again.
                              Sleeping Beauty

In a swirl of kissing contemplations, Katie
had to hurry to get ready for her date with
Rick. While it had been a couple of weeks
since their last official date, the two of them
had managed to meet the past two Tuesdays
at the fountain for lunch. Each time, Rick
had only half an hour. He always brought
Katie her favorite roast beef sandwich, with
mustard, and each time they had managed
to tuck in a few snuggle or splash moments.

As Katie dashed around her room to get
ready, romantic thoughts joined hands and
danced around gleefully in her imagination.
She was more than ready for a few mushy
moments with Rick. After reading the kissing quotations, she felt as if her cuddle
compartment needed to be filled up.

Katie sang while she was in the shower
and then went through her clean clothes

options in record time. Taking a few extra minutes to pay attention to how evenly her mascara was lining up on her eyelashes, Katie played with her rarely used eyeliner pencil. The results were pretty good. She missed not having Christy in her dorm room the way she had been last year. Christy would have a few tips at this point, and then she would send Katie out the door with a cheery boost of confidence.

As usually happened when Katie's thoughts drifted to her friendship with Christy, she opened the door to sadness. The sadness wasn't related to Christy but rather to what Katie had missed in her growing-up years. Because she wasn't fussed over or given any particular encouragement about how she looked, acted, or developed, in many ways, Christy became Katie's primary source of inspiration and instruction in those areas. Not that Christy deliberately tried to be a role model for Katie. The life lessons came naturally, blooming in the spring of their friendship.

Katie stopped to look in the mirror. "What a different person you might have become if it weren't for Christy."

As soon as she mumbled that thought, another thought came to her. This thought brought wings with it and seemed to attach those wings to a longtime heaviness in the corner of Katie's spirit. That heaviness was the sad, sighable sense that she never had been nurtured or mentored the way so many other women at Rancho had been. This time, though, when the thought settled on her, she saw how God had sent Christy her way to be that caring, nurturing friend. The invisible wings lifted the old heaviness of feeling neglected and fluttered away with it.

"You gave me everything I needed, didn't you, Lord? So what if my mother didn't excel in the pal department? You gave me Christy. You gave us to each other. All these years you were filling in the missing pieces for me, weren't you? You took care of my nurturing needs when I wasn't even paying attention. And now I have new friendships with Julia and Nicole."

The realization brought tears to Katie's freshly made-up eyes. "Oh, no, you don't!" she commanded the tears with a quick blink. "You little teardrops go back to where you were hiding. At least for now. I don't have time to redo my eye makeup."

Katie breezed past The Kissing Wall and past The Peculiar Treasures Wall. She paused by her photo just a blink and noticed Em still hadn't come up with a verse for her. All the other girls had verses. Maybe she would need to find one just to complete the wall at last.

Stepping outside Crown Hall into the late September evening, Katie smiled. The air was warm and carried the scent of dry grass. The sky was edged in a soft pink glow from the sunset.

Rick was walking her direction and wore an immaculately pressed short-sleeved shirt. He was the only guy she knew who ironed his shirts or sent them to the dry cleaner. He looked great. The best part, though, was the way his expression warmed when he saw her.

"Hello, gorgeous," he said with a half-grin.

Rick is so mushy right now. Eee! Romantic Rick. This is going to be such a great night!

24

Katie slipped her hand into Rick's as they walked to his car. She knew it was an excusable vanity, but inwardly she wished more women were around campus to see her promenade out to the parking lot with her dreamy date.

"I have something for you in the car," Rick said.

"What is it?"

"You'll see."

Rick's surprise was a huge bouquet of mixed flowers waiting for her on the passenger's seat. The color combination of the floral assortment and the fragrance from the day lilies was so intense his car was overwhelmed by the scent when he opened the door for her.

Katie was stunned at the size of the bouquet. "Did you clean out a whole floral shop?"

"No, I called in the order. I told them I

wanted a mixed bouquet of their best and most fragrant flowers, and this is what they created. I think they captured exactly what I asked for. It might seem a little over the top. A little on the bold, stunning, and dramatic side, but that's why they remind me of you." Rick closed her door and gave her a smile.

"Thanks." Katie didn't quite know what to do with the flowers. She felt like a pageant princess holding the huge bundle in her lap. If Rick's car were a convertible, she might have felt compelled to seat herself on the top of the backseat and wave to people as they drove by.

Rick put on some of his favorite music and kept glancing at Katie, smiling at her. "You look really good," he said.

"Thanks. So do you. Tell me about Arizona. How's the café working out? Are you going back there soon?"

"Not for awhile. We're in a holding pattern at the moment, waiting for more paperwork to clear. No more trips for me for a bit. I'm hoping that means you and I will be able to spend more time together." With a smirk he added, "That is, if you can manage to fit me into your schedule."

Katie reached over and playfully gave Rick's earlobe a tug. "Oh, I think I can manage to schedule you in occasionally."

"Good. I'm going to hold you to that."

Katie smiled contentedly. *It's been too long since Rick and I have been together. I'm really tired of being in the slow lane. We've made it through our first month of adjusting to a bunch of changes. The way I see it, we are overdue for our next DTR. I'm not going to start the conversation now, though. If Rick doesn't initiate a talk about our relationship at dinner, I will afterwards.*

Their short drive to Temecula brought them to the Thai restaurant where they found they would have to wait two hours to be seated in the bustling new eatery.

"Would you like to wait?" The hostess checked the seating schedule in front of her.

"What do you think?" Rick asked.

Katie shook her head. She didn't want to wait that long to eat.

As Rick ushered her back out to the car, Katie said, "I'm surprised you didn't call ahead."

"I did. They don't take reservations. I guess we'll have to go to Plan B."

"Okay, what's Plan B?"

"I don't know. I'm sure we can come up with something."

After ten minutes of debating options, they ended up driving through a fast-food restaurant, ordering hamburgers, and then hurrying to make it to a movie at the theater down the street from the Thai restaurant.

The theater was packed, and the film was disappointing. Katie described it as one of those comedies in which all the good parts are what you see in the trailers, but the film itself is a dud.

Added to that, the air conditioning didn't seem to be working in the theater. She and Rick had started the evening sitting close. By the end of the film, they both were feeling claustrophobic and weren't touching.

"What do you think?" Rick asked as they left. "Should we try the Thai restaurant now?"

"I'm not hungry enough for a sit-down meal," Katie said. "Are you?"

"Not really."

Even though they were outside, with the night air cooling them off, she still felt claustrophobic and edgy.

"I could go for some ice cream," Katie said.

"How about if we buy some at the grocery store and take it back to my apartment?"

Katie was surprised. She couldn't remember Rick's ever suggesting they go to his apartment.

"Is your roommate at the apartment?"

Katie asked. "I haven't met him yet."

"No, he went to a staff retreat this week-end. His name is Eli. I thought you knew him."

Katie shook her head. "I don't remember meeting him. How's it working out having a roommate?"

"Great. Neither of us is ever there, so I haven't gotten to know him very well."

"I suppose we could go to your apartment and have some ice cream. That is, under one condition," Katie said.

"What's that?"

"I get to pick the ice cream."

"Are you afraid I'm going to pick something you don't like?" Rick asked.

"What? Like something over the top and stunning and a little on the dramatic side?" Her grin was full of mischief.

Rick did a double take. "You don't like the flowers."

"I like the flowers. I just had to tease you."

He looked at her again. "No, you don't like the flowers, do you? Be honest."

Katie bit her lip and wished she hadn't made the revealing comment. "I love the intent behind the flowers, but to be honest, you could have picked a single California poppy from off the highway, and it would have meant just as much to me. Does that make sense?"

He nodded slowly.

"I'm not a real frou-frou kind of person, so the extravagance just feels . . . I don't know . . . extravagant."

"That's how the bouquet was supposed to make you feel. That was the message."

"Then I got the message." Katie smiled, but she couldn't tell if things were smoothed over with Rick so she added, "Thanks again, Rick. Really. Thank you for being extravagant."

"You're welcome." His eyes were fixed on the road ahead and didn't wander over to Katie with any sort of soothing look.

"I just like spending time with you, Rick. I want you to know that so you don't feel as if you need to lavish me with half of a floral shop to make our time together memorable."

Rick turned into the parking lot of the Sherman Brothers' Grocery Store.

"Why didn't you go to the Grocery Kart?" Katie asked.

"Why would I go there?"

"Sherman Brothers is way more expensive."

"Grocery Kart is a cavernous warehouse, and I don't feel like bagging my own groceries."

"Groceries? It's a single container of ice cream."

Rick got out and closed his door without answering.

"Okay," Katie said under her breath. "This is turning into a disaster!"

Note to self: Be nice to the poor guy. He's really trying. Stop spouting the first thing that comes into your mind!

They walked side by side into the grocery store. Katie decided on mint chip ice cream right away, but the brand she reached for came in a square container.

"Get the mint chip in the round container," Rick said.

"Why?"

"Ice cream in round containers tastes better."

Katie laughed. "No it doesn't."

"Just get the round one."

Katie gave Rick a cheeky look and picked up both the containers. She seemed to have forgotten about her most recent note to self. "How about this: We'll buy both and do a taste test. And you're paying. You'll see there's no difference between round and square ice cream."

"Fine, but your test isn't going to be valid." Rick led the way to the ten-items-or-less line.

"Why do you say that?"

"You're buying two different brands. They use different ingredients."

"No, they don't. Ice cream is ice cream." She picked up the square container after the woman at the checkout rang it up. Katie read off the first five ingredients. "Check your round ice cream, there, Doyle. I bet you anything the ingredients are the same."

The checkout clerk seemed to be repressing her amusement as she asked, "Would you like paper or plastic?"

"Plastic," Katie said. "And a couple of plastic spoons, if you have them. We can settle this right here and right now. As a matter of fact, you can be our impartial judge."

The woman held up her hand. "I make it a point to stay out of all marital conflicts."

"We're not married," Rick and Katie said in unison.

She looked surprised. "Brother and sister, then?"

"No," Katie said firmly.

"We're just . . ." Rick didn't have a defining term he could use.

Katie felt compelled to give one to this stranger, although she wasn't sure why. She wanted to say, "We're 'almost' a couple. This is an 'almost' date. Right now. We're on an 'almost' date. I know. Hard to believe. Not many couples go on dates, almost or otherwise, to the grocery store. Especially the Sherman Brothers' Grocery Store. But, hey, we're not like every other 'almost' couple."

Instead, Katie heeded her earlier note to self and kept her mouth shut.

The woman looked even more amused that neither of them could clarify their relationship. She held out the cash register receipt and said, "Well, you certainly fight like a married couple."

Neither Katie nor Rick seemed to find her comment romantic or worthy of a response. They strode together to the car, and Katie said, "Her comment was completely uncalled for."

"She's working late," Rick said calmly.

Katie turned and put her hand on her hip. "You're defending her?"

"I'm not defending anyone. I'm only saying, what does a person who works the late shift at a grocery store have to talk about?"

"It doesn't matter what shift she's working, it's all about customer service. Isn't that what you preach all the time at work?"

"Well, the Sherman Brothers' Grocery Store isn't the Dove's Nest. And I'm not the manager of Sherman Brothers'."

Katie slid into the passenger seat. "Next time, we're going to the Grocery Kart."

"No, we're not," Rick said.

Katie couldn't be certain, but it seemed that Rick slammed her door a little too forcefully. The overpowering fragrance of the flowers in the backseat was a sweet mockery to the tension between them as Rick revved up the Mustang's engine.

Nothing about this night was going the way Katie had dreamed it would.

Rick and Katie didn't say anything to each other during the four-block drive to his apartment. When they arrived, Katie left the flowers in the backseat but picked up the bag with the two cartons of ice cream.

Rick met her on her side of the car and took the bag from her. "Hey," his voice was low. He reached over and gently touched her shoulder. "Come on."

He leaned closer.

She felt herself calming down. It was crazy to pick a fight now. Katie eased up. With a rising sense of the comfortable rhythm they had shared during their long phone conversations over the past few weeks, she said, "Come on, yourself, Rickster. We have an ice cream taste test to conduct."

He put his arm around her shoulders, and

they started down the pathway to his apartment.

"You know," Rick said with an edge of tension still hanging in his voice, "if you and I are going to keep working on nicknames for each other, I think Rickster needs to be thrown out."

"Why?"

"It sounds like 'Trickster.' That's not me, Katie. It might have been back in high school when you started calling me Rickster, but that's not me anymore."

Katie realized his comment was true. Her high school nickname for him hadn't been born of warm and favorable thoughts.

"Okay, that's fair." She softened a little more. "Why do you think it's been so hard for us to come up with nicknames for each other? I mean, how long did it take for you to come up with 'Killer Eyes' for Christy?"

Rick stopped walking and turned to stare at Katie in the glow of the apartment complex lights. His jaw flinched. He didn't say anything, but instead started to walk again. Unlocking the door of his apartment, he held the door for her and then said, "Katie, does that bother you?"

"What?"

"That I called Christy 'Killer Eyes'?"

"No, of course not. Why should it? She

does have killer eyes."

Rick put the grocery bag on the counter of his small kitchen and turned to Katie. "Here's the question I'm trying to ask: Does it bother you that I had a thing for Christy?"

"No." Katie shook her head and kept her gaze steady as she looked into Rick's sincere, brown eyes. "It doesn't bother me. That was then. This is now. The key word in your question is, of course, 'had.' You *had* a thing for Christy. You don't still *have* a thing for her." She paused. "Do you?"

"No, absolutely not. That was high school. I definitely was infatuated, but I think 90 percent of it was because she was a challenge. She was the unattainable new girl. I've changed, Katie. You know that."

"Yes, I know." Katie put the ice cream in the freezer. She didn't want to mess around with her taste test challenge until both of them were back in a light-hearted mood. When she turned around, Rick still was looking at her pensively.

"There were a few others," Rick said in a stiff voice.

Katie didn't know if he meant a few other nicknames for Christy or a few other high school crushes. Either one, it didn't matter to her. This wasn't news. Katie had been around for the various seasons of Rick's changes. More than anything, she wanted their relationship to work. If it was going to work, she knew she had to be ready and willing to accept Rick on every level, just as she wanted him to accept her with all her flaws and quirks.

If they were about to move out of the slow lane, as Katie believed they were, then opening up to each other was a good thing. It was like using a turn signal. Rick was signaling a change. And Katie was ready.

What she didn't understand was why her stomach felt so upset at the moment.

25

Rick leaned against the kitchen counter opposite Katie in his small but tidy apartment and started with, "Do you remember last fall when I said I wished I could go back and change a couple of years of my life?"

"Yes."

"I did a lot of stupid things. I made some pretty bad choices."

"That was then, Rick. This is now."

"I know."

"You're not the same person you were back then. God has been changing you. He's forgiven you for whatever happened back then. You're free to move on to whatever is next." Katie almost added, "And it just so happens I'm what's next for you; so move on, buddy." But she held back because Rick's expression made it clear he had more to say. He seemed to be skimming over her grace proclamation and clenched his jaw.

"I want to tell you something, Katie, and

I need you to hear me out."

She nodded.

"One of the women I went out with the first year of college contacted me last week. I barely remember her." He paused. "Actually, that's not true. I want to keep being honest with you, Katie. The truth is, I remember the way she kissed. I'm a guy, okay? We remember those things. For a long time. It's like certain moments of physical contact just don't ever go away. They burn a memory in a guy's brain. But you see, the thing is, I don't remember her personality or the way she laughed. I didn't even remember her name until she called."

"How did she get your number?" Katie tried to keep her expression and voice steady.

"I don't know. She lives in Boston now."

Katie relaxed a little and attempted to communicate by her posture and expression that Rick could tell her anything.

"Here's the thing, Katie. Like I said, I didn't remember anything specific about her." He attempted a smile. "I have no idea what kind of ice cream she likes, let alone what shape of container she prefers. By my standards now and my current way of measuring a relationship, she and I didn't have a real relationship. Nothing like what you and I have."

Rick shifted his position. "I wanted to tell you this because I don't want anything or anyone from my past showing up one day and freaking you out."

He moved closer to Katie and touched the end of her hair, rubbing the copper strands between his thumb and forefinger. "What you and I have is real. You're very real. Everything you say and do is genuine."

"Well, not everything I say is real. Sometimes I exaggerate."

"Oh, really?" The lines around Rick's chocolate brown eyes softened.

"Yeah, and sometimes — just sometimes — I overdo things."

"Is that right?" His grin warmed his face as he slid his fingers under her chin and tilted her face up toward his.

For a moment the two of them stood fixed in place, gazing into each other's eyes. Katie felt her heart pounding.

Is this it? Is he going to kiss me? Here? In his kitchen? Is this how Rick intends to change lanes?

All the times Katie had imagined this defining moment of their relationship, it had been in a more dramatic setting. Her favored backdrop for this first kiss was the beach, preferably at sunset. Or in the mountains under sheltering tree branches that were heavy with snow. They would kiss, and then the snowflakes would magically flutter down, enclosing the two of them in a private snow globe of wonder.

Never in her imaginings did she picture the scenery around them to be the dark-stained cupboards and mushroom-colored walls of Rick's dull apartment kitchen.

Rick tipped his head closer to hers.

Neither of them spoke.

Don't analyze this, Katie! Just let this moment be what it is.

With her heart thumping all the way up into her ears, in stereo, and with her chin tilted just right, Katie lowered her eyelids like the lowering of the shades over the window of her soul. She could feel Rick's breath on her closed eyelids and anticipated the touch of his lips on hers.

But the kiss didn't come.

Peeling open her eyelids, Katie looked at Rick's dispirited expression.

"What?" she whispered.

"We should wait."

Katie's entire being slumped into an exasperated tangle of emotions. She turned away, took two steps to the right, and let out a huff. Then quickly turning back, she came at him. With her open palms, she shoved Rick in the chest the way she shoved the umpire at her last softball game. Her aggressive actions got her benched last spring.

Rick took her shove by stepping back and putting his hands up on top of his head. "I'm sorry. I . . ."

"Don't be sorry," Katie blurted out. "Just kiss me!"

"No, not yet," he said.

"Then when? Rick, it's been almost ten months. If not now, when?"

"I don't know."

"What do you mean, you don't know?"

His voice rose, matching Katie's intensity. "I don't know. It might be ten more months."

"No! You're killing me!"

"You think this is easy for me? Come on! I'm trying to do what's best for both of us. You have no idea how hard I'm trying here. Give me a break!"

"It's just a kiss, okay?"

"It's not just a kiss. It means something. It has to mean something. Don't you see? It means we're taking the next step, Katie. We're changing lanes, isn't that what you call it?"

Katie jutted her chin forward.

"Not every kiss comes with the purest of

intentions, Katie."

"You think I don't know that?" Even though Katie knew she should keep her mouth shut, she pressed forward. "You stole kisses from me twice, remember?"

"Of course I remember." His voice came out sounding like gravel. "I told you. Guys don't forget."

"Well, girls don't forget either!"

The air between them went dead. They stared at each other, as if daring one another to blink first.

"Katie, I promised myself the next time I kissed you I wouldn't steal a kiss from you. I would give you the kiss."

"So, go ahead." Her voice toned down to a whisper. "Give me a kiss, Rick. I'll take it."

Rick didn't move for a full thirty seconds. Maybe longer.

He finally let out a huff and rubbed his hand over the side of his jaw. "We shouldn't have come back here. That's my doing. I'm sorry. I apologize, Katie. I wanted something about this night to be special for us."

"Oh, this is ridiculous," Katie muttered. "Now who's dissecting everything down to the last molecule? Isn't that what you say I do? Well, if you ask me, I think both of us have overanalyzed this. We have put far too much significance on one stupid kiss. We set ourselves up for all this tension. We've made a solitary expression the apex of our whole relationship. We must be insane!"

"We're not insane," Rick said. "We're trying to do what's right."

"Then if we're trying to be so perfect, why not put a ban on all gestures of affection? I mean, what are we doing holding hands? How intimate is that? And what about the hugs? Maybe we should cut out all hugging while we're at it. You and I have had some pretty close and cuddly hugs, you know."

She paused only long enough to catch her breath. "With a stupid kiss, the only part of us that has to officially touch is our lips, right? With a hug, well, hey that's a whole lot more contact. A hug can be like, what, 50 percent of our bodies touching. Whereas with a kiss, two sets of lips make up only, what, like half a percent body contact. No, more like a sixteenth of a percent."

"Katie." Rick's voice was firm.

"No, don't try to hush me. It's time one of us got this out in the open, and I just have to say this. I think being in the slow lane stinks. We're humans, aren't we? Physical beings. Aren't we capable of controlling our stupid passions?"

"Our passions aren't stupid!" His voice rose.

Katie's voice lowered. "Okay, so our passions aren't stupid. That must mean we're stupid. Is that what you're saying? You and I are too stupid to be trusted."

"Katie, you're way off on this."

"Am I? Then why are we treating ourselves and our natural desires as if they're imbeciles and untamable? Isn't it possible for us to kiss each other and not go wacko? Are we saying we have zero self-control? That's only in the movies. In real life people manage to express their feelings of passion and affection — with a kiss, all right? — and they also manage to do it without ruining their virginity. Todd and Christy kissed before they got married, and they didn't get carried away or whatever it is you are so afraid will happen to us."

"Katie . . ."

"I'm not finished. You seem to think I'm so naive and inexperienced, but I'm not. I had some fairly significant moments with Michael when we were dating. Yes, that was back in high school, and no, I'm not saying he was my model for the ideal relationship or that I'm proud of what happened between us. But I am saying that if you think you're the only guy who has ever kissed me,

Rick Doyle, you are wrong. I know I'm only one of many on your kiss list so —"

"Katie, don't go there." Rick's expression toughened.

Katie backed down. "You're right. That wasn't fair. I'm sorry."

They remained in their opposite corners, unyielding.

Katie felt as if her whole nervous system was wired for an explosion at any moment. With thick, even words she said, "Here's the thing. You and I need to figure out how to be 'us.' We're not Doug and Tracy. We're not coming into this relationship with either of us claiming to be a poster child for purity. We're us. And I think we should decide what is right for us. That's all I'm trying to say."

"We did decide, Katie. We talked this over months ago. Why are you questioning all that now?"

"Because."

He waited for her to expand her answer.

"Because." Her voice was back to a whisper. "I really, really, really want you to kiss me. Now."

Rick didn't blink. He didn't move.

Katie stared back. Something overwhelmingly strong inside told her that if Rick wasn't going to give her what she wanted, she should march right over to his side of the kitchen and take it. All she needed to do was make three decisive steps.

She had seen plenty of scenes like this in the movies. One of the exasperated people, usually the guy, makes a bold move. He takes the girl in his arms; they lock in an eternal embrace. The camera comes in for a close-up of the kiss, and their hearts are sealed forever.

The next scene is always one in which the couple rides off merrily on a motorcycle or feeds each other sushi with chopsticks. That's what being together as a boyfriend and girlfriend was supposed to look like. Not all this ridiculous arguing in the kitchen.

Katie told herself she could do this. She could take the lead and cross the gap between them in three brazen steps. She would be right there, a millimeter away from his lips, and she would kiss him.

And when she did, she knew everything would change.

26

Katie could feel Christy staring at her from the passenger seat of Baby Hummer.

"So then what happened?" Christy asked.

"I took three determined steps."

Christy's eyes widened. "You did?"

"Yeah, but they were three big steps in the opposite direction. I walked out of the apartment."

"Oh, Katie." Christy's shoulders relaxed. "Where did you go?"

"Just around the apartment complex. I considered going to your apartment, of course, but then I wasn't ready to talk to anybody. So I just walked around and cleared my head."

"What did Rick do?" Christy's soft drink cup in her hand was dripping condensation on her lap.

"Nothing. Made me so mad! I wanted him to come running after me, you know? I thought he should scoop me up and make everything all better. But he didn't come after me. And that ticked me off even more. Nothing about that night went the way it was supposed to. I'm so sick of all the fairy tales. They're bogus."

"That's because you're not living in a fairy tale. What you're experiencing with Rick is real life, Katie. This is the true stuff relationships are made of."

"Yeah? Well, I don't like it. Why can't falling in love be sweet, dreamy, and happy like in the storybooks?"

Christy seemed to be trying hard not to let a grin take over her sympathetic expression.

"Oh, please. No," Katie said, catching Christy's look. "If you're going to tell me that true love really is dreamy and happy and that everything changes once you get married, I might be forced to inflict bodily injury on you, and no one would blame me."

"You don't know what I was going to say," Christy said stubbornly.

"I could guess. You had that here-today-gone-to-Maui look in your eyes, and to be honest, I can't handle any flippant platitudes right now about castles in the cotton candy clouds waiting for me on the other side of my purity vows."

"I wasn't going to tell you any flippant

platitudes. I don't think I even know any. What I will tell you, and you need to hear me say this, is that everything does change, in good ways and in bad ways. Everything in the relationship intensifies once you're married. All the quirks in the other person get quirkier. All the sweetness amplifies too. All the conflict escalates. You wouldn't believe the insane fights Todd and I have had in the past few weeks."

Katie leaned back. "Are you serious? You guys have been fighting?"

"Not all the time. But we've had a couple of Goliath-sized misunderstandings. Todd says we're adjusting to each other and figuring out how to be a married couple. I think he's right, but I still hate arguing with him."

"I can't picture you guys having arguments now. I mean, all the tensions are being released, right?"

Christy pressed her back against the car door and looked as if she were trying to decide how to answer. "Yes, many tensions are released. Physically, of course."

Katie noticed the way Christy's face took on that familiar understated glow she had whenever she talked about being married.

"It's not all about the physical part of the relationship, though, Katie. I'm sure you know that."

"Right now, I don't know what I know."

"Yes you do. You know what works and what doesn't work. You know what lasts and what fades away. You guys are doing really well, Katie. You are."

"I don't think so." Katie sighed and lowered the sun visor on the windshield of Baby Hummer. "Rick and I haven't talked to each other since Saturday night."

"You haven't?"

"Nope."

"Katie, it's Monday."

"I know."

Christy crumpled up the bag from Archie's Burgers that contained the remains of her now-cold french fries and uneaten last two bites of chicken sandwich. "Todd has this thing about not letting the sun go down on our anger. He won't let us go to bed mad. The sooner you and Rick talk, the better it will be."

"Or the worse it could be."

This was the first time Katie had pulled out all the details of that disappointing night and talked about them. She could see how the whole night would have gone differently if just one of them had bent a little.

"Rick and I could sit down and talk, but he might say, 'That's it. You're a nut case. I'm out.' "

"He might," Christy said, quickly skimming over the possibility. "Or he might say nothing has changed in his heart and in his head toward you, and he wants to move forward. Rick is a determined man. He has set his affections on you, Katie. I have a feeling it will take more than a tense argument over kissing to get him to change his interest in you."

"The man has a temper," Katie said. "But then, so do I. I guess we discovered how stubborn we both could be. We couldn't even agree on the shape of the ice cream carton. When I went back to Rick's apartment that night, I saw he had heaved both the cartons into the trash. They were sitting there melting, and I thought, *Fine. Whatever.* That's when he wanted to sit down and talk, but I told him I couldn't right then. So he drove me home in silence. I got out of the car, slammed the door, and left the flowers in his backseat. You've heard of mocking birds? Well, I think those were mocking flowers. Maybe the best thing was for us to reach an impasse."

"No, an impasse is never the best thing. It's been long enough, Katie. You need to talk to him. And I really hate to say this, but I have to get back to work."

"I know. I wish you didn't. I wish we could

run away for a while. Couldn't we go AWOL for the rest of the day? Sunshine like this shouldn't be wasted on the unappreciative."

"The weather is perfect, isn't it?" Christy agreed. "I love late summer days like this."

Katie started Baby Hummer's engine and headed back toward the Dove's Nest. "I mean it, Christy. Say the word, and I'll turn around. Why couldn't we just get on the freeway and keep driving until we hit the coast? We would go directly into the water and swim all the way to Catalina, and when we got there we would hike to the top of Mt. Orizaba. I'd show you my listening spot under the eucalyptus tree where I placed the twelve stones. Then we would get a pedicure or something really decadent like that."

Christy laughed. "You're definitely stressed, girl. You realize that, don't you?"

"Who, me? Stressed?" Katie crossed her eyes and made a funny face at Christy.

"Watch where you're going!" Christy reached for the steering wheel as Katie swerved toward the curb.

Katie returned her attention to the road. "I don't want to go back on campus. I have so much studying to do. I'm already behind in most of my classes. I feel like I barely had a break between summer school and the start of this semester. Do you know that when we went to the beach with you guys and Doug and Tracy that was the only time I went all summer?"

"We should plan another beach day while the weather is still so nice," Christy said. "That is, assuming you and Rick start speaking to each other again."

"Oh, right. There is that."

"Come on, why don't you go into the Dove's Nest now and talk to him?"

"No, he really doesn't like mixing business stuff with personal stuff. That would only cause another fight. Besides, I don't have time. I have to go to a Student Services council meeting."

"Student Services council?"

"Didn't I tell you? I agreed to be a representative for the senior class on the Student Services council."

"On top of being an RA?"

"Overachievers for Jesus! That's my new club. Wanna join?"

"Katie, that's not funny. You know you don't —"

"Before you say what I know you're going to say, the meetings are only once a month. Ruth at Student Services told me I have helpful opinions, and I think she's right.

My bias bank is always full. You know how much I enjoy sharing my views with those who are underprivileged in the opinion department. This is my chance to exercise those skills."

"I'm still not laughing. You know you don't have to do this, Katie."

"I don't go looking for these opportunities. They keep finding me."

"Well, when those opportunities find you, all you have to do is say no. It's a miraculous little word. Only two letters. Easy to remember. Repeat after me, 'No-o-o.' "

"Yeah, yeah, very funny. You don't have to lecture me, Little Miss College Graduate who got sick during graduation and right before her wedding because she was trying to do too much."

"Truce." Christy put up both her hands.

"Besides," Katie said with a swish of her flaming hair, "I can say no whenever I want." As an afterthought she sarcastically added, "I might not be the champion of no the way Rick is: 'No, I won't kiss you.' 'No, I won't bend the rules.' 'No, I won't further our commitment until I'm good and ready.' But I do know how to say no when it counts."

"Yes, you do." Christy reached over and took hold of Katie's arm before she got out of Baby Hummer. "Listen, I want you to know that I applaud what you did Saturday night. Walking out of Rick's apartment was probably the best choice you could have made. And I know this is all very idealistic and sappy, but I'm going to say it anyway. Katie, your days of being single will go quickly. One day you'll wake up, and you'll be married. You'll have the rest of your life to spend all those saved up kisses. The rest of your life, Katie. Remember that, okay? Trust me on this. You will be so glad you didn't compromise. All your noes will turn into a lot of happy yeses, and you'll be glad you didn't spend your kisses now."

Katie gave Christy a half-hearted smile. "Thanks for the old-married-lady advice, Mrs. Spencer. I knew you would find a way to slip those cotton candy castles into this conversation."

"You want to talk about castles and princes? I'll tell you something else, Katie. My opinion of Rick Doyle has gone up about a hundred points. He's showing you how much he cares about you. He's trying to establish a strong foundation for your relationship. That's pure gold. Very princely."

"I know."

"I have a thought about the flowers too,

but I'll tell you later. I have to get to work. Call me tonight, okay?"

"Chris?" Katie leaned over as Christy closed the door. Christy turned back and looked at Katie through the open window.

"Thanks. Thanks for always being there for me and for being my truth-teller."

Christy smiled. "I love you, Katie."

"I know you do. I love you too."

Katie drove back to Rancho feeling comforted and highly agitated at the same time. The comfort came from the strength she always gained from her heart-to-heart times with Christy. The agitation came from things being unsettled with Rick. Part of her wanted to go back, march into the Dove's Nest, and get the necessary conversation over with, whether Rick wanted to have it during working hours or not.

She knew that kind of approach would only cause more problems. At the core, she wanted resolution with Rick and not more tangles. She also knew she didn't want the relationship to end.

As she was leaving Baby Hummer in the parking lot at Crown Hall, Nicole called to her. "Katie, up here!" She waved from the rooftop patio. "Come up!"

Katie joined her at one of the patio tables on the rooftop. Nicole's laptop and three textbooks were spread across the table.

"I'm glad I saw you. I've been wondering how things are going. You would never know we lived on the same floor the way we keep missing each other."

"I know. It's been pretty intense. Everything is fine. The Kissing Wall turned out good. A little too good, maybe." In the back of her mind Katie had assigned some of the blame for the Saturday night showdown with Rick to the way she had feasted on The Kissing Wall words.

"I think it turned out great. So did The Peculiar Treasures Wall. I love the verse by your picture."

"Em was going to pick one for me. I haven't seen it yet."

"She did a good job."

"What time is it?" Katie turned Nicole's wrist her way to read the time on her watch. "I'll take a look at it before I head across campus for a Student Services meeting."

"Could you do a quick favor for me before you leave? Help me to move this table. It needs to be more in the shade."

They worked together, scooting the table over, and came close to the edge of the enclosed deck. Katie looked down on the parking lot. "You really feel like a bird in a nest up here, don't you? You can see everything that's going on, but no knows you're watching."

"I know. Cool, isn't it?" Nicole looked over the rim. "Hey, is that Rick? This is great. You can watch your boyfriend on his way to visit you. How fun is that?"

Katie's heart did a fish-flop. "He's not my boyfriend," she muttered. Every instinct told her to hide. She didn't think she could face him. Not yet.

Leaving Nicole on the roof, Katie dashed down the stairwell. She thought if she took the stairs instead of the elevator she could avoid running into Rick. Her plan seemed to work. That is, until she reached the lobby.

There he was, standing next to one of the chairs looking down at the screen on his cell phone.

Ducking back into the stairwell before he could spot her, Katie leaned against the wall and tried to think how she could get to the other side of the building without going through the main lobby. Then her cell phone rang.

Katie grabbed her phone and stared at it, paralyzed. Of course it was Rick. The high notes of his custom ring echoed loudly in the stairwell. Katie stared at the phone, trying to decide if she should answer and get this moment over with or let Rick leave a message. If he left a message, then she would at least know by the tone of his voice if he was still upset with her.

Jamming her phone back into the side pocket of her shoulder bag, Katie decided to wait it out in the enclave of the stairwell. Her phone stopped ringing on the third ring. It was supposed to ring five times before her voice mail picked up. Now Katie didn't know what to do. If Rick had hung up without leaving a message, she wouldn't be able to tell if he was upset. She also wouldn't know if he was still in the lobby, or if he had left.

She was about to slide open the door to peek when the door swung toward her. Katie leaned back just in time to avoid a collision. Rick stepped into the stairwell and stood only inches from her, looking at her with his hot cocoa eyes.

"You were loud," Rick said.

27

"I know. I was loud." Katie felt all her defenses against Rick melt into an invisible puddle there in the stairwell. "You're right. I was loud, I was rude, and I was way out of line last Saturday night and —"

"Katie, I was talking about your phone." A grin tugged at the corner of Rick's mouth. "The ringer on your phone was loud. I could hear it bouncing off the walls. That's how I knew you were in here."

"Oh."

Rick narrowed his eyes. "Katie, I don't want to fight like that with you. We have to work this out."

She nodded. "Are you saying you want to keep going?"

"Absolutely. Why? What were you thinking?"

"I was thinking a lot of crazy things." Part of Katie wanted to explain to Rick about The Kissing Wall and how thoughts had been directed to their next "first" kiss. Before they even got in the car Saturday night for their date and Rick had showered her with flowers, Katie's hopes were elevated. It seemed a moot point now. Better to go on than to discuss what went wrong and, as Rick would say, "dissect everything down to the last molecule."

"So why are you hiding in the stairwell?" he asked.

Katie flashbacked to the guy hiding in the wardrobe in Sabrina and Tasha's room. She was doing the same thing. In the pit of her stomach she realized that everything she raged against on Saturday night — the restrictions, rules, and guidelines — was born of an ancient fervor. Every rule ever established, from the beginning of time, invited mutiny.

"I guess I was hiding because I was afraid of how this conversation between us might go."

"Katie." Rick's voice was tender as he held out his hand. "Come on, we need to go for a ride."

"I have a meeting."

"When?"

"In about fifteen minutes."

"Okay, so we'll make it a short ride. Come on."

Katie took his hand, and they walked to the car. Rick opened Katie's door. Before she got in, she noticed something on the seat.

A single California poppy.

Her cheeks warmed. "Rick, where did you get this?"

"I have my sources." He looked pleased.

Katie twirled the poppy between her thumb and forefinger. "Thank you." She gave him a big smile.

"You're welcome. I take it that says more to you than the big mixed bouquet."

"Much more. Thank you, Rick."

He smiled. "Go ahead. Get in."

"I really am supposed to go to a meeting over at Student Services."

"In twelve minutes, right?"

She nodded.

His expression coaxed her more than his words. With his soft brown eyes, he gave her the you-are-the-red-headed-woman-of-my-dreams look.

Katie couldn't resist. "Oh, all right." She slipped into the passenger seat, and Rick closed the door. "Where are we going?"

"You'll see. Not far."

Rick drove to the upper campus. He stopped the car in the gravel parking lot by the meadow where Todd and Christy's wedding had been four months earlier. The meadow grass was now a dry, pale yellow. The palm trees rustled their hula skirts furiously in a strong wind that was kicking up its heels in its own dance steps.

Rick opened the car's trunk and took out an ice chest. Katie gave him a skeptical look.

"Trust me," Rick said. He led Katie across the meadow to one of the benches along the walking trail. The view from the edge of the plateau was breathtaking because the winds had blown away the smog and marine layer that usually hung over the coast. They could see all the way to Catalina.

"Wow," Katie said. "I've heard you could see Catalina from here, but I never checked it out on a clear day. This view is amazing. I never asked you, Rick, have you been to Catalina?"

"No."

"We should go sometime. I think you'd really like it. It feels so remote."

Rick was busy setting up something from the ice chest. When Katie looked down, he held out to her two bowls of mint chip ice cream.

She laughed.

"I believe you and I have some unfinished business."

Katie looked at both the bowls. The ice

cream was melting fast. "Are you going to tell me which one came from a round container and which one from a square container?"

Rick's grin was full of mischief. "No," he said. "You tell me."

"Okay, I will."

Katie took a spoonful from the first one. "Nice," she said.

Then she took a taste of the second one. "Hmmm. I'm not sure."

She went back and forth with a few more tastes of each and finally said, "This one," pointing to the first bowl.

"Really?" Rick said. "That's your final choice, then?"

"Yes. Which one was it? Round or square?"

"Check the bottom of the bowl."

Katie held up the bowl and saw a piece of paper taped to the bottom that read "Round." She read the answer reluctantly since round was Rick's preferred choice of ice cream containers.

"Is that so? Round, huh? Imagine that. So, are you telling me that ice cream in round containers is the best-tasting ice cream?" Unfortunately Rick looked really cute when he was smug.

"Yeah, yeah, yeah. Okay, you win. Get over yourself, Doyle. The truth is, they both tasted pretty good and . . ." Katie lifted the other bowl, expecting to see a tag that read "Square."

"Hey, this one says round too!"

She reached over and opened the lid of the ice chest, exposing Rick's taste-testing supplies. The ice chest contained one carton of ice cream. And it was round.

"Uh, Rickster — and I do use the name accurately — what's with the skewed taste test?"

He still was grinning irresistibly. "What can I say? I went to the highly recommended Grocery Kart, and would you believe, they only had mint chip ice cream in *round* containers? I would have set up the test with both options, but the Grocery Kart was uncooperative with the supplies."

"You're pretty happy with yourself, aren't you?"

He gave her a charming shrug, but his powers of persuasion had stopped working on Katie.

"Why did you do this? It was pointless. You set me up."

"It was supposed to be a joke."

"Yeah, a joke on me."

"Katie." Rick reached his arm around the back of the bench and leaned closer. "Hey, you're taking this the wrong way. I really intended to get both the round and the square boxes and finish the crazy taste test. The Grocery Kart honestly only had round ice cream. So I thought it would be funny to run the test this way. It was supposed to be a joke."

"You and I don't have the same sense of humor." Katie felt herself calming down as she thought through Rick's logic. The point was that he was trying to do something clever and fun. Yet in the same way the huge mixed bouquet hadn't sat well with her, the ice cream taste test didn't sit well with her either.

"You're right. We don't have the same sense of humor. You and I are opposite in a lot of ways. But you know what they say about opposites."

"Yeah, we attract each other."

Rick tugged gently at the ends of her hair, rubbing the fine strands between his thumb and forefinger. "Katie, you need to know that I'm trying here. I'm trying to figure out how to do things right in our relationship. I've put on the turn signal, as you called it, but nothing is going the way I thought it would."

"Do you think we're trying too hard?" Katie asked. "I mean, we rolled along pretty well the first part of this year."

Rick nodded. "I don't think either of us was as concerned then about what should happen next."

She drew in a deep breath. "You're right."

Rick paused and in a lower voice said, "I have to tell you, Katie, I'm in uncharted territory in our relationship. I've never continued a relationship this long. I don't know how to ease over into the next lane. I'm trying but . . . I don't know. Maybe we're not ready. Maybe we're not supposed to go anywhere beyond the great friendship we've had all these months. Maybe we're done."

His last line ran through her like ice.

"Do you think we're done?" Katie's heart was pounding.

"No, I don't. Not yet."

"I don't think we're done either."

"Good. At least we're not opposites on that point." Rick grinned.

Katie grinned back. "It seems like figuring out our relationship shouldn't be this difficult."

Rick laughed.

"Why is that so funny?"

"It's funny because every couple I know has to figure all this out for themselves. I think a few basic principles apply across the board, but for the most part, every relation-

ship is a signature piece. They're all different. God writes a different story for every
couple."

Katie let Rick's words fill the space between them. She thought of Julia's hot-on-
God's-heels theology and knew that the
only way for her and Rick to know what
was next for them was to stay close to the
Lord. He would make it clear.

"I do have one question for you, though,"
Katie said.

"What's that?"

"What are your plans for the rest of the
ice cream?"

Rick laughed and pulled out the container.
Sitting side by side, the two of them dipped
their plastic spoons into the round carton.
The wind had died down, and now a warm
breeze spun figure eights between them as
they gazed out at the ocean miles away.

"Remember when you were an elf?" Rick
asked.

"What?"

"In high school. You were an elf at the mall
during Christmas. Remember?"

"Oh, yeah. I almost forgot. Or should I
say, I tried to forget. Thanks for bringing
that memory back to the forefront."

"I've never forgotten how you looked that
day in the car with Christy."

"Do you mean in my Santa's little helper outfit complete with curly-toed shoes and pointed ears?"

Rick nodded. "You tried to hide from me that day too, remember?"

Katie recalled all too well the way she had scrunched down in the passenger seat of the car, hoping Rick would keep walking and not stop to talk to Christy. But he stopped, all right.

"Why do you think you hide from me, Katie?"

She knew the answer, but for a moment, she didn't speak it. It wasn't that she was embarrassed or shy. The truth was, she didn't trust Rick. She was afraid she would get hurt by either something he did or something he said. That fear, she knew, was linked to her past with Rick, but more importantly, it was connected to a lack of trust that pervaded her relationship with her parents.

"I'm not sure you want this much of an answer, Rick, but here it is. This is a big piece of me, and I don't know what you're going to do with it, but just remember you asked. The truth is, I can't bear the thought of being hurt by people that mean a lot to me. I avoid pain whenever possible."

Rick seemed to let her words sink in.

"Katie, have you forgiven me for hurting you in the past?"

"Yes," she said. "Absolutely."

"Do you trust me?"

She didn't answer right away.

Rick drew back. Taking a deep breath, he glanced at his watch and said, "I've made you late for your meeting. Sorry."

"I trust you," Katie said, trying to finish the suspended conversation.

Rick looked her in the eye. Katie could tell that her expression wasn't sincere enough for Rick to believe because his countenance fell as he studied her face.

"You should probably get to your meeting." Rick packed up what was left of the ice cream. "We can talk about this some more tomorrow. Do you want to meet for lunch by the fountain?"

"Sure. Same time?"

Rick nodded and headed for his car. "I'll see you then, Katie."

Katie hated this unsettledness. She didn't know what to do. The good thing was that she would see Rick tomorrow. They would talk some more. He said he wasn't ready for the relationship to be over, and neither was she. It seemed the only thing the two of them could do was to leave their conversation where it was, stalled in the slow lane, and come back to work on it more when they had the necessary tools.

As she made her way across campus, Katie realized she had left Rick's poppy on the front seat of his car.

28

Katie ambled through the rest of the day. She ate dinner with a bunch of girls from her floor and had a lengthy RA meeting with the rest of the staff at eight.

Julia pulled Katie to the side after the meeting and asked if she was doing okay. "You seemed pretty distracted during the meeting."

"I'm processing a lot of stuff. I'd like to talk with you about it sometime."

"Sure," Julia said. "I'm open tomorrow afternoon, if you want to set a time."

Katie was hoping Julia was available right then. Since she wasn't, Katie said, "I'll call you later and figure out a time."

Returning to her room, Katie stopped to talk with some friends in the lobby. It was after ten o'clock when she entered Crown Hall North and passed under the Peculiar Treasures banner. She decided that if she knew what was good for her, she would go to bed early for once. That one kindness would benefit her emotions greatly. She would meet Rick for lunch the next day with her heart a little more settled.

A note was waiting for her on the message board outside her door. "Katie, I need to talk to you. Vicki."

She erased Vicki's note and headed back down the hall. Knocking on Carley and Vicki's door, Katie waited for one of them to answer. She hoped it would be Vicki. Katie had managed not to run into Carley very often, and that was fine with her.

Neither Vicki nor Carley answered, so Katie left a note for Vicki and then stopped by The Peculiar Treasures Wall. She spotted the verse Em had posted next to her picture and drank the words as if they were water.

Katie realized she had been wandering from pool to pool all evening looking for a sip of refreshment. Her friends at dinner had provided nice conversation. Julia had invited Katie to connect with her later for a deeper conversation. Even the friends she'd just chatted with in the lobby were sweet and welcoming. But none of these sources had given her the quenching words she was looking for, whether she knew it or not. Her weary spirit was still thirsty.

Here in front of her on The Peculiar

Treasures Wall was the sip of hope she needed. It was only a small sip, but it made her smile.

> The Lord will guard your going out and your coming in from this time forth and forever.
>
> Psalm 121:8

She was definitely in a season of "going out and coming in." Most days she felt as if she were caught in a revolving door. The quirky twist of words that made Katie smile was the term "going out." When would Katie be able to say that she and Rick were officially "going out"?

To that long-standing question she had no answer. But here next to her picture was a promise that the Lord was guarding her, protecting her, directing her "going out" and "coming in." He would continue to guard her, "from this time forth and forever."

Of that truth she could drink deeply and be satisfied.

Returning to her end of the hall with a lightness in her step, Katie paused in front of The Kissing Wall and checked out the new photos that had been added. Someone had put up a photo of a wrinkled grandpa kissing the cheek of a pudgy baby. The new quotation next to it was:

If you are ever in doubt as to whether or not you should kiss a pretty girl, always give her the benefit of a doubt.
                                        Thomas Carlyle

Katie smiled.

Beside that photo was another new one. Katie looked closer at it. Then she stopped smiling. She recognized Carley as the one being kissed in the picture. Or at least Katie was fairly certain it was Carley. All that showed was part of Carley's face with one eye open, looking at the camera. The scruffy, unshaven guy who was kissing Carley had his face turned away from the camera and was blocking most of her face.

Katie didn't like the photo, but she didn't know why exactly.

Anyone on the floor could add a photo, kissing verse, or kissing poem to the wall, but Nicole and Katie reserved the right to have the final say as to what stayed on display. Katie knew that when it came to just about anything pertaining to Carley, her judgmental radar was on high alert. She decided she would ask Nicole to have a look, and the two of them could decide together if the picture was within the "innocent" parameters they had set for the pictorial selections.

Before crawling into bed, Katie indulged in her one little luxury. She went to her compact dorm refrigerator, pulled out a milk carton, took a bowl from the shelf above her desk, and poured herself a happy mound of Cocoa Puffs. Slipping under her cool sheets and wiggling her bare toes, Katie enjoyed her midnight snack in solitude.

When she first found out she would be alone in her dorm room as an RA, Katie wasn't sure how that would turn out. She knew she would miss Christy terribly. Now that she was well into the semester, though, Katie's biggest surprise was how much she needed the chance to be by herself every night. The solitude gave her an opportunity to think, pray, and process.

She was almost finished with her bowl of Cocoa Puffs when Katie remembered she hadn't printed out her two-page reading summary due for her first class in the morning. It would be easier to do the printing now than try to remember in the morning.

Slipping out of bed and clicking to the summary paper file on her laptop, Katie sent the file to her printer. While the paper was printing, Katie decided to check her email. That was always a dangerous decision when one should be doing something else, like sleeping.

She told herself she really should go to bed. Herself answered and said, "I will right after I read just a few of these."

Katie read and answered all her emails. She clicked open Tracy and Doug's series of photos of the "Awesome Danny Boy" and moved on to reading Sierra's blog about life in Brazil. She was well into listening to four new songs on a link Emilee had sent to her before she realized it was almost 2 a.m.

"You need to be done now," Katie told herself.

This time herself listened.

Katie's stimulated mind had drifted into dreamland for only twenty minutes when an image on the edge of her subconscious caused her to wake and sit bolt upright in bed. The image she saw in her barely-floating-on-the-surface dream was the photo of Carley from The Kissing Wall. The photo had been disturbingly familiar to Katie, and now she knew why.

Yanking open her dorm room door, with her eyes squinting at the brightness, Katie stood in front of The Kissing Wall. She blinked at the picture, trying to adjust her vision. To Katie, at that moment, there was no doubt in her mind. That full head of wavy dark hair in the photo belonged to Rick Doyle.

And he was kissing Carley.

Plucking the photo from its position of prominence on the wall, Katie took the picture into her room, put it under the light on her desk, and examined the shot. Without a doubt that was Rick's "Cactus Boy" unshaven cheek. That meant the photo was taken the day Rick got back from Arizona. The day Carley followed Rick to work.

Everything within Katie begged her to shake it off. This time she couldn't.

She picked up her cell phone and called Rick. But it was Christy who answered on the third ring. Katie realized she had pressed the wrong speed dial number.

"Katie?" Christy answered. "What's wrong?"

"Oh, Chris, I'm sorry! I meant to call Rick. I'm sorry I woke you."

"What's wrong, Katie? Are you okay?"

Katie noticed her hands were shaking. She blurted out, "I think Rick kissed Carley. She posted a photo of them on the wall across from my room."

"What? That's crazy!"

"I know. That's what I told myself. But I haven't been doing a very good job of listening to myself tonight."

"Katie, do you want me to come over?"

"No. It's the middle of the night."

"I know. But I'll come if you want me to."

"You don't have to."

"Actually, I do. Todd heard me talking to you, and he just went for the car keys. We'll be right over."

Now Katie felt embarrassed. This didn't need to be a community rescue. Katie felt she could settle the matter on her own. She just was so tired she couldn't figure out what to do next. Carley was the person she should be questioning, not Rick.

Scooting down the hall, Katie knocked on Carley and Vicki's closed door. Even for college students it was pretty late. When neither of them answered, Katie knew she shouldn't knock louder. This could wait until morning.

If only her pounding heart would go down a notch. Too much adrenaline this late at night rarely resulted in anything productive except maybe some fairly creative pages in term papers. She stood in the hallway in front of Carley's door and wondered about things she knew she never should be wondering.

Has Rick been playing me all along? All those smooth lines about waiting and doing what's right and wanting what's best for us . . . has he been lying to me? No. I don't want to even think that.

However, once she let that thought in, that was all Katie could think about.

What if he never really went to Arizona? What if he was just off with other girls and wanted me to think he was out of town? No, that's crazy. Don't go crazy, Katie. Stay with what you know to be true. Rick does care about you. He's proven himself over and over.

Katie felt as if a herd of green slugs of untruth was closing in on her with their razor-sharp teeth. She couldn't shake them.

He's not the guy you think he is. You tell yourself that he changed and he's not going to hurt you, but how do you know? He's hurt you before. Why wouldn't he hurt you again?

A knock on Katie's door was followed by a quiet turning of the knob. "Katie?" Christy entered. "Are you okay?"

"Yeah. No. I don't know. Thanks for coming."

"It's okay. Where's the photo?" Christy asked.

Katie handed her the photo, and Christy agreed that the guy in the photo was Rick. No question. And Carley and Rick were kissing.

Katie's spirits sunk deeper.

"You said Carley put this up on the wall. Is that right?" Christy asked.

"I'm assuming it was Carley."

"Have you talked to her yet?"

"No, I knocked on her door, but no one answered, and I didn't want to wake her."

Katie took a closer look at Christy's outfit. The odd combination distracted Katie for the moment. On top Christy was wearing one of Todd's oversized, navy blue, hooded sweatshirts, which Katie knew was a favorite article of comfort clothing for Christy. The rest of the outfit was what caught her attention.

"Why are you wearing a skirt in the middle of the night with your bunny slippers?"

"My feet were cold."

"Why didn't you wear sweats or something?"

"This was the first thing I grabbed. You didn't sound good."

"I'm not good. I can't think clearly. I don't know why I'm evaluating your choice of midnight mission-of-mercy apparel."

Christy's cell phone buzzed, and both of them jumped.

Christy looked at the text message. "It's Todd. He's waiting in the car. He just wants to know if you're okay."

Christy tapped a quick message back as Katie looked closer at the photo. "Todd had a thought on the way over here. Do you think there's any chance the photo was digitally edited?"

In her blaze of confusion, Katie hadn't thought about that possibility, even though it was the most obvious. She looked again at the photo. The background was full of inconsistencies in the lighting and the details. The line that traced Rick's hair looked uneven and speckled with white.

"I don't know that much about digital editing," Christy said, "but it almost looks as if Rick has been cut and pasted into the shot."

Katie wilted onto her bed. "I am such a colossal doof. You're right. He probably was. I can't believe I assumed the worst."

Christy sat down next to her. "Katie . . ."

Before Christy could offer words of encouragement, a knock sounded softly on Katie's door, and Vicki peeked in.

"Hi. I just got back from studying upstairs, and I saw your light was still on. Is this a good time?" Vicki stepped inside Katie's room and noticed Christy. "Christy, what are you doing here so late?"

"I just came by to see Katie."

"In your slippers? And a skirt?"

"She's wearing her standard mission-of-mercy outfit," Katie said. "I had a minor meltdown so I called her, and she came."

Vicki's gaze was fixed on the photo in Katie's hand. "Was your meltdown over the pictures?"

"Pictures?" Christy and Katie repeated in unison.

"Is there more than one?" Katie asked.

"Yes, there are a couple of other questionable pictures. I guess Carley hasn't printed them out yet."

"Why would she do something like this?" Christy asked.

Vicki looked at Christy and back at Katie. "You don't know?"

"Know what?" Katie asked.

Just then another knock sounded on Katie's door.

"This is crazy!" Christy said. "Dorm life was never like this when we lived in Brower Hall last year, Katie."

"I know. Welcome to Crown Hall North. No socially stunted women on this floor." Katie opened the door.

Nicole was standing there in a spa-style bathrobe and matching slippers. "Security just called me to see how much longer they should wait before your guest leaves."

"I didn't know security was waiting for

me," Christy said. "I'm sorry if they woke you, Nicole."

"It's okay. What's going on? Are you guys all right?" Even though it was the middle of the night, Nicole was still gracious.

Katie filled Nicole in on the situation with the photo. She showed Nicole the picture and said, "Vicki was just about to tell us why Carley would do such a thing as put up a photo like this."

"I thought you knew," Vicki said. "Everyone else on our floor knows."

"Knows what?" Katie looked at the three women standing in her room. "Will someone please tell me what's going on?"

29

"Photos like this are a Kissing Wall tradition," Vicki said.

"Why?" Christy asked.

"Yeah, why?" Katie echoed. "Is the tradition to try to sabotage perfectly good relationships of the other women on the floor?"

"No, of course not," Nicole said. "That's not the tradition. The tradition is to print out pictures of someone on the floor kissing someone unlikely, such as a movie star. Do you remember the photo last year with Kim kissing Kermit the Frog?"

Katie blinked but didn't answer.

"Or the one with Amy last year where she was kissing Spiderman," Vicki added. "That's the tradition. We've always had one or two photos on the wall of an unlikely couple, and everyone knew the pictures were fake."

"Not everyone," Katie retorted.

"That's why I left a note for you earlier today. I saw the photo, and I thought you should know about it before Emilee finished it in case you didn't want it up."

"Emilee? Em put this picture on The Kissing Wall?"

"I don't know exactly who put it up. Em asked Carley last night in our room to do a picture of her with some country western singer. I don't remember which one. While Carley was doing that digital mockup for Em, she decided to do one of her with her boss. When I saw her working on it, I told her I didn't think it was a good idea. I didn't think you would appreciate it."

"You're right. I didn't."

"But, Katie, you need to know it was meant as a prank. Not as something mean. It was a joke. That's all. Think of it as being on the same level as last year when you put my shoes in the oven."

Katie fell silent. She had nothing to say to Vicki's comment. She knew all about how great an inside joke can seem at the moment and then how ridiculous it can turn out later. The revelation gave her new sympathy for Rick and his attempt at a joke with the ice cream.

"Okay, I'm tracking with you guys now. I still don't want this one up on the wall,"

Katie said.

"I agree," Nicole said.

"Me too," said Vicki. "That's why I was trying to talk to you before it went up. I'm sure if you tell Carley she'll be fine with your taking it down."

"We can talk to her tomorrow," Nicole said. "Or rather, later today since tomorrow already is today."

"Carley can do the picture of her with Dean instead," Vicki offered.

"Who's Dean?" Katie asked.

"He was her boss at Casa de Pedro where she worked for awhile this summer. I heard her say the photo of Rick was a higher resolution so that's why she went with it."

"Casa de Pedro," Christy murmured.

Katie turned to her. "I know. Doesn't a chimichanga burrito sound good right now?"

Nicole laughed. "How can you think of food at this crazy hour?"

"It's a gift," Katie said.

"Do you guys want to go for burritos?" Vicki asked. "Because I'm up for it, if you are."

"Yes," Katie said. "But I really need to get some sleep so I better pass."

"I need to call campus security," Nicole said.

"You can tell them I'm leaving," Christy said. "I'll pass on the burrito too, Vicki, but it does sound good. I'd love to go with you guys another time. Call me if you make plans another night. Maybe a little earlier in the evening."

"No, I think we'll wait and call you after we're sure you've already gone to bed," Katie said. "That way we'll be sure you'll show up in another smashing outfit like this one."

Christy smiled. She got up from Katie's bed and adjusted the big sweatshirt as Nicole and Vicki left the room and headed down the hall.

Katie thanked Christy for dashing to her aid and scrutinized her outfit one more time. "What do you have on under there?"

Christy grinned in a shy sort of way. "Nothing."

"Nothing as in nothing-nothing? Or nothing as in none-of-my-business, nighty-night nothing?"

Christy grinned and left her answer at that. Turning to leave Katie's room, she said, "Oh, and Katie?"

"Yeah?"

"Try to get some sleep. This is too much stress for your senior year. And you've only just started."

"I know," Katie said. "You and I have a lot to catch up on. Do you want to try to get together later this week?"

"Sounds good. Let's check our schedules and see what we can work out."

Katie waved as her original Peculiar Treasure friend shambled down the long hall in her funky outfit. Then Katie returned to bed exhausted. She was sure she would wake up early enough for class, so she didn't set her alarm.

The good news was that Rick called at 7:15.

The bad news was that Rick called at 7:15.

"Hey." Katie's voice was slow and groggy.

"I heard you had a rough night last night."

"Yeah, how did you hear? Todd?"

"Yes, he drove me to the airport this morning."

"Airport." Katie propped herself up on her elbow. "Are you going back to Tempe?"

"Yes, it's last minute. My brother was able to set up a meeting, and I just found out this morning. My plane leaves in forty minutes. I wanted to call before I left to tell you we'll have to reschedule our lunch by the fountain."

"Oh, yeah. Okay. Sure." She was finding it difficult to think clearly this early.

"We'll have to reschedule the rest of our

conversation too."

"Yeah, we can talk later. We definitely need to talk some more."

"I agree."

An easy pause followed before Rick said, "Katie, I have a huge favor to ask you."

"Okay."

"Is there any chance you could go to the Dove's Nest around five this evening for about an hour and help Carlos with a special order? I agreed to provide pizzas for a large soccer awards night at the community center. They have someone coming by at 6:30 to pick up the order, but I wasn't able to schedule enough staff to handle the prep. I've called everyone else. You're my last option."

"Sure, I'm free tonight. I can do it."

"That's great."

"By any chance is Carley going to be working?"

"Yes, why?"

"Didn't Todd tell you?"

"Tell me what?"

"About last night."

"He said you called Christy in the middle of the night with a problem on your floor, and the two of them came over for about half an hour. That's all he said."

Katie sat up in her bed and gave Rick a

crash summary on the previous night's events, complete with some of the inner dialogue she had wrestled with over whether she should distrust him.

"Wait a minute," Rick said. "Let me get this straight. The picture was a joke, but you thought it was real?"

"It looked real. At least when I first saw it. I was really tired."

"But you honestly thought I might have kissed Carley." Rick's words were slow and deliberate. That wasn't a good sign.

"It was a prank, but I didn't get it. I'm still really groggy right now, and I don't know why I'm telling you all this, especially when you're about to board a plane. I guess I just need to resolve this awkwardness between Carley and me before I go the Dove's Nest tonight. But that's my problem, not yours. I'll take care of it. Have a good trip. Sorry to splurt all this out right before you leave."

The other end of the phone was very still.

"Are you there, Rick?"

"Katie, I need you to answer honestly one question."

"Okay."

"Last night, did you think I might be cheating on you?"

She couldn't find her voice to answer him.

The honest answer was, "Yes, for a few minutes, at least," but she didn't want to say that.

"Katie . . . I, I don't know. After all these months, and everything you and I have been through, if you still have serious doubts about me, I don't know what to do anymore. I mean, if you still don't trust me . . ."

"I trust you," she said quickly.

"I want to believe that. But, Katie, you just told me that when you had a chance to either doubt me or trust me, your leaning went toward doubting."

"I know. I wavered. It was late."

"Yes, but Katie . . . I don't know what to say right now. I keep thinking you and I are further along in some of the foundational parts of our relationship and then . . . I start to wonder if you're ever going to completely forgive me and start trusting me."

A heavy silence kept Katie's phone attached to her ear like glue. Even after Rick said, "I need to think about all this. We need to talk when I get back from Arizona in a couple of days," and then hung up, Katie still sat there holding the phone to her ear.

Forcing herself out of bed to make it to class, Katie shuffled down the hall for her usual morning routine. She found Carley in the bathroom washing her face.

"Vicki told me," Carley said before Katie had a chance to say anything. "You know it was supposed to be a joke."

Katie nodded.

"Vicki said you were pretty upset."

"I was."

"I'm sorry, Katie." Carley turned to look at her.

Katie nodded again. It was the only acceptance of an apology she felt she could give at that point.

Two other girls entered the bathroom. Carley left, and Katie showered. For a long time she didn't move from under the showerhead. The water poured over her, and Katie wished it could baptize her heart and clear her mind.

None of the scenarios or explanations running through her thoughts seemed to offer any defusing of the dilemma with Rick. She said over and over that she trusted him, but in her heart she kept waiting for something to go wrong. She expected to be let down. The longer they were together the more devastating she expected the break-up to be.

What is wrong with me? I'm a mess. Why can't I trust Rick? He consistently proves his loyalty to me and his commitment to our relationship, but I keep trying to sabotage it.

What's my problem?

For the rest of the day Katie was in a funk. She didn't want to eat. She couldn't pay attention in class. She avoided people she usually hung around with. At noon she remembered that if Rick hadn't gone to Arizona, they would be eating lunch together at the fountain.

She tried to call Christy. Voice mail picked up, and Katie said, "Call me when you can. I'm helping out at the Dove's Nest at five. It would be great if you had some time to talk after 6:30 or so."

When Katie arrived at the Dove's Nest at 4:45, she still hadn't heard back from Christy. Checking in the Ark Bookstore, she found out that Christy had left for the day.

It felt strange going into the kitchen and reaching for a clean apron. Carley came into the back and said, "Carlos mentioned you were coming in. I hope you're not still mad at me."

Katie wanted to spout off with something like, "Why should you care?" Instead she said, "I don't know, Carley. I'm not doing very well right now. Can we talk about this later?"

"Are you upset because of the picture of Rick and everything?"

"Yeah. Everything."

"I told you I was sorry."

"I know. I get the whole thing about the photo being a tradition and a prank. But you know what?" Katie hesitated. She realized how much her words in moments like this could get her into trouble. Deciding she couldn't hold in any longer what she was feeling, Katie said, "Can I just say something? Ever since last May it feels as if you have been trying to come between Rick and me. I don't know if that's all in my head, and I'm just having serious distrust issues, or if something is going on between you and me that I don't know about."

Carley looked down.

"Have I made all this up, or is something going on?"

Slowly lifting her chin, Carley said, "Do you remember what you said to me at the fall pizza night at Brower Hall a year ago?"

Katie scrunched her eyebrows. She didn't even remember the fall pizza night, let alone anything she might have said.

"I can tell you don't remember, but you were really bubbly about going to somebody's house where you and all your friends had this big sleepover. In the morning you made omelets with Rick, and you were so excited that Christy was engaged."

"Right, I remember all that. But I don't

remember the pizza night or saying anything in particular to you."

"We were standing by the door, and I said, 'Your life is so perfect, Katie. I wish I could trade with you.' And you said, 'Yeah, right. As if you could pull off that one.' " Carley's expression displayed her hurt as she recounted the conversation.

"I don't remember saying that. But I can tell that I hurt you, Carley. I'm sorry. I spout off far too often and say things I shouldn't. I'm sorry." Katie felt regret for whatever it was that caused such a wound in Carley, but she was having a hard time figuring out why her words had caused such pain.

"It's okay," Carley said. "I should probably apologize to you because I think I got carried away with the challenge."

"The challenge?"

"You said, 'As if you could pull that one off.' People have been saying that to me my whole life. So I guess I took the challenge too far. It started out as a stupid sort of game, and then it became an obsession, I guess. I was jealous. You've had such a completely perfect life and —"

Katie stopped her right there. "Oh, no! My life has been far from perfect. Believe me, if you had even an inkling of how I grew up . . ."

Katie's expression must have turned fiercer than she expected because Carley looked startled and almost frightened.

"You know what, Carley?" Katie pulled her emotions and her words way back. "Have you ever heard the saying 'Hurt people hurt people'?"

"No."

"I think that's what you and I somehow got caught up in, and it's really wicked. Others have hurt us both, and we both have hurt others. You don't want my life, trust me. I don't want to hurt you with my flippant comments. Honest. Do you think the two of us could start fresh?"

Carley nodded. A soft expression replaced the stunned one. "I'm sorry," she said.

"I'm sorry too."

They exchanged fresh smiles and for the next hour and a half worked as a team, cranking out an Army-sized supply of pepperoni pizzas.

30

When Katie returned to Rancho Corona after working at the Dove's Nest, she still felt heartsick about Rick. She wanted to call him to talk over her exchange with Carley and to tell him how everything had changed while the two of them were working together. She didn't call him, though.

Changes to the relationship were likely only to occur when she and Rick could sit down for a heart-to-heart. Until then, all she could change was herself.

With that piece of truth, Katie headed to Julia's apartment. Her door was open, and steel guitar music floated out into the hallway. Katie tapped on the doorframe, and Julia looked up from the couch. That's when Katie noticed that Julia was on the phone.

"I can come back," Katie said, mostly mouthing the words.

"No, come in. I'm on hold with my credit card company. I was overcharged for some-

thing last month. As a matter of fact, I'm not in the mood to hassle with them right now. I'll call back later."

Julia put down her phone and gestured for Katie to sit across from her on the love seat.

"I was going to call and set up a time to talk," Katie said, "but my day got a little wacky."

"I heard about the picture on The Kissing Wall," Julia said. "Is everything settled with that?"

Katie nodded. She gave Julia an update on her conversation with Carley at the Dove's Nest. "What kills me is that I don't know how many times I've said the wrong thing and hurt people."

"I think most individuals understand your humor and your pithy statements, Katie. This thing with Carley is a little unusual. You handled it well."

"She was the one who initiated the apology, really. And I know I didn't handle things very well with Rick this morning."

"What happened?"

Katie gave Julia an overview of her conversation and her feelings about Rick; then, before she knew it, Katie had poured out her heart.

A few minutes into the conversation Julia

shut the door to make sure they had privacy. Five minutes in, Julia handed Katie a box of tissues. Twelve minutes in, Katie felt worn out and miserable. Julia, however, looked calm and ready to give Katie some insight.

"So what should I do?" Katie asked. "Assuming that Rick will ever speak to me again, how can I convince him that I trust him? What he said is true. I keep expecting him to disappoint me or betray me or something. You don't think I'm an absolute nut case, do you?"

"Absolutely *nut*," Julia said with a smile.

"Clever. I feel like something is wrong with me. I mean, why can't I trust him?"

"You said you forgave him more than a year ago. Is that right?"

"Yeah. I told you about the letter he sent me. That's when I forgave him. That was way before I saw him again at the Dove's Nest. In his letter, he asked if I would forgive him for being a jerk and for not treating me with the respect I deserved."

"And you forgave him then?"

"Yes."

"But you're still expecting him to hurt you."

Katie nodded. "Do you think maybe I didn't truly forgive him? Is that why I'm just waiting for him to blow it?"

"Only you know whether you truly forgave him."

Katie thought for a moment. "I did. I know I did. It was like there was this invisible measuring scale in my head. I took all the stuff I held against Rick that was weighing down one side of the scale and asked Jesus to incinerate it. The scales were even then. Like nothing was left to weigh down my thoughts or feelings about Rick in an unbalanced way."

"That's a great way to explain forgiveness," Julia said.

"I didn't come up with the illustration," Katie said. "I heard a guy use it in one of my Bible classes. The picture stayed with me. I took off of the scale in my mind all that stuff with Rick."

"In your mind," Julia repeated. "But what about in your heart?"

Katie wasn't sure what Julia meant.

"Let me ask you this. How did Rick hurt you? I'm not asking what he did. What I'm asking is for you to identify the injury. For instance, did he steal from you?"

"No, he used me, tricked me, and basically betrayed me." Katie was stunned at how instantly the accusations against Rick popped out of her mouth.

Whoa! I may have forgiven him, but I cer-

tainly haven't forgotten!

"I think you just moved from your head to your heart." Julia's expression softened, as if Katie had accomplished something difficult. When Julia spoke again, it was with tenderness. "The way I see it, when we're hurt at the heart level, the forgiveness and healing have to happen in the same place the injury took place. Rick didn't hurt your mind; he hurt your heart. That's where you have to go to forgive him all the way.

"Now," Julia said, taking a deep breath, "I have another question for you. When you look around in your heart, I'm wondering, what did you do with the injuries Rick caused you? Did you give them to Jesus to incinerate?"

Katie felt a thud in her chest. The answer to Julia's question came at her with certainty. It wasn't as if she knew the answer in her head; she knew this answer in her heart.

"I kept some of them."

Julia nodded slowly, offering Katie a comforting look.

"I didn't throw them north or south or east or west or anywhere, did I? Instead of throwing the hurts away, I held onto some of them. Here." Katie tapped her heart. "I never realized I did that. When you asked me what I did with the hurts, I just knew.

They're still with me. I've been saving them."

Katie looked down at her curled-up fingers. "I don't know why I'm saving them. It's like having a box of hand grenades in the corner. I say I don't want to blow up anything, but I know I have them on hand just in case I need to use them."

"For self-defense," Julia said.

Katie nodded. "For self-defense. That's my life pretty much. Right there. Be prepared to hide or to have ammo when you get too hurt by those closest to you."

"Such as your mom?" Julia asked.

"You picked that up, huh? Yeah, I don't have much of an emotional connection with either of my parents, but especially with my mom. I keep expecting her to be a real mom, you know? And she's just herself."

"Would you say that you have forgiven your parents?" Julia asked.

"Forgiven them for what?"

Julia didn't answer. She looked at Katie with singleness of purpose.

Katie knew she was the only one who could name her childhood, heartfelt hurts. "Do you mean I should forgive my parents for abandoning me emotionally?"

Julia gave Katie a cautious yet affirming look. She seemed to be waiting for Katie to state the obvious.

"I guess I just said it, didn't I? I guess the answer is no, I haven't forgiven my parents. And I haven't completely released Rick either."

For a moment they sat quietly, letting the painful realizations sink in.

"I'm looking at a couple of scales in my heart right now," Katie said. "I thought those scales were empty and in balance. Maybe they are in my head. But in my heart, they're weighted down. So how do I get rid of this toxic stuff?"

"You said it earlier. Ask Jesus to take it and demolish it. Do you want to pray with me about all this now?"

"Yeah." Katie closed her eyes and said, "Dear heavenly Father, please forgive Rick for the stuff he did to me and —"

"Katie." Julia touched Katie's arm, interrupting her prayer.

Katie looked up. She never had anyone interrupt her when she was praying before. Julia was shaking her head.

"You're just saying the words, Katie. It sounds like you took an express elevator from your heart back to your mind. God knows your heart. He's already there. You need to go back there. All the way to your heart's core."

Katie swallowed. She knew what Julia meant. Katie knew where her heart's core was — it was a place she avoided. That spot was covered with scars from the hurts she had experienced. And those scars were covered up with boxes of grenades.

"Do you want to deal with this now?" Julia asked gently. "Because you don't have to, if you're not ready."

"Yes, I do. I don't want to carry all this deadly ammo for another moment. God forgave me of so much. I know he wants me to forgive other people the same way he forgave me. He doesn't store up a box of lightning bolts from all the stuff I've done to hurt him. You know, he's never hurled past stuff at me. No, I want to deal with this now. I feel as if I've been hoarding these hurts like a treasure in this cave in my heart. This junk is not a treasure."

As Katie spoke, she cried. Julia teared up as well.

"You're there now," Julia said with a smile. "You're at your heart's core. This is honest. This is true. Now, go ahead, tell God what you were starting to pray earlier."

Without closing her eyes this time, Katie cried silent tears and spoke aloud. "God? Great God, I know you're here. I know you're listening to me. I'm sorry I've held onto this garbage for so long. I don't want it. Take it. Throw it away. Far away. I want to release Rick completely. I want to release my parents completely. From my heart . . ." Katie drew in a quavering breath. "From my heart, I choose to forgive Rick for tricking me and for betraying me. From my heart, I choose to forgive my mother and my father for abandoning me and hurting me emotionally. You want them to be forgiven completely just as you completely forgave me. I want what you want. Do one of your amazing God things. Set them free, and set me free."

Katie leaned back and closed her eyes. She felt as if she were riding on a wave or soaring like a bird. A free bird. Never had her heart felt so light.

"Wow," she said softly. She looked at Julia, who was smiling and crying at the same time. That's when Katie realized she was crying too. She laughed. "We look like it's raining while the sun is shining."

Julia chuckled, and the two women hugged.

"This is good stuff," Katie said. "I feel great right now!"

Julia reached over and gently pressed the palm of her hand against Katie's cheek. The gesture was a loving mother one, the kind

Katie longed for but never had received.

"Don't ever forget this moment, this feeling. I'm sure you won't," Julia said. "God's truth really sets us free, and I think we're never closer to his truth than when we choose to forgive others the way he forgave us."

That night, before Katie went to bed, in the solitude of her room, she wrote in her journal. The exercise was a rare experience, but then, what she had experienced that day was rare.

I feel as if the treasure chest at the core of my heart had long been overflowing with stored-up pain, hurts, and disappointments. That place is now emptied of the garbage and ready to be filled up with true treasures. Every day God sends Peculiar Treasures my way, but I haven't been able to hold onto many of them because I had no room in my heart to store them. Now I do.

Rick is definitely one of those Peculiar Treasures, and I feel as if I finally have room in my heart for him. The right kind of room, and the right kind of reasons to move forward in our relationship.

But I really think I need to wait until he makes the next move. I'm ready to wholeheartedly trust him. He needs to be willing to wholeheartedly trust me now too.

If Rick and I move any further in our relation-ship, then I think it's going to be a result of God's prompting Rick to make the lane change, so to speak. If Rick decides to refer to me as his girlfriend, then I'll know for certain he's not holding against me any of my mistrust mess.

Katie felt so much peace. She knew she didn't have to run after Rick to try to explain in a thousand tumbling words why she felt the way she did or to try to convince him to overlook her lack of trust. The old hurts were gone. She and Rick would be able to pick up where they had left off. She just knew it. Only now it would be different between them. Rick would no longer have to keep proving himself to Katie, and she would have room in her heart for love to grow.

That's what she thought on Tuesday after her glorious time with Julia. By Wednesday evening, Katie was thinking about calling Rick since she hadn't heard from him. By Thursday after her last class, Katie felt as if she couldn't stand the silence between them any longer. The doubts kept coming at her, but she fought them off as valiantly as if she were fighting a dragon.

Maybe, in some ways, she was fighting a dragon. A very ancient one.

31

On Friday, after Katie's last class, she put on her favorite pair of jeans and the top she had worn on check-in day since she remembered that Rick had noticed it and said he liked it.

Climbing into Baby Hummer at 8:05, she drove down the hill, practicing what she would say to Rick when she saw him. He had sent her a text three hours earlier that read, "HOME 8P TALK?"

Katie smiled as she walked down the apartment complex path on the way to Rick's front door. This could only turn out well. She was in the best place she had ever been spiritually and emotionally. She finally was ready to take her relationship with Rick seriously and enter in with the same interest and enthusiasm he had expressed to her over their months together.

I think all this stuff had to happen so God could clean out my heart. Now I'm ready to be open to him and to Rick. You are so good to me, Lord. Thank you for what you've done in my heart. Thank you for what you're going to do in my relationship with Rick. I trust you.

Katie found herself grinning. *That's the foundation of any lasting relationship, isn't it? Trust. Complete trust. In that case, let me say again, Father God, that I trust you.*

She was at Rick's apartment door and could hear music from inside. Filled with hope and confidence, she pressed the doorbell. Then, remembering how Christy's doorbell still didn't work, she knocked and took a step back.

The door opened, and there stood the last person she expected to see. Goatee Guy.

"What are you doing here?" Katie checked the number on Rick's door to make sure she had the right apartment.

Goatee Guy grinned. "Hi."

"What are you doing here?" Katie repeated.

"I live here."

"No, you don't. Rick lives here. Where's Rick?"

"Arizona."

Katie felt her knees wobble. "He said he was going to be back tonight at 8."

"I don't know his schedule. Do you want to come in and wait for him?"

"No." Katie turned to make a beeline for Todd and Christy's front door. Pounding hard on their door, she swallowed back her stunned feelings.

"Katie, how's it goin'?" Todd, wearing a lobster-shaped oven mitt on his hand, opened the door. He snapped his fingers open and closed, as if the oven mitt were a puppet. Katie knew the mitt had been a wedding gift from Christy's aunt and uncle, but she thought Christy had taken it back to the store during one of their returning sprees.

"Hi. Are you guys having dinner or something?"

"No." Todd swung open the door the rest of the way. Katie could see Christy's aunt and uncle sitting on the love seat, looking at Christy's wedding album. "We ate already, but if you're hungry, we have plenty. Come on in."

"Oh, no. I was just . . ."

Christy was standing behind the love seat. When she saw Katie, she came to the door.

"Hi. Why don't you come in?" Christy asked.

"I didn't know you had company."

"It's okay. They just returned from a cruise and stopped by on their drive back to Newport Beach."

"Is that Katie?" Bob called from inside the apartment.

"Hi." Katie waved at both of them.

"You're just in time for dessert," Bob said. "Todd was going to pull the pie from the oven. Are you going to join us?"

"No, I better go. It smells good, though."

"It's awfully drafty with the door open, don't you think?" Marti said to no one in particular.

Christy looked at her aunt and then back at Katie. Over her shoulder Christy said to Todd, "I'll be right back." Then she stepped outside the apartment, closed the door, and looked closely at Katie. "What's going on? Are you okay?"

"I don't know. I was doing great, you know, like I told you in the email I sent you yesterday."

Christy nodded. "That was an incredible email about what happened when you prayed with Julia. I showed it to Todd. I hope that's okay."

"Yeah, sure. Fine."

"I'm sorry I haven't been able to get together with you. It's just that —"

"Don't worry. I didn't come over because you and I haven't had a chance to talk. I came to see Rick. But now I'm flustered. He texted me to meet him at eight to talk, but he's not home. Goatee Guy answered the door at Rick's apartment."

"Goatee Guy?"

"I don't know his name. I guess he's Rick's new roommate."

"That's Eli. I thought you met him at our wedding."

"How do you know him?"

"He and Todd lived together in Spain. Katie, are you okay?"

Katie had flipped one of her hands in the air and then placed it on the top of her head. "Yeah, I'm okay. This is just bizarre. So, are you going to be around tomorrow after work?"

"Yes."

"Can you and I go out to dinner or something?"

"Sure. What do you think about going to Casa de Pedro?"

"On one condition. You have to promise you will stop me before I eat an entire, giant chimichanga burrito by myself."

"We'll split one," Christy said.

"Perfect. We can catch up on everything then," Katie said. "You probably should get back to your aunt and uncle and the pie."

Christy giggled and leaned close. "Did you see the lobster oven mitt?"

"Yeah. I thought we returned it a couple

of months ago."

"We did! Todd reminded me that it came from Bob and Marti, and I had to run to the store on the way home to buy one. At least I still had gobs of credit at the kitchen store."

"Your secret is safe with me."

Christy reached out and gave Katie a hug. "I know it is. You're my favorite Peculiar Treasure, Katie. You know that, don't you?"

"And you're mine." Katie hugged her back. "I'll see you tomorrow around 5:15 at Pedro's."

"Can't wait!"

Katie took the long way back to the apartment parking area so she wouldn't have to walk past Rick's apartment and risk seeing Goatee Eli. She decided to go back to Rancho and wait for Rick to call. His plane could have been late, or he could have decided to do something before talking with Katie, like checking for ants in a variety of not-yet-checked locations at the Dove's Nest.

To Katie, the really great thing at the moment was that her heart felt free. She had no trouble assuming all the right sorts of reasons Rick wasn't home or why he hadn't called. She trusted him. It was a refreshing, freeing, completely different entry point for all the thoughts she had about the two of them.

Unlocking Baby Hummer's door, Katie settled into the driver's seat. As she glanced out the windshield, she saw something under the wiper. It wasn't a ticket. It was a flower. A pink bougainvillea blossom like the ones that grew up the side of the apartment complex. Katie decided it must have blown there. She sat for a moment before starting the car, thinking about the huge bouquet of flowers Rick had given her on their disaster date.

A few days ago, Christy had expressed a thought about those flowers in an email to Katie. Christy said Rick's giving Katie lots of flowers was possibly one of the safe ways he could express his passion and his interest in her. Christy suggested that, since the two of them weren't expressing their feelings with kisses, that Katie should be receptive and appreciative of any and all of the ways Rick expressed his emotions, including luxurious, overdone bouquets.

"Think of the flowers as being in lieu of two dozen kisses," Christy had written. "What is it you quote from that movie about the orphans? 'Take it and be thankful!' That's what I think you should do from now on if Rick gives you flowers or anything else.

Take it and be thankful."

Katie knew she would view Rick's expressions toward her with more appreciation now that her mistrust of him was gone. Her affection for him and his unique way of doing things was growing.

She only hoped it wasn't too late and that he hadn't given up on her. Quietly, in her heart, she didn't think their relationship was over. Not yet. Katie felt a lot of hope about what was going to happen between Rick and her. She couldn't explain why; she just felt hopeful.

Katie checked her cell phone. Something she realized she probably should have done right away. She had two messages from Rick. As she read his first text message, a set of car lights flashed in her rearview mirror.

It was Rick's Mustang.

Katie pulled the keys from the ignition and walked across the lot to Rick's car. She had her phone in her hand, trying to read his message. Rick remained in the driver's seat and rolled down his window.

"I see you got my message."

"I'm just now reading it. It says your plane was late, and you want to get something to eat." Katie took her gaze off her phone and looked at Rick. He was looking at her with that I-can't-get-you-out-of-my-heart gaze.

"So what do you think?" he asked.

"I wouldn't mind going for a drive somewhere. It's a nice night."

"Hop in, Zing."

"Zing?" Katie slid into the passenger's seat and repeated, "Zing?"

"Yeah, Zing. What do you think of that?"

"Zing, huh? I'll have to ponder that one."

Rick pulled out of the parking area.

"I met your roommate," Katie said.

"Did he ask you out?"

Katie studied Rick's profile as he kept looking straight ahead.

"No, he didn't ask me out. Why did you say that?"

"He wants to."

"Why do you say that?"

"He told me he thinks you're extraordinary and something else."

"Something else?"

"Yeah, some other word. Oh, yeah, 'unforgettable.' That's what it was. He thinks you're unforgettable."

"And what did you tell him?"

"I told him if he thought you would ever go out with him that he would just have to learn to live with disappointment."

Katie tried not to grin too broadly that Rick had used one of her flippant phrases in response to Eli.

Rick turned up the music and thumped his open palm on the side of his door in time with the song. Everything felt back to normal. They still needed to talk. Katie wanted Rick to know she trusted him. She wanted to tell him how she had put aside all the ammo she had been saving just in case she needed to use it on him. The old hurts were gone, and she was free. She wanted him to know.

"I thought we could try the Thai place. I'm guessing it won't be too difficult to get in at nine o'clock. With or without neckties."

"Sounds good. How was Arizona?"

"Hot."

"How's the project going?"

"Great. Are you ready for my news?"

Katie bit her lower lip. If he was going to say he was moving to Tempe, she didn't want to hear his big news.

"What's your news?" she asked cautiously.

"We hired a manager, and the building code cleared. My part in the project is just about over."

"So you're not moving to Arizona?"

"Nope. But I do get a portion of the profit share, and in about two years I should have enough to open another café somewhere, if everything goes well."

"That's very good news."

They got out of the car and walked into the ornately decorated restaurant where they were seated in a sequestered booth. It was the perfect spot for a private conversation.

Rick took a quick look at the menu. Katie took a long look at Rick. He put down the menu and caught her gaze. His eyes fixed on hers, and for an intense moment neither of them spoke.

A grin slowly tugged at the corners of Rick's mouth. He said, "You decided you're ready to trust me, didn't you?"

Katie blinked in surprise. "How did you know?"

"I see it. I can tell. You're different. You're looking at me like you believe in me."

"I do. That was going to be my big announcement. You can really tell just by looking at me?"

"You're an open book, Katie."

"That's right. You think I have no bile, don't you?"

"Guile," Rick corrected her. "You have no guile, Zing."

The busboy stepped up to their table and filled the water glasses. As soon as he stepped away, Katie said, "Zing, huh? So, where did you come up with that nickname?"

"Is it growing on you?" Rick asked.

"Maybe."

"When I was in Tempe, I was telling my brother that you and I were having some challenges. I didn't go into any detail, but I asked what he would counsel me to do at this point in our relationship."

"And what did your brother say?"

"He asked, 'Does she still make your heart go zing?' And I thought 'Yeah, even in the middle of all this stuff, Katie still makes my heart go zing.' "

Katie smiled.

"You do, Katie," Rick said. "Even if I'm an enigma sometimes and even when these challenges come at us, you make my heart go zing."

A clever twist of words came to Katie. She narrowed her eyes. "You know, an enigma is like a maze."

"Okay," Rick said, as if not following her logic.

"So maybe I should call you, a 'Maze.' "

Rick didn't look too thrilled with his potential nickname.

"Because if you're a 'maze' and I'm a 'zing,' all you have to do is put us together, and we become 'amaze-zing!' "

Rick laughed. It was so good to hear laughter that came from his heart all the way out. He reached across the table and said, "Katie . . ."

He didn't finish his thought. Instead, he leaned forward, looked her in the eye, and gave her a fabulous wink. She was sure it was the most romantic and memorable wink any woman had ever received anywhere on planet Earth at any time.

If Rick shouldn't, couldn't, or wouldn't give her affirmation of their relationship in the form of kisses, she willingly would take his flowers, his words, or his heart-melting winks. Yes, she would take it and be thankful. Very thankful.

The waitress stepped up to their table. Katie could feel herself blushing.

"Have you had time to decide?" the waitress asked.

"I think so," Rick said. "More than enough time probably. But we both needed time to be sure." He closed his menu and leaned forward. "I'll have whatever my girlfriend is having."

Katie froze.

This was it. Rick had just changed lanes in the middle of a Thai restaurant with very little warning. Or maybe the truth was, he had been turning the blinker on and off for months, but this time he was ready; he moved effortlessly over to the boyfriend-girlfriend lane. The way it should be when the timing is right.

In response, Katie closed her menu, looked at Rick and said, "I'll have whatever my boyfriend is having."

The waitress lowered her pad. "Okay, then. I'll come back when you two know what you really want."

As she slipped away from the table, Rick said, "I think we both know what we really want now."

"Smooth lane change, Doyle."

"You like that?"

"I like you."

"I like you too. More than ever."

Rick reached across the table and took Katie's hand in his. With a gesture more romantic and gallant than she had ever imagined, Rick lifted her hand to his lips. He lowered his eyes and kissed the back of her hand.

This kiss, given with all the true affection and most sincere intent of a valiant heart, was their fresh-start kiss. Katie smiled. At that moment, she had every reason to believe that when it came to "make-my-heart-go-zing" moments with Rick Doyle, this was only the beginning.

Dear Peculiar Treasure,

That's what you are, you know. You are God's Peculiar Treasure. His love for you is deep and abiding and filled with "mercy moments." He reveals his mysterious ways to you every day. He never stops loving you. You are his first love and he always wants you. You *are* God's Peculiar Treasure.

I have to tell you something. When I first started writing this book about Katie, I was very emotional. For a variety of reasons, it had been seven years since I'd last written about these characters. I felt like I'd been given a gift. The gift was the chance to spend many weeks inside a corner of my imagination where Katie, Christy, and the rest of the God-Lovers gang gathered and told me what they'd been doing since I was last with them. I love being with all these characters again. It feels like a tender privilege. I can't wait to start writing the next story about Katie.

The verse I was pondering when I started writing this book comes from Galatians 6:4 in *The Message:*

"Make a careful exploration of who you are and the work you have been given, and then sink yourself into that. Don't be impressed with yourself. Don't compare yourself with others. Each of you must take responsibility for doing the creative best you can with your own life."

I think the words "creative best" are what captured me when I first read this verse. God certainly did his creative best when he designed each of us and ordered our days. We are given the opportunity to take responsibility and do our creative best with our lives. What a privilege!

My question for you, dear Peculiar Treasure, is what do you see God doing in your life right now? Are you hot on his heels, seeking him and eagerly getting as close to him as you can? Oh, how I pray that you are! Keep trusting in the Lord with all your heart. You'll never regret it.

With a full heart,
Robin Jones Gunn
www.robingunn.com

ABOUT THE AUTHOR

Robin Jones Gunn is the much-loved author of the Christy Miller, Sierra Jensen, Glenbrooke, and Sisterchicks® series, with over 3.5 million books sold worldwide. Robin loves to travel and often speaks locally and internationally. She and her husband live near Portland, Oregon, where the view outside her window is green all year round.